Praise for QUICKSILVER:

"Dan Brown for younger readers. . . Smart
entertainment, deftly done"
Financial Times

"A superbly constructed and vividly depicted tale
of ley lines, ancient prophecies, interplanetary communication
and a dog called Elvis . . . this is a superbly absorbing
old-fashioned thriller"
Daily Telegraph

"It is easy to like the three protagonists,
who deal with their unusual lot with plenty of good
humour and a sense of adventure"
Myshelf.com

"Sam Osman's debut is in the Susan Cooper vein,
with a dash of Anthony Horowitz's supernatural thrillers. . . If
you love stone circles, planetary alignments, Atlantis myths
and ancient history, then curl up with *Quicksilver*"
The Times

"Warmly enjoyable . . . the combination of old-fashioned romp
and galactic villainy will delight and entertain girls and boys"
Philip Womack, *Literary Review*

"A heart-warming story, for those that like their fantasy
or adventure with a bit of fact. Immensely enjoyable"
Bookbag.co.uk

"Told at a cracking pace"
Lovereading4kids.co.uk

"An exciting fantasy adventure that
crackles with mysterious power"
tBk magazine, Spring 2010

SERPENT'S GOLD

SAM OSMAN

MARION LLOYD BOOKS

First published in the UK in 2011 by Marion Lloyd Books
An imprint of Scholastic Ltd
Euston House, 24 Eversholt Street
London, NW1 1DB, UK
Registered office: Westfield Road, Southam, Warwickshire, CV47 0RA
SCHOLASTIC and associated logos are trademarks and/or
registered trademarks of Scholastic Inc.

ISBN 9781407105765

A CIP catalogue record for this book
is available from the British Library

Printed by CPI Bookmarque Ltd, Croydon, Surrey
Papers used by Scholastic Children's Books are made from
wood grown in sustainable forests.

1 3 5 7 9 10 8 6 4 2

This is a work of fiction. Names, characters, places,
incidents and dialogues are products of the author's imagination
or are used fictitiously. Any resemblance to actual people, living or dead,
events or locales is entirely coincidental.

www.scholastic.co.uk/zone

For Charlotte, Murdo and Lily
with love

"Everything is determined, the beginning as well as the end, by forces over which we have no control. It is determined for insects as well as for the stars. Human beings, vegetables or cosmic dust, we all dance to a mysterious tune, intoned in the distance by an invisible piper."

Albert Einstein

The itch, the snitch, rheumatic and the gout,
If the devil puts them in you, let these waters take
them out.
If the devil does his dancing on the roads that lead
to life,
Take a needle from these waters to relieve the world
of strife.
If the devil's doorway opens and his demons join the
dance,
Then seek across the oceans for a spur and spear
and lance,
For the devil he is clever and the devil he is sly,
And the roads grow sorely restless when the devil
passes by.
But you'll not hurt him with your weapons till your
will's a whetted spear,
For the will's the only weapon that the devil's
dancers fear.

Folk rhyme engraved above the
healing well at Thornham

CONTENTS

PART ONE
The Devil's Doorway

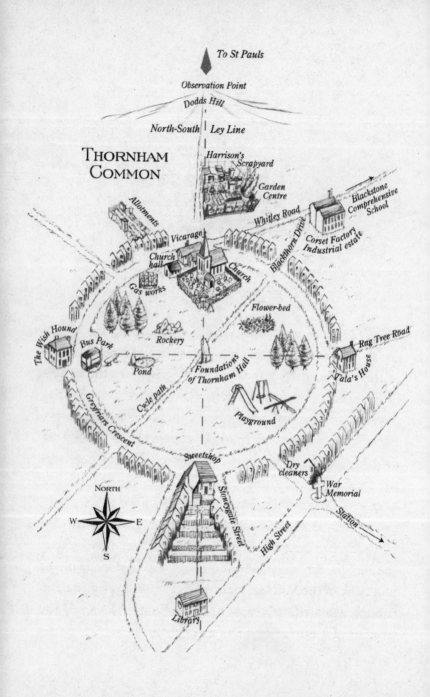

1

The Beast

There was malice in the damp morning air. Wolfie Brown could feel it on his skin and smell it in the stale, gritty winds whirling litter down the gutters of Greyfriars Crescent. He swung his empty delivery bag over his shoulder and jumped back on his bike, eager to get home, eager to get away from the smears of blackened mist drifting low over Thornham, wringing all the colour from the landscape and turning the trees and the tower of St Michael's Church into grimy smudges of grey.

The Browns had owned the sweet shop on the south side of Thornham Common for generations. The then Lord of the Manor, Sir Edgar de Monteneuf, had given them the plot back in the Middle Ages, when this sprawling London suburb was a village surrounded by thorn woods and the remains of a Bronze Age stone circle still towered over its common grazing land. Wolfie was looking out across a view he knew so well he could have drawn it in his dreams, yet suddenly it felt strange to him, as if the sitters in an old family photograph had shifted their poses very slightly, transforming the known and familiar into something deeply unsettling.

A violent jolt shook the jagged scrap of gold hanging at his throat. It was half of a golden star that had once belonged to his father. Fumbling beneath his jumper, he grasped the spikes. A flesh-searing heat sprang from the metal, as if he had plunged his hand into the otherworldly furnace in which the star had been forged. It tuned his senses to the living forces of the cosmos and now its red-hot pulser signalled danger. He felt no pain, only a bitter, blood-numbing dread that his mother was in peril. Racing across the common he bumped his bike through the back gate of the shop. He saw her framed in the kitchen window as she pushed back her hair and disappeared into the storeroom, yet the fear in his star was spiralling into panic. Feverishly he cast around the cluttered yard. The lid had been knocked off the dustbin, and over by the outhouse a large terracotta planter lay broken in a pool of compost. Wolfie froze. Slowly his eyes travelled upwards from the mess. A black bin liner flapped eerily from the outhouse roof. He stood there straining his ears for the swish of wind-blown plastic, but the undulating darkness made no sound. The air stilled. Out of the pool of black appeared two slanted, amber eyes. They stared at him, unblinking

4

and defiant. A long, pendulous tail uncoiled, twitching lazily. Wolfie laid down his bike and edged backwards. This was not a bin bag. It was a panther.

The lustrous creature was beautiful, yet Wolfie's flesh crawled as if he were looking at something foul and rotting. A rancid smell of earth and blood and stagnant water floated on the breeze. He held his breath to keep from retching. The back door flew open. Barking loudly, his dog Elvis bounded out, massive and supple as a wolf; in a flash of grizzled fur he leapt on to the outhouse roof. The panther swung its savage stare from Wolfie and faced the great mongrel without fear, merely dropping its blunt head below its shoulders and flexing one razor-clawed paw. Elvis moved closer, his lean body tensed. For a moment the two beasts eyed each other, as though across a deep divide that neither was able to bridge. And then, in one sinuous movement, the panther turned and sprang into the air, soaring high over the wall into Stoneygate Street.

Elvis dropped clumsily back into the yard. His tail drooped. Crouching low, he padded over to Wolfie and together they stared up and down the empty street. A falling shower of blue sparks fizzed from an overhead cable – and as if snapped from a trance, Wolfie grabbed the dog's collar and pulled him into the kitchen.

"Mum!" he yelled.

Clutching her dressing grown, Sarah Brown hurried through from the storeroom. "What was all the barking about?"

"There was a panther . . ." panted Wolfie, ". . . on the outhouse."

She ran to the window and took in his bike discarded by the gate, the rubbish spilling from the open dustbin and, with a little squeeze of sadness, the smashed planter. She glanced quizzically at her son.

"Honest, Mum. If you don't believe me look at Elvis."

The huge dog was pacing and whining, clearly spooked.

"I'll ring the police."

She made the call and ran outside in her slippers. It was silly, she knew, to feel so upset about a broken plant pot, but she had bought it when she was an art student and paid for it with the money from the first painting she had ever sold. The man on the market stall claimed it was Native American; a Navajo blacksmith's quenching pot. Sarah had no idea if this was true but she loved the way the fine pattern of wavy lines snaking beneath the glaze seemed to echo the ripple and hiss of hot metal slicing through water.

She had been feeling tired and a bit feverish for days and now, as she carefully rubbed the shards of earthenware clean with her fingers, a dull ache crept into her skull. She carried the pieces into the outhouse, wondering if she could glue them back together. With a sigh she swept the scattered compost into a pile. Stooping to rescue a single half-chewed stem from the mess, she cradled it in her palm and brought it inside.

"Looks like your panther took a fancy to my Saravita,"

6

she said. "Thank goodness the rest of the cuttings are in the airing cupboard."

Within fifteen minutes, Constable Mike Mott was rapping on the shop window. As Wolfie unbolted the door the policeman gave him a long hard look. There was something strange about this kid. His eyes weren't exactly shifty, just a funny shade of green flecked with yellow. Mott found them oddly disturbing.

"This way," mumbled Wolfie.

An ear-splitting screech burst from Mott's radio. He jabbed the buttons and ducked into the kitchen, tripping over a bundle of newspapers and a paint-splattered palette propped against an artist's easel. The smell of warm dog and melting sugar, the mismatch of flowered china on the dresser and the torn leather sofa pulled up in front of the fire, stirred echoes of childhood visits to his grandparents' house. But Mott was not a sentimental man and the cluttered cosiness of the Browns' kitchen did nothing to dispel his suspicions that this skinny kid with shaggy hair was up to something. A panther in Thornham? Forget it. Still, he had to go through the motions.

"Morning, Madam. Are you Sarah Brown?"

Sarah looked up from stirring an enormous pan of fudge. "Yes, Officer. Can I get you a cup of tea?"

"No, thanks. Did you see this animal yourself?"

"No, I was in the storeroom."

Avoiding the solemn gaze of the huge dog lying by the hearth, Mott turned to Wolfie.

"Name?"

"Wolfie Brown."

"Age?"

"Twelve."

"Where did this sighting take place?"

"In the yard. The panther was on the outhouse."

"Time?"

"'Bout . . . half past seven."

"What were you doing out so early?"

"Paper round."

"Hmm . . . how big was this . . . cat?"

Wolfie spread his arms. "Pretty big."

"Colouring?"

"Black and really shiny."

"What shape were its ears?"

"Small . . . maybe a bit pointy."

"Tail?"

"Long and kind of curled up at the end."

"Any other distinguishing features?"

Wolfie stared at the floor. How could he describe the malign presence of the creature or the revulsion he had felt when it looked at him?

"It smelt funny," he muttered.

"Did it make any noise. . .?"

"No."

". . .do any damage?"

8

"It knocked over a lovely old plant pot and ate my herbs," said Sarah.

"Hmm. Did it stay on the roof?"

"No," said Wolfie. "When my dog came out it jumped into the street and just . . . disappeared."

Mott clicked his biro and looked sternly at Wolfie. "Look, son, wasting police time is a serious offence."

Sarah slammed the saucepan on to the back burner.

"I can assure you that Wolfie is telling the truth," came a gruff voice from the doorway. "I saw the panther quite plainly from the bathroom window."

An elderly man in a brown and red plaid dressing gown had stepped into the kitchen.

"Your name, sir?" asked the constable, meeting a pair of bright blue eyes set beneath thick white eyebrows.

"Remus Forester. I lodge here."

"Occupation?"

Mr Forester straightened his shoulders. "I am the proprietor and editor of a magazine called *The Earth Mysterian*."

Here we go, thought PC Mott. "This wouldn't be some kind of publicity stunt to increase your magazine's sales, would it, sir? Because as I just told this young man—"

"How dare you, constable," bristled Mr Forester. "*The Earth Mysterian* is renowned worldwide for its fair and factual reporting of anomalous events."

"In that case, sir," said Mott, momentarily chastened,

9

"can you add anything to the lad's description?" His pen hovered hopefully.

"Only to confirm the numinous beauty of the beast and to say that an animal such as this is probably a link between the world we know and a dimension sadly beyond our understanding."

The constable stared at his pad as if he had lost the ability to blink. "Right you are, sir. That's a great help. Thank you." He snapped the notebook shut and stuffed it in his pocket.

"This may throw some light on your investigation," went on Mr Forester, sifting through the pile of pamphlets on the dresser and pressing one into the policeman's hand. "This is a short introduction to ley lines, the paths of energy coursing through the cosmos whose actions may well lie behind this morning's manifestation."

Wolfie was gazing at the old man, obviously shaken by his words. A dark wiry girl came running into the kitchen, pulling her unbrushed hair into a ponytail. Roused by the turmoil in her own broken star, she shrank back in horror at the sight of the policeman.

"It's OK, Tala," Wolfie said quickly. "I saw a panther in the back yard."

"You're kidding."

Mott studied the girl. What was she looking so guilty about? She'd got the same funny eyes as the boy, but she was too foreign-looking to be his sister and that accent was definitely American.

"Did you see anything, Miss . . . er?"

"Bean . . . no . . . sorry. I was asleep."

"Live here . . . do you?"

"No."

Wolfie shot her a look of warning, which was not lost on Mott.

"I mean, yes. I'm staying here . . . while my uncle's away . . . on . . . business," said Tala, flustered.

Mott put on his cap. There was definitely something fishy about this lot. That batty old lodger, two kids who were obviously hiding something and that hippy dippy woman who'd been looking daggers at him for the last ten minutes.

"What you saw was probably an oversized domestic cat. But I'll just take a look around outside."

Wolfie joined Sarah at the window and watched Mott kick the pile of compost, poke the contents of the dustbin with his truncheon and stride away trying to kill the screeching crackle from his radio.

"He didn't believe a word you said. I've got a good mind to make a complaint," Sarah said crossly. She noticed a fine crack in the corner of the windowpane, pointing like a crooked finger to the sky, and as she reached out to touch it a jag of pain burrowed deep into her brain.

PC Mott might have been a little less dismissive of Mr Forester if he had seen him explaining his theories on last Friday's edition of the TV programme *World Watch*.

11

on over the cause of the mysterious
that erupted last week over the South
of Thornham," the host, Julian Forsyth, had
to the studio audience. "Meteorologists
the light show to colliding space debris. However,
subsequent reports of unusual electromagnetic activity all
around the world, ranging from sporadic power cuts,
electrical fires and mobile phone interference to clouds of
sparks appearing over certain ancient structures including
Stonehenge, Machu Picchu and the Great Pyramid at Giza,
accompanied by an *eight hundred per cent* increase in
magnetometer readings at these sites, have raised the
question, *Is something fundamental happening to the earth's
magnetic field?* Conventional scientists confess themselves
baffled. However, members of the so-called earth mysteries
community are claiming that it was the light ball at
Thornham that triggered these unexplained phenomena and
that it's all to do with something called 'ley lines'."

"With us in the studio to explain this controversial
'alternative' view is Remus Forester, editor of the
specialist journal *The Earth Mysterian*."

Tala and Wolfie shifted down the sofa to make way for
their friend Zi'ib, who had come round specially to watch
the programme. This tall thin boy with dark skin, thick
wiry curls and green, gold-flecked eyes just like theirs also
wore a broken star around his neck.

"I'm glad Sarah made Mr Forester trim his eyebrows," he
grinned.

12

"Yeah, but look, he's got odd socks on," groaned Tala.

"Remus Forester, can you tell us exactly what ley lines are?" asked Julian Forsyth.

"Well, Julian, they are lines of natural earth energy that criss-cross the world like the veins of a living organism and channel the forces that enable our planet to support life. Without them the earth would be merely a lump of dead rock."

"So if this 'earth energy' actually exists, why are we only hearing about it now?"

"Mankind has known about it for thousands of years under different names – life force, cosmic breath, chi, prana, celestial fire, dragon energy, ley energy. . ."

Tala began to relax. Mr Forester was doing fine.

"Our early ancestors lived in harmony with this force, developing ways to channel, harness and regenerate it using a complex network of megaliths and stone circles activated by complex rituals. There is even evidence that they actually used the earth energy to power their civilizations – employing it to heal the sick, fertilize the soil, transport thought, heavy materials and possibly even people, across considerable distances. They also had an innate sensitivity that enabled them to engage with the energy – what we now might call a sixth sense. Sadly, in most of us that ability has atrophied through disuse, although traces of it remain in those who are lucky enough to be able to dowse."

"So how do these ley lines, these channels of energy, relate to the explosion of light at Thornham?"

"Allow me to give you some context here, Julian. Earth mysterians are divided on the precise make-up of the ley system. However, I adhere to the view that the earth is part of a wider system of planets capable of supporting life, scattered across a dimension of the cosmos which has been called the Wilderness Between the Worlds. Not only are the individual inhabited planets veined by ley lines, they are linked together by a web of *interplanetary* leys to create one vast connected entity."

Julian Forsyth, well known for his combative interviewing style, remained unusually quiet.

"Now, on planets where there are no *conscious* beings – for simplicity's sake, let's call all such beings people – the energy runs freely through the leys in total harmony with the flora and fauna it has brought into existence. But as soon as you get *people* on a planet things get complicated. Their consciousness actually saps the life force. That's fine as long as those conscious beings use the methods I mentioned earlier to husband and regenerate it. However, if the population forgets the secrets of that regeneration technology the energy begins to dry up. Sadly, Julian, that is exactly what has been happening to our world." His voice grew grave. "Centuries of abuse and neglect of our ley system have substantially depleted the earth's energies, jeopardizing our planet's very ability to support life. If those energies ever disappear completely, it will be like pulling the plug on a life support system."

A roving camera swept the faces of the audience. Some

14

frowning, some shaking their heads, others open mouthed. All were silent, transfixed by Mr Forester's strange theory.

"Not only would that mean catastrophe for us, it would have grave consequences for every planet on the cosmic grid."

"In what way?" murmured Julian.

"Imagine the cosmic leys as the wires on a string of old-fashioned fairy lights. If one bulb dies, the flow of power along the whole set is interrupted."

"So how does that relate to the events at Thornham?"

Mr Forester drew a long breath. "I believe that the explosion of light over Thornham Common signalled the release of an unimaginably massive injection of cosmic energy into the ley grid that we can only hope has snatched our planet back from the brink!" He paused, his ruddy face alight as if marvelling at the wonders he was relating. "According to many dowsers and geomancers who have contacted *The Earth Mysterian*, the world is now glowing with levels of fresh, raw, vibrant energy not seen since the Bronze Age. It is as if the power supply has been turned up from two volts to two thousand volts. In my opinion, it is this influx of energy that is causing the strange phenomena taking place at key nodes on the earth's ley grid."

"Why would something like that happen at *Thornham*? Why not some important ancient site?"

"Thornham may look like an ordinary London suburb, but its common is the point where eight of the country's most important ley lines meet in a perfect star shape. Our ancestors recognized the extraordinary significance of that convergence of power lines by marking it with a stone circle much larger even than Stonehenge. Sadly that circle was destroyed long ago. Possibly deliberately."

He turned to stare earnestly into the camera. "Now that our precious planet has been given a second chance we must learn from such catastrophic mistakes and restore our ancestral rapport with the forces of the cosmos! We must repair and replace the stone energy receptors our megalithic forebears erected across the landscape and seek out the fragments of their lost technologies hidden in the ancient texts, myths and folk ceremonies that have managed to survive! SILK, the Society for the Investigation of Lost Knowledge, is planning a major conference and a series of nationwide seminars to discuss the way forward, so please visit their website to see how you can get involved."

Julian Forsyth fingered his collar.

"Finally, before I take questions from the audience, what do you think triggered the regeneration of these 'earth energies'?"

"I really don't know. I wish I did. All I can say is that unlike the forces of electricity and gravity, the power in the leys has memory and intent – consciousness, in fact. It strives constantly to keep the ley system going by using human beings as instruments of its will. So it is possible that, knowingly or unknowingly, human beings were involved. Even so, that doesn't explain how this energy was sourced or created. However, a number of *The Earth Mysterian*'s readers have been doing their own detective work and the magazine will be publishing their findings later in the year."

Wolfie, Tala and Zi'ib went rigid, appalled and suddenly afraid. What if someone discovered that *they* had saved the leys? What if it came out that three human children had been born for the precise purpose of repairing the centuries of ignorance that had brought the planet to the brink?

That task had torn their lives and families apart. Now they huddled on the sofa, fearful for their secrets. But other dangers were threatening their young lives. Outside on Thornham Common, a germ of darkness was slowly taking root beneath the earth, spreading its negative vibrations through the flow of energy that these three reluctant guardians of the earth's ancient forces had sacrificed so much to revive.

"Um, Mr Forester," Wolfie said, after PC Mott had left and Sarah had gone to get dressed. "Why did you just tell that policeman the panther might have something to do with the energies in the leys?"

"Because," said Mr Forester, "I have a horrible suspicion it may."

"But how?" Wolfie said. "All that new energy's s'posed to be a good thing and that panther felt, I dunno, bad and creepy."

"The vast infusion of fresh energy now coursing through the leys is like a torrent of life-giving water pouring into a dried-up network of rivers. In itself a wonderful thing. But if something were to poison one of the tributaries. . ." He broke off, visibly perturbed.

"What could poison energy?" Tala asked.

"You'd be surprised. Traumatic events, shifting underground fault lines, even portals opening up from other dimensions can all affect the vibrational frequency of the energies, turning them from positive to negative and creating what is called a black stream. These black streams can cause serious upset, and manifest themselves as all sorts of disturbing phenomena."

Wolfie paled. "You mean that panther isn't real?"

"It's real all right. Elemental beasts have always woven their way into our lives. It's just that the forces that give them life are the dark mirror of those that animate the world we think we know."

Wolfie met Tala's shocked gaze as a dank, spirit-sapping foreboding vibrated through their stars.

"Can't this black stream be cleaned?" demanded Tala.

"Well, yes, and in most ancient cultures there was a priestly elite who knew how to turn negative forces positive again. But they had to keep their knowledge secret because in the wrong hands it could also be used to turn positive forces negative."

Tala frowned. "Who'd want to do that?"

"Oh my dear, seekers of wisdom have been tempted to

misuse their knowledge since time began. It's human nature. I'm sure there have always been those who would happily contaminate the earth's whole ley system if that enabled them to control it. Sadly, the need for secrecy means that all but a fragment of the old cleansing technologies have been lost. However, I shall get straight on to the Society for the Investigation of Lost Knowledge. Some of their members have achieved excellent results with purifying mildly tainted pockets of energy."

"What if this is more than a mild contamination?"

"Then we might have a serious problem," the old man said quietly.

The uneasy silence was broken by the snap of the letter box in the shop. Tala jumped up nervously and clattered around making Elvis's breakfast.

Sarah came in scrunching up a letter. "When will that smarmy estate agent get it into his head that I do *not* want to sell this shop." She frowned at the heavily smudged postmark on a second envelope and skimmed its contents. "Oh, thank goodness. His mobile's been off for weeks. I know there's been trouble with the phone networks but I was beginning to think he'd had an accident." She waved the typed sheet at Tala. "It's from your Uncle Matthias."

Tala hacked at a lump of meat. "Yeah? What's he say?" But she knew exactly what the letter said. She had written it herself.

"Something's come up on some mineral survey he set up for the government and he's going straight on from Alaska to sort it out. It all sounds a bit hush-hush. He wants to know if you can stay on here till he gets back. That's fine with us, isn't it, Wolfie?"

"Sure," Wolfie mumbled.

Neither he nor Tala were devious by nature and the strain of so many secrets and lies was making them brittle and wary.

Tala's "Uncle Matthias" had brought her from America to live in Thornham when her father suddenly vanished. But the children had discovered that Matthias was an imposter who was unlikely ever to return, and they feared that if anyone found out she had been abandoned she would get sent straight back to the States.

Right now there was far too much at stake to let that happen.

2

A Letter from the Ancestors

Watery light spilled from the window of Wolfie's cramped attic bedroom on to a layer of socks, bags, dog biscuits, shoes, pens and sweet wrappers, thick as a forest floor. His drawings covered the walls, clothes scattered his bed and Tala's inflatable mattress and all her stuff were squashed against the chest of drawers. On the little iron mantelpiece stood a portrait of Wolfie's father, Arion. It had been painted by Sarah just before he had disappeared over a decade before. Father and son had the same shaggy fair hair and green eyes but Arion's piercing stare held a fiery certainty that flashed only rarely beneath Wolfie's pale lashes. Beside it, Tala had propped a battered snapshot of her father, Jack, taken on their last fishing trip together, wedging it beside a little box made of polished black stone that had once belonged to her mother.

"Something bad's happened, hasn't it? My star's been going crazy," Zi'ib said, clambering through the trapdoor.

Wolfie nodded. "I saw a panther on the outhouse."

"Blimey. What was it like?"

"It smelled funny and it felt really . . . evil."

"Mr Forester thinks it's an elemental – a manifestation of negative forces created by one of the ley lines getting contaminated," added Tala.

Six months ago, Zi'ib had been living with his mother in a small desert village in Sudan, unable to speak a word of English, unaware of the existence of ley lines, Thornham, Wolfie or Tala. But the power in the leys had fractured every belief he had ever held about himself or the nature of the world, and so he just sat there, dreading what she might say next.

"It's OK," Tala said hurriedly. "Mr Forester says there's people at SILK who can sort it out . . . probably."

Elvis gave a lusty snore and turned over with his massive paws in the air. To the outside world he was a huge lumbering stray who had been lucky to find a home at the sweet shop. To Wolfie, Tala and Zi'ib he was a clever, loyal, mysterious creature who had appeared from nowhere to guide their quest to save the leys.

"Do you think elementals can manifest out of *positive* energies as well as bad ones?" Tala said, scratching the great dog's enormous ears.

22

"It would explain a lot," said Wolfie, thoughtfully.

"Did Sarah buy the story about Matthias?" Zi'ib asked.

"For now," Wolfie said. "But how long before someone starts sniffing round, asking where he is and why he hasn't paid his bills?"

Tala fished a wad of papers from under her pillow. "Well, before I get packed off back to the States we'd better get on with our letter. I've done a draft but say if you want to change anything." She started to read the letter out loud.

TO THE DESCENDANTS OF WOLFIE BROWN,
TALA BEAN AND ZI'IB BAKRI,
DO NOT SHOW THIS TO ANYONE!!!
When strange things started happening to us we found messages from our ancestors that helped explain what was going on, so we are doing the same for you. Our story will shock and frighten you and you will probably tell yourself it is a hoax. It is not. Everything in this letter is true.

First you need to know that we each have a parent who is an explorer from another world.

Wolfie looked at the portrait of his dad. That terrifying discovery had tipped him out of the life he knew into a mysterious reality he still struggled to understand. "Couldn't we . . . you know, break it to them gently?"

"No," said Tala, briskly.

23

They are: Tala's mother, Kara; Zi'ib's father, Zane; and Wolfie's father, Arion. The world they came from is called Lupus (the ancients called it the Lands of the Wolf) because of the wise wolves that roam its mountains. Our Lupan parents disappeared when we were babies and no one knew they were Lupans or where they had gone. We only found out ourselves a few months ago. But don't worry, Lupans are totally normal except they've got green eyes with gold flecks and know the Wisdom of the Stars. If you've got eyes like that, or you've always had a feeling there was something different about you, it's because of your Lupan blood.

The boys nodded in silence.

The other side of our families were wise men from ancient tribes of this world. Wolfie's mother, Sarah, is descended from Druids from Thornham in England, who practised the Wisdom of the Forests. Tala's dad, Jack, is descended from the shamans of Mount Shasta in California who knew the Wisdom of the Mountains. Zi'ib's mum's ancestors were priests from Meroe in Northern Sudan who knew the Wisdom of the Nile.

"I've put in our family trees." She held up the page so they could see.

Arion (Lupan) – Sarah (English)   Jack (American) – Kara (Lupan)

/   /

Wolfie   Tala

Zane (Lupan) – Shadia (Sudanese)

/

Zi'ib

The second thing you need to know is that there are lines of energy called ley lines that criss-cross the inhabited worlds and link them together.

She showed them her sketch of the world's ley grid.

We don't know how they work but it's like they are alive and they connect people and events across time and place to make things happen. At first you think it's just coincidences linking you to things that happened ages ago or miles away but it's not, it's what's called a "kinnection". The ancients called it "turning the tides of fate". The whole ley grid is controlled by Spheres, which are pieces of a star that exploded millions of years ago and still float round the cosmos.

The Lupans used to keep one of these Spheres in their meeting chamber under a crystal dome. Their scholars never managed to decode all its secrets, but they did work out how to use its power to travel the leys and open gateways to other planets at places like Thornham, Shasta and Meroe, where the ley lines meet in an eight-point star shape that looks like this:

The Lupans also make star-shaped golden medallions that tune you into the ley energies. They use these stars to link teams of interplanetary explorers with "ties that bind through darkness unto death" and enable them to communicate across the cosmos through something called the Link of Light. When it is working properly the Link of Light is amazing and lets you feel other star bearers' feelings as well as see them and talk to them.

Our parents broke their stars in two and left half for

each of us, but without the Sphere the Link of Light doesn't work properly. All we can pick up are the vibrations from the leys and each other's feelings (which can be a bit embarrassing). Weirdly the stars also give us the mastery of tongues and number, which means we can speak zillions of languages and do maths and computing and things we used to be rubbish at.

The early civilizations of the earth developed ways of storing and renewing the energy in the leys using megaliths and special rituals. But when that wisdom got forgotten the earth's energies started to dry up and weaken the whole cosmic grid. So our Lupan parents were sent to earth on a mission to save the leys and that's why we were born.

The ancient Lupans had chosen our ancestors to be guardians of three sacred stones that contained the secret of how to use the Spheres to turn the tides of fate. That knowledge was so powerful it would release a massive store of cosmic energy if ever the stones were brought together. Our guardian ancestors hid these stones away and left messages explaining that only their descendants whose blood mingled the wisdoms of the earth <u>and</u> the stars could find them.

It was all part of a scheme to stop a cult of power-crazed Lupan scholars called the Manus Sacra from getting their hands on the secret of the Spheres. They believed that they had been born to rule the cosmos and despised all other beings in it. (They called them "unworthies" and "lesser mortals".) Most of the Manus Sacra had been

27

expelled from Lupus but their leader, Therion, and some of their cleverest scholars were still there, secretly controlling the exiles and waiting to steal the Sphere, bring it to earth and take over all the inhabited worlds.

When the Manus Sacra found out we existed they got rid of our parents one by one. They lured Wolfie's dad Arion and Tala's mum Kara back to Lupus and closed all the gateways so they couldn't return to earth. Then they had Zi'ib's mum Shadia abducted and no one knows what's happened to her.

Zi'ib's eyes burned. His thoughts of his mother were so vivid that sometimes he thought he glimpsed her out of the corner of his eye, but when he swung round all he ever found was shadow.

The men who took her shot Zi'ib in the leg. He nearly died but a charity brought him to England for treatment and now, thanks to the healing power in the Thornham leys, he can run much faster than he did before.

The Manus Sacra cast Zi'ib's and Tala's dads into the Wilderness Between the Worlds, which is like a nightmare wasteland between the inhabited planets. They got out, but the wilderness did terrible things to both of them. Tala's dad...

A whimper of misery escaped Tala's lips as she read out the words "*...is in a coma in a hospital in America...*"

The paper dropped from her hand. After a moment, Zi'ib picked it up and took over.

. . .and Zi'ib's dad Zane is here in Thornham. He survived better because Lupan explorers are trained to cope with hostile environments, but he's really weak. The only one the Manus Sacra left alone was Wolfie's mum.

Wolfie flinched. For the second time that morning fear for his mother shot through his limbs.

When the leys brought us together from across the world to look for the Stones of Knowledge the Manus Sacra started worming their way into our lives and spying on our search. Zi'ib got fostered by one of them – Godfrey Peasemarsh, who'd been living as the vicar of Thornham for years. Another one called Ridian Winter pretended to be Tala's long-lost Uncle Matthias. He brought her to live in Thornham. We found out that the real Matthias was a Lupan explorer on the same mission as our parents, and that Ridian Winter killed him and stole his identity over a decade ago.

We followed a trail of clues that led us back to Sudan and Shasta, but the stones themselves were all hidden in Thornham. One was the hard stony seed of a Lupan herb that grows in Wolfie's back yard. We call it Saravita and his mum uses it for flavouring fudge. One was a pink

granite obelisk and one was the leg of an old bench on
Thornham Common. We couldn't move it so we had to
bring the other stones to it.

But the exiled Manus Sacra were there waiting for us.
They were about to snatch the power in the stones when
Wolfie's dog Elvis arrived—

"Put in that we think he's an elemental manifested by the
positive energies," said Zi'ib.

Tala made a note.

...with half the dogs of Thornham and chased them
towards the ruined foundations of an old manor house
that used to stand in the middle of Thornham Common.
Just as they got there, the exiles vanished as if they'd
been swallowed up by the earth. At that same moment
the wise wolves of Lupus smashed through the crystal
dome above the Lupan chamber. They chased off the
Manus Sacra leaders who had been standing by ready to
steal the Sphere and bring it to earth. Seconds later the
stones came together as if drawn by some strange
magnetic force. There was a massive explosion of light
and suddenly the leys were brimming with energy again.
But in all the commotion on Lupus the Sphere drifted
away through the hole in the crystal dome.

Zi'ib's dad says that the Manus Sacra were sucked
down into a dimension that the ancients called the nether
void, which is way more horrible even than the

Wilderness Between the Worlds. Unfortunately, Ridian Winter was away in Alaska when all this happened so he escaped and we have no idea where he is or what he is up to.

You need to know all this because our bloodlines are destined to be guardians of the leys for ever. So be warned. If a series of weird coincidences brings you together like they did with us, it'll be a sure sign that the leys need your help. We'll hide our stars somewhere safe for you before we die but it won't really matter what we do with them. If you need them they will find you.

We hope to be able to stay together long enough to recapture the Sphere of Lupus and bring Arion and Kara home. After that, who knows what will happen to us. But as you'll find out, the bond between the bearers of the broken stars is stronger than time or space.

So good luck.

Yours sincerely,

Your ancestors,

Wolfie Brown, Tala Bean, Zi'ib Bakri

PS We're attaching extracts from an old book called the *Book of Light* so you can read up on the history of Lupus.* And a photo of Elvis, because he (or a dog that looks just like him) keeps turning up through the centuries to help guard the leys.

* See Appendix 1

PPS Don't forget. Never <u>ever</u> reveal your Lupan blood to anyone. Zi'ib's dad says this world has replaced wisdom with fear and if the authorities found out that someone was part Lupan they would stop at nothing to silence them and <u>everyone who knew about them</u>.

The three children felt the terrible weight of that warning. They yearned to share their secret with Mr Forester, whose friendship and research into ancient truths had helped them at every turn. But for his safety as well as their own they knew they never could.

"Do you think our descendants will get what we're on about?" Wolfie said.

"Yours'll be too dumb, but don't worry, mine can explain it to them," Tala said, dodging the pillow he hurled at her.

Zi'ib grinned. "Now we've got to work out someplace to hide the letter so that only they can find it."

Wolfie was impatient. "You and me can do that later. We're going to spend every minute we've got left together, getting Dad and Kara back from Lupus."

3

A Second Sighting

Sergeant Woodall handed PC Mott a mug of coffee. "Find your panther?"

"Barking mad, the lot of 'em," muttered Mott, typing up his report.

"That Sarah Brown came down the station years back saying her bloke had gone missing. Nice woman, but she wouldn't have it that he'd done a bunk. Kept on about the place being locked from the inside and how he couldn't have got out without her knowing."

"Yeah, well, there must be something in that fudge she makes because this time it's the kid and her crazy old lodger who are in la-la land." Mott slapped Mr Forester's pamphlet on the desk. "He gave me this, said it might 'help with my investigation'. Listen to this: 'Everything in the cosmos, all matter, force, thought, sound, mind, memory and experience are manifestations of one universal power, differentiated only by differing rates of vibration and rotation.' I'd like to see the super's face if I put that in my report. Oh yes, and according to them, this panther had been eating pot plants. What panther's going to ignore the chicken carcass hanging out of their dustbin and eat a load of leaves?"

Their radios beeped. Mott's blotchy face turned pallid as a crackly voice instructed them to proceed immediately to St Michael's Church, where a large leopard-like creature had been seen skulking in the graveyard.

On the other side of Thornham, Wolfie, Tala and Zi'ib stared glumly at the noticeboard on Wolfie's wall. At the top he had pinned the headline **Operation Arion and Kara**, written in Sanskrit so his mum wouldn't understand it. Beneath it glittered a painting of a Sphere so cleverly shaded in dabs of gold and silver it seemed to leap from the paper and hover in the air. Over the last few days, all they had managed to add to their plan were four action points.

1 **Capture Sphere**
2 **Restore Link of Light**
3 **Find out how to open gateway**
4 **Bring Arion and Kara back from Lupus**

"I went through Mr Forester's pamphlet about Spheres again last night and there's absolutely nothing in it about capturing them," Wolfie moaned.

A siren wailed in the street below. Rushing to the window, Zi'ib spotted a police car screeching round the crescent towards St Michael's Church. "Come on. Maybe they've found the panther," he said, eager to take a rest from the brain-battering problem of capturing a lost fragment of star matter. The others followed him outside and as they neared the ruined foundations of Thornham Hall they sensed something deeply oppressive seeping through the grass and spilling out along the major ley line that ran due north towards the church and south towards the shop. Tala ventured slowly along its path, testing its strength. It rose, it rested, rose again with the rhythm of her breathing, washing a sickening chill through all their stars.

"Don't!" Wolfie cried, dragging her away, and they ran in a wide arc towards the churchyard.

"You kids stay right where you are," roared PC Mott, blocking the lychgate. "Oh. It's you again." He glowered at Wolfie and Tala and stared at Zi'ib, astonished that a black kid should have those funny eyes as well.

"Has someone else seen the panther?" demanded Wolfie.

Mott eyed him suspiciously. "The woman that cleans the church."

"What, Mrs Poskitt?"

"Know her, do you?"

"Yes, she. . ."

The policeman bore down angrily on Wolfie. "Right, this has gone far enough. When I find out what's going on *you* are going to be in *very* deep trouble. Go on, stand back, the lot of you. You can't come in here."

"We haven't done anything," protested Tala.

"I said clear off."

The children slipped round to the side of the lychgate and peeped through the wooden struts supporting the steep little roof. Sergeant Woodall appeared with a tall, thin-faced woman in a raincoat. Patting the halo of pale curls peeking from beneath her headscarf she sat down heavily on the narrow wooden seat and called to a large white poodle who was sniffing the gatepost.

"Sit, Monty, good boy."

Monty flicked his pompommed tail and bounded off to rub noses with Elvis.

"Now, madam," said Sergeant Woodall, "could you give us a description of this animal."

"I can do better than that," said Mrs Poskitt, fumbling for her mobile. "I'd just rung my Sid to see if he fancied a bit of haddock for his tea when I smelled this funny smell, like there was trouble with the drains. I looked round and there it was, under the old yew tree. It gave me a right turn. I said, 'Sid, it's either the devil himself or there's a bloomin' leopard staring right at me,' and he said, 'Quick, Vera, take a photo.' So I did." She held up the phone with a mixture of pride and relish. "Look at that, the Beast of Thornham!"

Two amber eyes stared out of a blur of darkness on the tiny screen. As Wolfie stood on tiptoe to get a better view Zi'ib and Tala felt the hollow whisper of his fear.

Masking his surprise in a burst of efficiency, Mott began to bark into his radio, calling for backup.

"I wouldn't bother if I were you," said Mrs Poskitt, folding her arms. "Soon as Monty started barking it scarpered."

"We can't take any chances, Mrs Poskitt," said Sergeant Woodall. "Do you know who'd have a key to the lychgate so we can close off the graveyard?"

"You're in luck. It's me looking after *everything* since the vicar went missing." She handed him a bunch of keys. "Churchwarden thinks he ran off with that stuck-up librarian, Leonora Grindle, 'cos she's done a bunk an' all. But who'd run off with Reverend Peasemarsh? Not exactly George Clooney, was he?"

"If you don't mind, Mrs Poskitt, I'd like to forward this photo to the station," cut in PC Mott.

"You be careful, that picture's worth money. I'm sending it to the *Thornham Gazette*." With a sudden smile, she saw Zi'ib peeking through the wooden struts. "Hallo dear, how are you getting on?"

"Fine, thanks, Mrs Poskitt."

"I've still got some of your washing – it's all done. You can pick it up any time, though lord knows what I'm supposed to do with the vicar's baggy old smalls."

Sergeant Woodall wagged a thoughtful finger at Zi'ib. "I *knew* I'd seen your face before. You're the kid the vicar was fostering. You were on that telly documentary looking for your parents. . . Didn't your dad crack the code of some ancient language, then disappear?"

Zi'ib nodded shyly. He was getting used to being recognized by complete strangers who insisted on telling him his own life story.

"His dad's back now, didn't you see the piece in the paper?" put in Mrs Poskitt. "Mind you, he looks like death warmed up. Lost his memory by all accounts, doesn't have a clue where he's been."

"Well good luck to you, son, you've had a tough time," said Sergeant Woodall. "But you'd best be off while they search the area. This animal could be dangerous."

The children backed away, feeling quivery and unsettled, as if their bones had ceased to sit comfortably inside their skin.

"Let's see what Dad thinks about it," Zi'ib said. He whistled to Elvis and they ran down the crescent.

Across the common a man in overalls was fixing a bright yellow "Under new management" sign to the front of the Wish Hound pub, while beneath the grass something dark and unknowable trembled through the soil, searching for minds and matter on which to feed its gnawing hunger.

4

Nobody's Shadow

Sarah swallowed some aspirin and hefted a sack of sugar on to the table. Following the discovery of her grandmother's secret recipe, the success of Brown's Traditional Fudge had been a lifesaver for the shop's precarious profits. Today she couldn't afford to let her headache stop production.

Outside on Greyfriars Crescent the children met Mr Forester. His frown darkened at the news of Vera Poskitt's encounter with the panther. "A second sighting so soon? That doesn't bode well at all. They do say bad news always comes in threes."

"Why, what else has happened?" Tala asked.

"I've had a rather depressing letter from the *EM*'s accountants. My TV interview brought in a lot of new subscriptions but I'll still be lucky to find any office space I can afford."

When Britain's leading journal of alternative earth sciences had announced its sudden closure, Mr Forester had been appalled. He made an immediate and impetuous decision to save it, cashed in an insurance policy and bought it out. However, the reality of taking over an ailing magazine was proving far more stressful than he had imagined.

They parted at the corner of Rag Tree Road. The children turned into the drive of number forty-five, the dilapidated villa that Tala had once shared with Ridian Winter. It had been her idea for Zi'ib and his father to stay at the abandoned house, and sometimes she daydreamed that it was she and her mother Kara living in those dark, musty rooms, taking tiny steps towards the intimacy they had never known.

"Dad!" Zi'ib crashed through the front door, tossing his key on to the hall table, the way he had seen kids do on TV. Still struggling to accept the truth about his long-absent father, he kept trying different ways of acting around him, searching for something that felt, if not normal, at least real.

"In here!" croaked a voice.

Elvis trotted ahead into a large shabby sitting room that smelled of damp. On the mantelpiece stood a framed black and white photograph of Zi'ib as a toddler on the knee of his mother, a pretty, smiling Sudanese woman in a softly draped *tobe*, his father standing proudly at her side.

Zane Bakri struggled to stand up, barely recognizable as the tall powerful man in the photograph. Ten years spent wandering the Wilderness Between the Worlds had left him gaunt and stooped, threading his dark hair with grey and hollowing the flesh from his cheeks. Only his eyes were fiery and alert: eyes that, like those of every Lupan, were green and flecked with gold. He rested them for a moment on his son, before turning his ruined face to Wolfie, a gilded flash of metal glinting at his throat.

"What frightened you?"

Wolfie trembled. He had seen Zane Bakri nearly every day for the last two weeks yet still he was overawed by this other-worldly bearer of a broken star who shared every beat of his emotions.

In a rush he blurted, "I . . . I saw a panther. . ."

Zane closed his eyes.

". . .and then Mrs Poskitt, who cleans the church, she saw it too."

Zane listened gravely as Wolfie explained Mr Forester's disturbing theory.

"Remus is quite right," he said. "Have you three been picking up a growing melancholy in the air?"

They nodded, warily.

"I sensed the changing vibrations days ago and I've been waiting to see what sort of manifestations the black energies would produce."

Zi'ib threw himself into a chair. "I don't get it," he cried bitterly. "We nearly kill ourselves reviving the leys and now it turns out we've just made everything worse!"

"When you released that vast store of natural energy from the Stones of Knowledge, you revived the fading forces of the earth. But energy is a form of vibration, and it is only the frequency of that vibration that determines whether the energy stays positive or turns negative."

"I still don't understand."

"Everything in the cosmos — light, sound, people, thoughts, mountains — is made of tiny ever-dancing particles. By changing the rate of their movement you change the nature of those entities."

"How can one thing change into another?" Zi'ib said sullenly.

Zane ran his hand through his hair. "Think of water. It can manifest as mist, a running stream, it can boil and bubble, steam, condense, cool and freeze into a lump of ice. Yet its particles haven't changed, merely their activity. So basically, Zi'ib, all that positive energy you released has the potential to turn bad and resonate at a negative frequency that can cause severe emotional and physical damage and take the form of negative elemental creatures."

"It's all right. Mr Forester says he knows someone who can sort this black ley out," Tala said.

Zane said quietly, "The skill of one wisdom or even one world will not be enough to reverse what is happening here."

Dread crept through the children's stars, pulsing to the quickening drum of their hearts.

"I sensed from the pitch of vibration that this was no ordinary contamination. Two realizations in such quick succession of a creature as powerful as a panther can only have been caused by intensely powerful negative energies. These forces come from the nether void. They must have escaped when it opened to swallow the Manus Sacra."

"So who *can* put it right?" said Wolfie, his voice wavering. *Not us. Please, please, don't say us.*

"Only minds attuned to the four great wisdoms of this world *and* the Wisdom of the Stars would have any hope of. . ."

"No!" cut in Tala.

". . .of healing such a contagion."

Zane's words, although spoken gently, had smashed their hopes like a hammer on porcelain.

"We're not doing *anything* till we've found the lost Sphere and brought Dad and Kara back from Lupus," Wolfie said, suddenly fierce.

"In the eternal battle for cosmic balance our plans and dreams count for nothing, Wolfie."

"Why us? There must be someone else who can do it."

"The wisdom flowing through your veins makes you uniquely attuned to the subtleties of vibration necessary to cleanse these negative energies."

"OK," Wolfe said, grudgingly. "But first we capture the Sphere."

"If you brought a Sphere into a world tainted by the void you could never use it to open the gateways. Because the Sphere itself would become contaminated. Then it would only respond to beings either born of darkness, or who embrace darkness."

The look on Zane's face was curdling Wolfie's insides. "What does that mean?"

"Embracing darkness means allowing negative vibrations to permeate your thoughts and actions so that you, in turn, become an instrument of malice and discord."

Wolfie stared at him bleakly. Yesterday everything had seemed simple. They had revived the leys. They were going to find a way to bring his dad home. Now there was all this stuff he didn't understand about darkness and light and negative and positive vibrations fouling everything up. Tears welled in his eyes.

"Why? Why does it have to be like that?"

Tala was crying openly, and Elvis laid his grizzled head on her knee.

"The secrets of the Sphere lie in realms of understanding hidden even to the greatest scholars," said Zane. "But remember, the battle between light and dark is in constant flux. Just as a trace of darkness lurks for ever in the light, so the light sows seeds of its own salvation in the damage wrought by darkness. Seek out those seeds and open your minds to the messages of the positive forces. They will be trying to lead you to the lost secrets of the ancient energy healers by any means they can. The rest will be up to you."

"The rest of what?" demanded Zi'ib.

"Of the necessary tools and methods. The contaminated energies from the void are far more dangerous than anything ordinary healers had to deal with. You will need to gather all their knowledge and more to fight this battle."

Wolfie's frustration flared up inside. Why couldn't his own dad be here to help him? Why was Zane just sitting there all cold and logical, spewing out this stuff like some kind of machine? "You *are* going to help us?" he said.

Zane's face clouded and they felt something oddly akin to shame shuddering from his star. "I will do everything I can to help you, but the wisdoms of this planet are alien to me. You three alone have the power to wipe out this contamination. But first, you must find the will. That is the most powerful weapon you possess, for consciousness, like everything else, is vibrating energy."

"What if . . . we fail?" demanded Tala.

"Then gradually the whole of the earth's energy grid will become infected, until only beings without conscience, kindness, affection or altruism will thrive." His face twisted in pain. "Believe me, such planets exist. I have seen them."

Once, long ago, he had spent time on such a world, convinced he would be immune to the pull of darkness. Little by little the black forces had dripped into his head

45

and sullied his mind. If it had not been for Tala's mother Kara, he might never have found the will to escape, and from that time on he had lived with the fear that he might succumb again.

"How long have we got?" Zi'ib asked, gloomily.

"Like any infection it begins slowly, almost imperceptibly, speeding up as it takes hold. I would predict that if it is not cleansed within the waxing and waning of two moons its grip on the world will become too strong even for you to reverse."

"So we've got no choice." Tala's head dropped wearily.

"Darkness takes on many guises and those born to fight it can never escape their destiny," said Zane.

"Well, let's hope we don't get carted off to some secret government lab before we even start," Wolfie said bitterly. "With all those earth mysterians poking around trying to work out what revived the leys someone's sure to find something that points to us."

Zane was unperturbed and explained the plan that had been forming in his mind. If the children helped Mr Forester with the magazine, they could intercept any letters from earth scientists that got too near the truth. They might also find important fragments of lost Knowledge that readers sent in relating to cleansing infected ley lines.

"So you see, Mr Forester's impulsive purchase of the *EM* might even have been prompted by the positive energies themselves," he said more cheerfully. "Why don't you email the letters page and start a discussion about dark leys? Put a post on the message board."

"OK," Zi'ib said unenthusiastically.

Wolfie felt like an insect flailing in sticky resin, sinking deeper every time he reached for a way out.

"There's another problem," he said. "Mr Forester is broke. If he can't find some really cheap office space he'll have to give up the *EM*. Then anyone could take it over."

Zane prodded a patch of damp spreading up from the skirting board. "If he did a few repairs he could use this place. It's big enough. Why don't I tell him I've contacted Matthias and he's willing to let the magazine base itself here on a temporary basis?"

"What if Ridian turns up?" said Wolfie.

"I'm sure any plans he had for this house are futile now that the rest of the Manus Sacra have been destroyed."

Zane was unwilling to admit how troubled he was by the thought of Ridian Winter at large in a world contaminated by the forces of the nether void. He walked to the door. "I'd better get back to my manuscript," he said. "But remember, time is against you."

"OK, OK," Zi'ib said, powering up his laptop. "We'll write to *The Earth Mysterian*."

They were confused and angry and it took them nearly half an hour of quibbling and commenting about the style of the letters to the *EM* before they agreed on a single short paragraph.

Dear Sir,

I have come across a major ley line that appears to have become infected with dark energy of a particularly rare and pernicious nature, which may take more than usual methods to cleanse. I am therefore collecting details of energy healing practices from all around the world in the hope that a combination of approaches may prove effective in this case. I would be grateful for any information your readers can supply.

"That should do it," Zi'ib said.

"I'm not leaving it there," Wolfie said, pulling the laptop towards him and typing fast. "We've got to find out more about Spheres – and we haven't got time to wait."

My extensive research into the lost technologies of the ancients has also led me to believe that the inhabitants of certain highly advanced worlds once travelled freely across webs of interplanetary ley lines, using fragments of primal matter known as "Spheres" to open gateways to other worlds. If anyone has come across references to these Spheres, particularly the technologies relating to their capture, or has practical suggestions as to how modern scientific techniques could be applied to their recovery, I would be very interested to hear from them.

"That's good," Tala said, reading over his shoulder.

48

"Who do we sign it from?" Wolfie's fingers hovered over the keyboard.

"Some name that sounds like a serious seeker of lost wisdom without being anyone real," Tala said. "Maybe something foreign."

Zi'ib began plucking words meaning nothing and nobody from the infinite storehouse of languages accessed by his broken star. "Niemand, Nessuno, Nada, Kein."

Tala shook her head. "Too obvious."

"Zip, Zilch, Nil, Naught, Personne, Nemo," suggested Wolfie.

"Nemo's a fish."

"Nikto?" said Zi'ib.

"Nik-to." Tala rolled the syllables across her tongue. "Not bad," she said, "But it needs something mysterious to go with it . . . Kresla, Sombre, Dunkel."

They rattled words around like dice, pairing them at random.

"Got it!" cried Tala. "Nikto Scuro!"

"No," said Wolfie, suddenly sure. "Nikto Senki. It's kind of like Nobody's Shadow."

He could feel Tala's urge to argue so he quickly typed in *Yours sincerely, Nikto Senki*. He flexed his fingers. "Hang on for just two minutes, Mr Senki, and we'll set you up your very own Hotmail account."

Up on the top floor, Zane sat hunched beside a little electric fire, rewriting his book on the lost language of

49

ancient Meroe. He had little appetite for the task, but stranded as he was on this strange backward world with a son to support, it was the only way he knew to make some money.

When he, Arion, Kara and Matthias had arrived from Lupus in search of the Stones of Knowledge, Zane had joined a team of archaeologists led by Professor Yassir Salah, who was excavating the ruined cities of the Meroites in Northern Sudan. No earthly linguist had ever deciphered their ancient language, but for a Lupan explorer in possession of the mastery of tongues, interpreting Meroitic was as easy as reading the *Thornham Gazette*. Eventually, on the walls of a ruined temple, he had found what he was looking for – a telling of the story of the hiding of the stones and the decree that only children whose blood mingled the wisdom of two worlds would be able to find them. He had begun writing a book that revealed the secrets of the Meroitic language, hoping that his translations of the inscriptions would prompt seekers of lost wisdom to join the fight against the Manus Sacra. It was a near-fatal mistake. The Manus Sacra had destroyed his manuscript and cast him into the Wilderness Between the Worlds. Now, despite everything that he, the children, the other explorers and their partners had suffered at the hands of those power-crazed fanatics, he was deeply relieved that the book had never been published. The ancient civilizations of this world had readily accepted the reality of alien life, but he had been shocked to discover how entrenched in fear and ignorance its modern inhabitants had become. Every day since his escape from the Wilderness, he had woken up dreading what might happen to Zi'ib, Wolfie and Tala if their Lupan heritage were ever discovered.

And so in this new version of his manuscript he had omitted the inscriptions relating to the children of mingled blood and left just enough ambiguity in the decipherment of the Meroitic hieroglyphs to baffle anyone who sought to translate them for themselves.

With a tap at the door, Wolfie, Tala and Zi'ib came in looking surly and confused.

"You said only minds attuned to the Wisdom of the Stars and the *four* great wisdoms of this world would have any hope of healing these dark energies," Zi'ib said.

"I did."

"Between us we've only got three: the Wisdom of the Forests, Mountains and Rivers."

"There is a fourth wisdom of this world. The Wisdom of the Winds. Its secrets were scattered even before your guardian ancestors agreed to hide the Stones of Knowledge."

"So we're stuffed, even before we start," Zi'ib said.

"Fragments will have survived and by your wisdom you will know them. I suggest you begin your search in Thornham. It's an important power node. Just as modern power stations keep their fire-fighting equipment on site, so local energy healers would have hidden their tools close by in case something went wrong." Zane's bony hand sought his star. "Promise me you will stay on your guard. Dark energy protects itself by sowing discord among those who seek to purify it. It feeds on their weaknesses and negative emotions. But worst of all, it tempts the wise with dreams of power."

Wolfie and Tala barely remembered leaving Zane's presence. Half an hour later they stood staring helplessly at three new action points on their noticeboard. The notes about capturing the Sphere had been relegated to the bottom of the list.

Cleanse Dark Ley
1 **Find fragments of Wisdom of the Winds**
2 **Look for messages from positive energies**

Slowly the magnitude of the task the positive energies had flung at them began to sink in.

Tala took herself off to the window and as she gazed at the path of the ley that ran north-south straight through Thornham Common, the thought of its evil black stream enveloping the world in darkness and discord swallowed her down into a swirling rush of despair. For a moment she went under, choking, gasping, drowning, certain she could never fight so vast and terrifying a threat. A pang of longing sent her spluttering to the surface.

If she didn't eradicate this contagion she would never see her mother again.

By focusing on that one thought she stopped feeling small and powerless. She pressed the jagged outline of her broken star, imagining the matching half hanging at Kara's throat, somewhere on a distant world.

"Don't worry, Mum," she whispered, "I'm going to do this and then I'm going to bring you home."

5

Someone like Stefan

On the south bank of the River Thames stood the old Battersea power station. Its turbines had been silent for over twenty years and its four great chimneys stood cold and smokeless against the London sky, yet the building retained a haunting majesty. It had recently been purchased by Zemogen International, world leader in alternative energy research and supply, and the first stage of the power station's conversion into their new headquarters was almost complete. A glittering eco dome had replaced the dilapidated roof and the chairman and directors had already moved into their expensively refurbished offices on the top floor, facing the river.

On the floor beneath, in the far northern corner where scaffolding still blocked the view, the chairman's twin brother, Stefan de Witt, Head of Special Projects, sat at his desk, engrossed in a slim pamphlet entitled *A Switch in Time − Controlling the Cosmos: Forester's Theory of the Nature and Action of Celestial Spheres*.

Stefan drew his finger across a diagram of a web of ley lines criss-crossing the earth and reaching out across the cosmos to a scatter of far-flung planets. His face alight, he traced the pattern of tiny Spheres clinging like dewdrops on gossamer to some of the outlying threads. Forester's work impressed him. He knew from bitter experience just how difficult it was to promote ideas that did not fit into the mosaic of accepted thought.

The intercom buzzed.

"Mr de Witt, your 11.30 with the chairman has been cancelled."

"Thank you, Paula." Furious, he glared out at the muddy waters of the Thames and caught the reflection of a balding, disappointed man consumed by slow-boiling resentment.

The intercom buzzed again.

"Mr Winter to see you, Mr de Witt."

Stefan frowned. "He hasn't got an appointment."

"He says it's urgent."

"All right." Stefan buttoned his jacket and smoothed his hair. "Send him in."

He had always felt intimidated by Zemogen's high-powered Head of Development. It was not just that he was an eminent geologist as well as an astute businessman. There was something disconcerting about his brilliant mind, his perpetual air of disdain, his piercing green eyes and his uncanny understanding of every aspect of the energy industry.

Ridian Winter appeared in the doorway, immaculate as ever.

"Ridian, always a pleasure. How was Alaska? Johann's pet thermal project still on course?"

"My trip to Alaska involved a confidential project of my own." Ridian sat down in one of the deep leather armchairs. "In fact, that's why I'm here. Clear your diary for the rest of the day."

Stefan retreated to his desk. "I can spare you twenty minutes. After that I've got back to back meetings."

"We both know that's not true, Stefan."

"I beg your pardon?"

"This executive office and your fancy title don't fool anyone. As far as your colleagues are concerned you're just another of the chairman's charity cases. One minute he's waving cheques at orphans, the next he's giving a seat on the board to a failed academic who just happens to be his twin brother. It all boils down to the same thing: good old Johann de Witt, billionaire philanthropist, to the rescue. No wonder you hate him."

"Johann gave me this job because he values my ability to think out of the box," Stefan said stiffly.

Ridian raised a dark eyebrow. "That last confidential memo you emailed him was *certainly* 'out of the box' . . . what was it now? Oh yes: 'Given the right receptors, the harvesting of the earth's recently restored ley energies could supply all the world's power needs now and for millennia to come?' His secretary leaked it. It's still doing the rounds. The technicians love a good laugh."

"What do you want, Winter?"

"I want you to stop deluding yourself. Johann may invest in your schemes for algae-powered engines and bladeless wind turbines but he never even opens your endless reports about earth grids and ley lines." Ridian's voice grew soft and insidious. "That's because he has no idea just how 'special' your projects could be. I, however, read all your reports with care and I'm also well acquainted with your academic work. Your evidence for the ancients of this world learning sophisticated technologies from alien beings really caught my attention."

Stefan blushed. That was the paper that had brought his academic career crashing to an end.

"You see, I too have an interest in alien life forms." Ridian slipped a memory stick into Stefan's computer and tapped the keys.

"What are you doing?"

"Academe rejects you. Your colleagues at Zemogen deride you. But do exactly as I say and you will soon be taken very seriously indeed." A picture appeared on the screen, showing two blobs of crimson-fringed white, one large, one tiny, glowing against a jet black sky. "This photograph was taken from a private observatory in Chile. The large mass on the left is the star GQ Lupi. The smaller companion mass on the right is a planet."

"I fail to see—"

"Astronomers call that planet GQ Lupi b. The ancient world knew it as the Lands of the Wolf. But what do its *inhabitants* call it?" Ridian paused. "Well, Stefan, *we* call it Lupus."

Stefan eyed him sourly. "If this is supposed to be a joke, Winter, it's in extremely poor taste."

"I assure you, Stefan, this is no joke." There was not the slightest glimmer of amusement in Ridian's cold green eyes and his poised demeanour gave no hint that he was anything but sane. Stefan's mind spun. For years he had nurtured a belief in the existence of alien beings. Was it possible that he was encountering one in his own office? A feeling new to him, half terror, half excitement, shivered down his spine.

"Why are you telling me this?" he demanded.

"Because I have a problem."

"What sort of problem?"

"One that involves three children and the future of the inhabited worlds." Silencing Stefan with a raised palm, Ridian flicked his eyes across the desk. "I see you received the copy of Forester's monograph I sent you."

"You sent me?"

"Of course. Have you acquainted yourself with his theory of celestial Spheres?"

Stefan nodded weakly.

58

"And did you contemplate, just for a moment, what it would be like to possess a Sphere; to hold the power of the leys in your hands; to open gateways to other worlds or even to use its secrets to turn the tides of fate?"

Stefan stared at his hands, recalling the powerful spell Forester's pamphlet had worked on his burnt-out dreams.

"Forester's theories come very close to the truth. I know this because until last week, Lupus possessed a celestial Sphere. Due to some rather unfortunate circumstances, that Sphere is now floating somewhere in the Wilderness Between the Worlds. I want *you* to help me retrieve it." He paused to allow Stefan time to absorb the significance of this offer. "Unfortunately, those children I mentioned stand in our way."

Stefan's doubts were dissolving before Ridian's steady gaze, giving way to a splutter of questions. "Who are these children? And if you're a . . . a Lupan, what are you doing here?"

Ridian pressed the intercom. "Hold Stefan's calls for the rest of the morning, would you, Paula? And bring us some coffee."

The Manus Sacra's ancient motto *The Chosen shall prevail* had sprung from their unshakeable belief that they had been chosen by the powers of the cosmos to wield dominion over all the inhabited worlds. This conviction had sustained them through centuries of hardship, suppression and exile. Their reward, however, had not been victory but annihilation, a shock that had plunged Ridian into despair. For days after the rest of the Manus Sacra had been cast into that dark dimension, known to the ancients as the nether void, he had been paralysed with grief. A return to Lupus would mean certain incarceration by those pompous imbeciles who had hounded the Chosen for centuries, yet the thought of living out his life among the backward fools of this world filled him with revulsion.

He had flown back from Alaska and holed up in his flat in the Barbican, harried by the spectre of what might have been if those half-bred brats had not destroyed centuries of sacrifice and planning. The Manus Sacra would now be in possession of the Sphere of Lupus, using all the resources of Zemogen International to establish their control of the world's ley grid.

The flat was modern and luxurious, much more to his taste than that crumbling monstrosity in Thornham, but he could not eat and dared not sleep, for his dreams were tossed by the storm of fear and destruction that his Lupan star had picked up from his Manus Sacra masters before their Link of Light had gone dead. He knew that the nether void drained spirit from matter like whey from curds. He also knew that while the Manus Sacra's physical bodies would have perished instantly, their conscious minds would be condemned to drift for ever in that churning abyss of desolation.

By day he stared down at the London streets, gripped by

fury that the ignorant, unworthy passers-by were free to live their useless lives while the greatest scholars of all time had been consigned to the darkest pit of the cosmos. By night he lay awake, frenziedly reshaping fragmented recollections of his masters' last desperate thoughts. Yet even amidst their terror, he had sensed their frantic attempts to cast gusts of tainted vapour from the void. But why contaminate the earthly leys? Was it purely revenge against the world that had thwarted their ambition? Questions wheeled round and round his fuddled head until on the third night, a strange and startling thought burst through the fog.

Had his Manus Sacra masters been sowing the seeds of their own salvation?

Freighted by desperation, the powerful engine of Ridian's brain hurtled into wild uncharted territory.

Could the dark energies *of* the void be used to free their disembodied minds *from* the void? And, once released, was there any reason why those magnificent intellects could not be downloaded into worthless human units to allow the Manus Sacra to live again?

Mankind had barely touched the edges of the alchemy necessary to perform such feats, yet he was sure that the matchless minds of his leaders – Therion, Godfrey and Leonora – were even now applying themselves to the problem. If only he could restore the Link of Light they would show him how to push the bounds of science to the limit.

Problems sprang to his mind only to be batted away by the force of logic:

To restore the link he needed the Sphere.

Therefore he would recapture it.

To draw the Sphere down to the earth on a thread of *positive* energy would take years and require much wisdom of this world that was alien to him. To draw it down on a thread of *negative* energy would be much swifter and simpler. But if he brought the Sphere into a world contaminated by the void, he would need to embrace the power of dark energy to control it.

And then, as if a veil had been snatched from his eyes, he saw the great plan of destiny unfolding before him and he felt a throb of wonder at the mysterious workings of the cosmic energies. Far from betraying the Manus Sacra by allowing them to be consigned to the nether void, he was now convinced that those unfathomable powers had in fact been preparing the Chosen for infinite greatness. A greatness sustained not by the hidebound forces of light but by the unfettered forces of darkness!

The words of the Manus Sacra anthem roared through his head, filling his heart with renewed hope and strength.

> *So many moons have waxed and waned*
> *Since we the Chosen few were free.*
> *We watch sweet Wisdom's power profaned*
> *By worthless vassals, foul to see.*
> *Yet we a sacred oath have sworn:*

That pure-bred blood once more will rise.
And when we greet that golden dawn
The worlds shall cower before the wise.

Nothing would stop them this time. Not the power of the positive energies and certainly not the meddling of those children of mingled blood.

Alliances that Ridian would have scorned a week before now became vital to his plans. Confiding in Stefan de Witt was a risk, but as Ridian sat in his office, sipping coffee, he was shaping a carefully edited version of the truth that played to Stefan's weaknesses. He presented the Manus Sacra as visionaries, persecuted for their brilliant minds and denied their rightful control of the inhabited worlds by an ancient conspiracy of Lupan and earthly guardians.

"We needed a place of safety, somewhere we would be free to test the limits of Knowledge. We chose this planet long ago and I've spent decades putting schemes in place and preparing the way for their arrival."

"Why here?" said Stefan, hoarsely.

"Because of this."

Ridian tapped the computer. On the screen appeared a world map that told a story of a lost time; an intricate lacework of dots, more complex than the circuit board of a computer, indicating the vast network of megalithic stone structures that had once girded the earth.

"As you so rightly conjectured, it is quite possible to

power a whole world with earth energies by artificially enhancing the planet's naturally occurring grid of ley lines and power points." He pointed at the screen. "This map shows the scattered remains of just such a system. These are stone energy receptors installed by the ancients of the earth in order to channel, harness and regenerate the world's natural forces."

Stefan blinked and twitched as if emerging from a desolate shadowland into the burning brightness of day. Everything this man was saying confirmed the theories he had struggled all his life to prove.

"The Manus Sacra plan to revive and augment this forgotten grid using the infrastructure of Zemogen. Beginning with Britain, we'll gradually expand the network globally and beyond. And once we have the Sphere and its secrets in our possession we won't just power the inhabited worlds, we will control them."

Stefan's thwarted ambition stirred with life. "Where are the rest of the Manus Sacra?"

"They are waiting patiently on the fringes of the cosmos while I finalize the arrangements here."

"What do you want from me?"

"In the short term I want you to take over the acquisition of certain nodes on the energy grid. At these key points where the leys meet you must oversee the replacement of lost stone circles with modern energy receptors. However, when the Manus Sacra arrive we shall need someone with a profound understanding of earth energies to front Zemogen for us – someone who has always been willing to sacrifice prestige and privilege for the sake of truth. Someone . . . like you, Stefan."

For the first time that morning Stefan challenged Ridian's gaze. "Powering a planet with natural energies isn't just about infrastructure. The ancients spent hours performing complex rituals – that's how they activated vital node points. They walked the ley paths and used the power of focused thought to regenerate the energies. Even when the original techniques were forgotten, the constant treading of the pilgrim roads kept at least some of the paths alive. How can you possibly replicate that kind of mass engagement today?"

Ridian smiled slowly. "Sport."

"What?"

Ridian clicked up a slide showing ariel shots of two circular structures placed side by side. One was of the tall grey boulders of Stonehenge, the other was of a state-of-the-art sports stadium.

"The ceremonies performed at modern sports stadia are every bit as intricate and fraught with meaning as those performed by ancient peoples at their circles of stone."

"Oh, come on. You can hardly compare the two," Stefan said.

Ridian eyed him coolly. "Think about it. The Bronze Age masses and the crowds of modern sports' fans flock to a revered circular space, all psyched up to experience something beyond the ordinary. They fix their attention on an inner area marked out for a special purpose and, collectively, they will an elite group of skilled individuals to achieve a desired outcome."

Stefan's brow grew moist and his mind began to race as the crazy brilliance of Ridian's plan sank in. "How are you going to harness all this psychic force?"

"I've been using Zemogen as a front to develop a major sports sponsorship scheme for some time. The project will enable us to build expertly camouflaged energy receptors right on key power points all across the country."

Stefan goggled at him, overwhelmed by the vastness of Ridian's vision.

"With all this in place why are you so worried about three kids?"

Ridian's voice grew colder. "They are descended from the guardians. Their powers are greater than they know and maturing every day. They must be monitored carefully. However, I have no intention of wasting their unique abilities. When the first phase of my plans has been completed they will play a key role in the implementation of my long term strategy."

"And if they refuse?"

"Then a degree of coercion may prove necessary."

"Who else knows who you are and what you're up to?"

"I brief everyone I employ on my private projects on a need-to-know basis. You are the only one who has any inkling of the overall plan." He studied the tip of his polished shoe. "I assure you that I shall be very, very selective about those I include in the later stages of the scheme, but I guarantee that your role will be pivotal. So, are you with me?"

Dazed, Stefan shook Ridian's outstretched hand.

"There is one more thing you can do for me," Ridian said. "Get on to the Society for the Investigation of Lost Knowledge. Offer them the Zemogen HQ as a venue for their forthcoming conference. Don't worry, I'll square it with Johann. I might even host a small reception in the evening for some specially selected delegates."

Beneath his elegant suit, Ridian was sweating with the effort of toadying to a man like Stefan de Witt. But it would only be a few weeks until the noble mind of one of the Manus Sacra was downloaded into Stefan's body. Keeping up this charade with Stefan and all the other unsuspecting human units was going to be a lot less taxing than the months he had spent playing "Uncle Matthias" to that wily little savage, Tala Bean.

In a distant corner of the Wilderness Between the Worlds, a Sphere of primal matter bobbed and twisted on a stream of cosmic energy, buoyed up by the glittering play of fathomless secrets rippling from its core. Like a child's balloon, slipped from its moorings, the Sphere had drifted through the shattered crystal dome above the Lupan Chamber. And now it was weaving a thread of darkness through the hopes, wiles and stratagems of those who yearned to harness its power, creating undreamed-of patterns in the gauzy fabric of fate.

6

Labs for Life

On Monday morning, the *Thornham Gazette* brought out a special edition with a pull-out "Beast of Thornham" supplement. Wolfie hated supplements because they weighed down his newspaper delivery bag and he particularly hated this one because it had a huge blow-up of Mrs Poskitt's panther photo on the cover.

As he cycled through the gates of Blackstone Comprehensive School, the playground was electric with rumour. Clumps of excited children gathered and dispersed like bacteria on a Petri dish, sharing ever more outlandish stories about the "beast".

"It belongs to an Arab princess who's offering a ruby-studded dagger to anyone who captures it alive," announced Jessica Albright.

"My uncle says it was part of a secret experiment and

the army's got to hunt it down before it creates a race of feline mutants," insisted Freddy Willis.

By far the largest crowd were seething around Marcus Harrison, whose father ran the scrapyard on Dodds Hill. His family's underworld connections were a source of constant admiration to Marcus's friends, who were lapping up his claim that the panther had been smuggled into England by an exotic animal dealer who had been mauled to death trying to stop it escaping. Wayne Snaith came running over waving a copy of the *Gazette*.

"Says here Paper Boy saw it in his back yard," he cried, incredulous. The crowd closed in on Wolfie, hungry for sensation.

"Go on then, what was it like?" demanded Gavin Wicks.

"Erm . . . black and shiny, bit like a . . . bin bag," mumbled Wolfie.

With a collective sneer the crowd moved off to gorge themselves on tales of Arab royalty, army manoeuvres and savaged animal smugglers.

Wolfe slipped away to join Zi'ib and Tala, who were sitting on the wall behind the recycling bins poring over the aerial shot of Thornham spread across the centre of the supplement. Zi'ib traced the little black cat symbols that marked the location of each panther sighting: the sweet shop, the old foundations ot Thornham Hall, St Michael's Church and Dodds Hill. Each place was a key point on the main ley line that cut north-south through the common.

"It's like the panther's been marking its territory," murmured Tala, feeling suddenly sick at the sight of the black cat symbol stamped on the dear old sweet shop.

In assembly, the headmaster, Dr Harker, sought to dampen the mounting hysteria, insisting that the creature could well be a fox or a large cat. But he advised everyone to stay alert, warning them not to take any unnecessary risks. Then he blew his nose and grasped the lectern. "This unfortunate business has rather overshadowed some excellent news we received late on Friday. I'll leave Mr Pegg to explain."

A stocky blond man stepped on to the stage. Like most of the teachers at Blackstone, Terry Pegg, the head of sport, usually sloped about the building with an expression of weary resignation. Today there was a definite spring in his step. He was joined by George Pinkney, who taught geography. "Stinky Pinkney", as he was known to his pupils, was a mousy, unkempt man. He was affable and overweight and if any of his pupils ever thought about him at all, it was to feel sorry for him.

Mr Pegg beamed. "At the end of last term a consortium of major companies calling themselves Labs for Life announced that they would be offering a generous sponsorship package to one lucky school per county. Mr Pinkney and I volunteered to prepare Blackstone's application over the Chrstmas break. To our delight, and I have to admit surprise, we have won."

His announcement met with stunned silence. Blackstone never won anything.

"In the first stage of the partnership, they will build us a state-of-the-art sports complex."

He clicked a remote control. Sparks shot from his laptop. After a moment's muttering and fiddling, a computer-generated view of an elegant sports pavilion appeared on the screen behind him. The building was crowned with a striking Labs for Life logo – two sloping L-shapes of flame set one above the other like a fiery yellow lightning bolt. *Click*. A four-lane athletics track popped up, curved around a huge statue of a young athlete, arm raised to throw a discus. "The consortium will purchase extra land in Whitley Road to accommodate a six-lane sprint track with full athletics facilities."

"Now, any questions?" said Mr Pegg.

Mr Grimes, who taught maths and history, stood up. "What is this consortium going to receive in exchange for their generosity?" he asked drily.

"Ah, Mr Grimes, always the cynic," replied Terry Pegg with a tight smile. "Yes, there is a quid pro quo. Blackstone has to sign up to be a guinea pig for the renewable energy system they are developing. The eighty-six selected schools will be the first institutions in the world to benefit from this revolutionary technology and once it is tried and tested they hope to expand the initiative worldwide."

"Do you know why we have been chosen? Blackstone is hardly renowned for its sporting *or* its academic excellence."

71

"Perhaps they recognized our potential," said Mr Pegg testily. He turned back to the body of the hall. "The Labs for Life sporting events will begin immediately and they're particularly keen to develop strong track and field eventers. Anyone interested in coming along to the tryouts please sign the list on the main noticeboard. However, I'd like to see Raj Patel, Megan Taylor, Marcus Harrison, Wayne Snaith and Zi'ib Bakri in my room after this assembly."

Ten minutes later Zi'ib was standing outside Mr Pegg's office, trying to ignore Marcus, who was eyeing him as if he were a piece of scrap in his father's yard.

"Hey, Charity Boy, heard your dad got parole," sniggered Wayne, thrusting his spotty face at Zi'ib, who stared straight ahead wondering how many punches he could get in before they floored him.

Marcus flicked his fringe. "Nah, he wasn't in the nick, was he, Charity Boy? He just ran off 'cos his kid was such an ugly loser."

He and Wayne cracked up laughing.

"Care to share the joke, Marcus?" Mr Pegg swept past and unlocked his door. "Thought not. Come in, everyone. Now, I believe that you five have exactly the kind of sporting potential our new sponsors are looking for."

"No way," said Marcus, making for the door. "Come on, Wayne."

"That's a shame." Terry Pegg turned on a TV monitor. "Before you go, I wonder if you could help me identify these intruders caught on the school's CCTV over the Christmas holidays."

Two hooded figures crept past the camera. For one brief grainy moment their faces were caught in close up. One was smattered with angry spots, the other had close-set eyes and a dark floppy fringe. Something moved in the distance and they broke into a run.

"See the astonishing agility as they clear that six-foot fence," said Mr Pegg, admiringly.

Marcus curled his lip. "Could be anyone."

"It will be much clearer when we get the footage enhanced. Now, if you'd care to reconsider, I'm sure that you and Wayne could excel at the high jump, hurdles or even the pole vault."

Marcus and Wayne sloped back to their seats.

"Now, Megan, your street dancing performance at the Christmas disco indicates that you've got the makings of a first-class gymnast. And Raj, you're a demon bowler on the cricket pitch so I want you to have a go at shot put and javelin. Zi'ib, I wasn't aware that you had *any* sporting ability until I spotted you chasing a dog the size of an antelope across the common. Amazing. Particularly given your recent injury. I want you to train for the hundred metres."

"I can't, I, er . . . the doctors won't let me."

"Reverend Peasemarsh sent me a note before Christmas saying the hospital had declared you fit for all activities. You've got real ability, Zi'ib. I'm sure you wouldn't want to let Blackstone down."

"S'pose."

"The first Labs for Life sports day is in Wiltshire in three weeks' time, so get your parents to sign one of these release forms and return it to my pigeonhole as soon as possible. There'll be training sessions every Tuesday and Thursday lunchtimes."

He opened a plastic crate. "Help yourselves to some of this kit. There's tracksuits, shorts and T-shirts."

Zi'ib rummaged for a tracksuit in his size. As he pulled one out, his thumbnail ripped on the little golden lightning bolt embroidered on the chest.

Ridian Winter paced his office, seeing always before him the faces of those three guardian brats. He knew Zane Bakri would be urging them to heal the black ley at Thornham; after all, they were the only beings on the whole of this backward planet with the wisdom to do it. They must be stopped. He needed those negative forces. Without them he could not capture the Sphere or draw the minds of the Manus Sacra out of the void. Since he also needed the children alive to complete the second stage of his scheme, he would have to content himself with merely neutralizing their power. First he needed to remove Zane Bakri from Thornham. That would not be difficult.

His thoughts passed through a twisting labyrinth of strategies, hitting dead ends at every turn.

Forget the children's strengths. Focus on their weaknesses.

For all their extraordinary wisdom those guardians were still lesser mortals, impaired by sentiment and desperate to be reunited with their parents. Perhaps at this very moment Tala and Wolfie were dreaming of capturing a Sphere and using it to unlock a cosmic gateway to bring Arion and Kara back from Lupus.

A path began to open before him. Dreams and desperation! That's what he would exploit. Slowly, surely he gathered the makings of a plan.

Somehow he must convince the children that the best way to capture a Sphere was by using dark energy. Difficult! Zane Bakri would have told them that that would contaminate the Sphere and that old busybody Forester who had just taken over *The Earth Mysterian* would be warning them against the evils of meddling with dark forces.

Unless . . . well, unless this information reached them through someone whose influence outweighed even that of Bakri and Forester.

There was no one.

What about a message from the past? A fake inscription in Meroitic perhaps, purporting to be from one of their guardian ancestors?

Too clumsy, too impersonal. The messenger had to be able to manipulate the children subtly, over time.

A *voice* from the past?

Wasn't there some kind of psychic who wrote for *The Earth Mysterian*? Dame something or other. He googled her. Dame Esmé Hiram Glottis. A "past life regressionist", she called herself. What if Dame Esmé suddenly discovered a former self who had been one of the children's guardian ancestors? One of the very sages who had first hidden the Stones of Knowledge? He smiled. If the priestess Kandass of ancient Meroe spoke to them in a lost language that only they understood, that should convince them she was authentic. He buzzed his PA and requested an immediate background check on Dame Esmé.

The preliminary report arrived within two hours, revealing that Esmé not only wrote for *The Earth Mysterian*, she was also one of its financial backers. How very useful. The dark energies were with him! There was no doubt in his mind of that.

Glistening in the lamplight, the crystal dangled from the silver chain in Zi'ib's hand, poised for instruction. Spread beneath it on the attic floor lay a map of Thornham marked with the enormous star of leys that branched from the site of the lost stone circle on the common. There had been a time when Wolfie, Tala and Zi'ib had been frightened by their preternatural ability to dowse the ley energies with pendulums and rods, but now it felt like just another of their senses, sharpened and attuned to forces they did not understand but were learning to accept.

A shiver shook their stars as the gleaming facets of the crystal focused their concentration like a magnifying glass intensifying the rays of the sun. Instead of the familiar sharp tingle of positive energy they felt stabs of gloom shooting from the pendulum.

"Please, show us how far the negative energies have spread," faltered Zi'ib and slowly the crystal began to swing along the axis of the ley, dipping south to the sweet shop and moving steadily north through the old foundations of Thornham Hall, the church, Dodds Hill and up to the swimming baths.

"The taint's spread at least a mile already," Tala said, her voice trembling. "But why only northwards?"

"There must be something at the shop stopping it spreading south," said Zi'ib.

Wolfie saw Elvis stiffen as if sensing danger. His consternation broke the connection.

"Where's all this help Zane said the positive energies would be giving us?" he moaned.

Tala gazed out at the sliver of new moon, thin as a nail paring in the night sky. "I dunno, but we're not going to hang around waiting for it to turn up."

"Mr Forester said on World Watch there might be hints of ancient technologies left in local myths and ceremonies," said Zi'ib. "So come on, what are the traditional customs of Thornham?"

Wolfie shrugged. "Mostly spraying graffiti on the railway arches and setting fire to wheelie bins. There is this raising of the giants thing some time around now, but it's just a load of old codgers prancing round..." his gaze flicked to the window, a frisson of associations shaking his star, ". . .the common."

Tala said in a grave, quiet voice, "A processional rite that takes place on the site of the ancient stone circle can't be a bad place to start."

7

PiZazz

The big old-fashioned fridge in the kitchen at number forty-five hummed noisily as Zi'ib poked through the shelves. "What about egg and chips?" he suggested to his father.

Over the past two weeks he had grown to love this time after school: deciding what they would eat, cooking it while Zane asked about his day, the gentle clatter of cutlery and plates. But tonight his star was in turmoil. Something had happened, he had sensed it all day.

Zane said, "Don't worry, we're going for pizza."

No! Zi'ib reached for the eggs, clinging to their nightly ritual. "I'd rather stay home."

Zane touched his son's arm. "Zi'ib. Look at me. I've heard from an aid project in western Sudan. Your mother may have been seen in a refugee camp on the

Chadian border. The lead is tenuous but I have to follow it up."

Although Zi'ib had dreamed of this moment from the day of his mother's abduction, the edge in his father's voice made his lip quiver. "When do we leave?"

"I'm sorry, Zi'ib, I have to go on my own."

Zane's words were dissolving Zi'ib's fragile world. He'd only just been reunited with his father and now he was losing him again. "You're ill, you need me to come."

"I can't take you. It's too dangerous. The camp was attacked. Some of the aid workers were killed and the refugees fled into the bush."

"How are *you* going to survive in the bush?" Zi'ib's voice was tight and shaky. "Look at you, you can hardly stand up."

"It isn't just the danger. You have a job to do here."

Zi'ib slammed the fridge shut. "I don't want to cleanse that stupid ley, I don't want to be a guardian. I want to find Mum! And don't you dare start on about it being an honour to be chosen to fight the dark. It's crap and you know it!"

Zane stood firm against this onslaught of misery. Seeing it was useless, Zi'ib slumped into a chair. "How long . . . will you be gone?" he choked.

"As long as it takes to find her. You mustn't worry. I'll get stronger as soon as I'm away from Thornham."

"How can you know that?"

"The dark vibrations are sounding in my blood so I can

barely think or breathe." Zane lowered his head, ashamed. "You see, once long ago I visited a dark world and almost succumbed to the negative energies, and now they are seeking out my weakness, defiling my thoughts. I . . . I don't trust myself to stay."

Zi'ib stepped back, shocked by his father's admission. Then he turned away, not a guardian but a kid again, alone, afraid. Where could he go? There was no room at Wolfie's and he dreaded the thought of sleeping on his own in this creepy old house.

"Don't worry. I've had a long talk today with Sarah and Mr Forester. He is going to move in here, Tala will have his old room and I've ordered bunks for the attic for you and Wolfie. We're taking them all out to eat, to say thank you. Now come on, wash your face and get your coat."

PiZazz, the new pizza parlour in the back of the Wish Hound pub, flickered with candlelight and buzzed with diners eager to try out Thornham's latest attraction. Wolfie and Tala watched Zi'ib squeeze through the tables towards them, his eyes red and his hands thrust deep in his pockets.

"Just a small side salad for me," Sarah said when the waitress came to take their orders.

Wolfie studied his mother's face in the candlelight, shocked to see how run-down she looked. A thin thread of fear tightened around his thoughts.

Zane raised his glass and said, "To you, Sarah, my

heartfelt thanks for all your kindness to me and my son. And to you, Remus. Long may *The Earth Mysterian* flourish under your firm and steady hand."

Everyone clinked glasses and Mr Forester took a sip of wine. "Without your kind offer, Zane, there would *be* no magazine." He swirled the liquid in his glass. "The more I think about it, the more convinced I become that the leys themselves had a hand in entrusting me with such propitious premises, right on the eastern entrance to Thornham's lost stone circle. It makes me feel like an ancient priest, just as you, Sarah, are the priestess of the southern entrance."

Sarah smiled and shook her head.

"I'm quite serious, my dear." He set the salt and pepper shakers and the vials of oil and vinegar in a square, tapping them in turn. "Imagine these to be the vicarage, the sweet shop, this pub and number forty-five – built on sites that once marked the northern, southern, eastern and western entrances to the stone circle. Now that the earth is once more brimming with energy it's imperative that these cardinal nodes are held by those who will keep them pure."

"I'm not sure I'll be much help there," said Sarah.

"That's where you are wrong. You have made the shop into a loving home. What better way to keep the contaminated energies at bay? But I'm very worried about the vicarage. Mrs Poskitt heard they're going to sell it and buy the next vicar a bungalow on Blackthorn Drive." He glanced over his shoulder. "And I'm a little concerned about the new owners of this pub." He tapped the word PiZazz on the front of the menu. "Apart from their inability to spell, no one seems to know much about them."

The candle flame flared briefly, catching the gold in the children's eyes before guttering into a tendril of black.

Mr Forester raised his glass. "And so, my thanks to you, Zane, for giving the *EM* a home." His voice caught in his throat. "And here's to the success of your trip to find Shadia. Our thoughts go with you."

Zi'ib stared at his plate. Although the uncertainty about his mother was horrible, certainty might be unbearable. In the warm glow of the restaurant, surrounded by people he had grown to trust, he eventually managed to force down a few bites of pizza.

"I'll be in and out of the shop for meals and so forth but I do hope you'll all be popping round to see me," said Mr Forester. He smiled awkwardly at Zi'ib. "In fact, I wondered if you might come over and help with the *EM* website. The last editor was developing an interactive ley line map, which is quite beyond me."

"OK," murmured Zi'ib.

"And I could do some illustrations for you," said Wolfie.

"I'd really like to have a go at writing something," Tala said quickly. "How about I have a go at a report on that giant raising ceremony they do on the common every year?"

"All right," Mr Forester said, "let's put your talents to

the test. The giant raising takes place next Monday. Write me eight hundred words on giant raising past and present. And Wolfie, I've commissioned a piece on the connections of the de Monteneuf family with the Knights Templar that could do with an illustration. What about a sketch of the de Monteneuf tombs in St Michael's Church?"

That night, Zi'ib dreamt his father was lost once more in the Wilderness Between the Worlds. He glimpsed Zane's wraith-like figure silhouetted against a crag of emptiness and watched it slowly crumple and fall into the gaping dark. Zi'ib shouted "Baba, Baba!" and drove himself on until his lungs burned, but the tracksuit Mr Pegg had given him was dragging him back, clinging to his body like slimy seaweed, crushing him beneath its weight. He woke up screaming. Zane came running and held him tightly for a long, long time, murmuring that they would probably only be parted for a few weeks and that he would phone whenever he could. It was no good. Neither of them could shake off the terrifying spectre of Zane's last disappearance at the hands of the Manus Sacra or the pain of their long, lonely years of separation.

Zane left the next day, rushing to the airport at dawn in a taxi. Wolfie, Tala and Zi'ib cycled home from school that evening beneath darkening storm clouds that swelled and scudded like shapeless unspoken fears. A rickety green van with goggle headlamps and a long low bonnet shot out of a side street, nearly knocking them over, before hiccoughing away down Whitely Road. Wolfie zoomed ahead to tell the driver to get his eyes tested, and was horrified when Elvis poked his head through the passenger window. Pedalling crazily he drew level with the driver. It was Mr Forester, who waved genially and hit the brakes.

"Where'd you get the van?" panted Wolfie.

"It's one of the assets of *The Earth Mysterian*. The garage wouldn't release it until I'd settled their bill."

"Where'd you get the money?"

"I sold some advertising space. Some huge company have paid up front for a double page spread every month for a year." He tooted the horn. "Hop in. I'll take you for a spin."

Dumping their bikes in the back, they clambered in and the van wheezed across town, heading for Dodds Hill.

At the traffic lights they drew up beneath a vast billboard image of the Grand Canyon. The only lettering was a deeply shadowed fissure that etched the shape of a huge black Z through the sunlit rocks.

"That's the poster version of the ads I'm running in the *EM*," Mr Forester said. "What is it the company call themselves, Zumofen? Zomochem? Can't remember. I've got their letter in the office."

"What do they make?" asked Zi'ib.

"Renewable energy of some sort. Their whole campaign

is based on marvellous photos of the world's most dramatic landscapes. They're obviously out to make an impact."

As the lights turned green the storm broke, hammering raindrops on the roof of the van. Oncoming headlights loomed misty and blurred through the sweep of the windscreen wipers. They reached the brow of Dodds Hill. A weird crackling rippled the air. With a curdling howl Elvis hurled himself across Mr Forester's lap. He lost control, the van slewed round, hung for a sickening second on one wheel and smashed with a grinding crunch against the kerb. On the opposite pavement, a flash of blue fire snickered up the shaft of a telegraph pole, sending a burst of sparks sputtering along the trembling cables. With a screeching and tearing of wood the pole crashed across the road and slammed down in front of the van, still spitting darts of flame. All around them cars screamed to a halt. Unhurt but quaking, the children scrambled out of the van. Choked by a sickly sulphurous smell, they gazed at the smouldering pole. A patch of darkness shaped the air like a splash of liquid velvet. Two sparks of amber glared from its depths, fizzing with menace before melting into the gleam of headlights dancing on the wet tarmac. Everyone stared down the hill at the dark expanse of the common spread below. The soft glow of the distant sweet shop only confirmed what they already knew. The fallen telegraph pole lay directly in the path of the dark ley.

No one spoke as Mr Forester reversed the van and took the long way back to number forty-five. No one commented when he stopped off at the butcher's to buy Elvis a very large rump steak.

"Don't worry," he said shakily, handing round mugs of sweet herbal tea. "The people from SILK are doing their best to find someone who can purge these negative energies, and failing that we'll put out an emergency appeal to all the delegates at their forthcoming conference."

The children stared silently into their mugs, wishing they could take comfort from his words.

8

Dame Esmé
Hiram Glottis

Dame Esmé Hiram Glottis took the 4.00 train from Victoria to Thornham Junction and set off briskly down the gum-spattered pavements. She had expected rather more of this planetary power centre, but it seemed that Ridian's reports of a badly infected ley were true. The whole place had a nasty oppressive atmosphere that threatened to bring on one of her migraines. The decrepit exterior of number forty-five did nothing to improve her mood. She took a deep breath, rang the bell and flicked a chip of crumbling concrete from the step with the tip of her umbrella.

An elderly red-faced man opened the door. She cast a glance of chilly appraisal over his tweed plus fours and crumpled jacket.

"Remus Forester?"

"Yes indeed. Dame Esmé, thank you so much for coming all this way."

"One can learn an awful lot by bearding a person in their lair."

"Quite so."

Mr Forester cast a glance up the stairs. Tala leaned down to give him an encouraging smile. The boys had retreated, giggling at the bizarre concoction of silk and net perched on Esmé's head like an abandoned bird's nest.

"Lead on, Mr Forester," commanded Esmé. "My time is precious."

"Snotty old bag," fumed Tala.

Dame Esmé advanced into the sitting room and met the unnerving gaze of an enormous grubby dog.

"Is that animal safe?"

"Elvis? Oh yes, perfectly."

Her nostrils flared, picking up the smell of damp.

"Am I to understand that you propose to run *The Earth Mysterian* from *here*?"

"That's right," replied Mr Forester, closing the door. He looked about him, as if seeing the grim decor for the first time. "I have some young friends who have kindly offered to help me decorate. Do sit down. Would you like some tea?"

Dame Esmé plucked off her gloves. "In a moment. First, I wish to know how this miserable state of affairs has come about."

"Sadly, the last editor fell victim to declining sales, rising costs and some very unwise personal investments. I couldn't stand by and watch the *EM* go under so I bought him out." He smiled nervously. "With the continued support of generous backers such as your good self, I am sure I can make it work."

"And what are your aims for the magazine?"

"My aim, Dame Esmé, is to change the world by changing its priorities. I'm very worried about the electromagnetic activity occurring around ancient energy receptors. The massive influx of fresh earth energy now firing off the broken circuitry is already beginning to disrupt the modern networks that channel our electricity, broadband, radio waves and heaven knows what else. If we don't repair the old system there will be chaos. The earth energy could end up destroying the whole infrastructure of the so-called developed world until only the societies who live by the power of natural forces would be able to function. Harmony would be restored, but at what cost?

"My first policy for the magazine is therefore to spearhead a programme of mass re-education to restore the neglected systems and technologies of the ancients."

"Hmm. And how do you propose to achieve this laudable goal?"

"By commissioning contributors able to marry the wisdom of the remote past to the cutting edge of modern science."

She smiled inwardly and leaned back in her chair.

Forester's sense of mission and desperate need for funds made him as malleable as dough.

Born plain Muriel Peebles, Dame Esmé had been orphaned as a child and raised by a mean-spirited aunt. Muriel, however, was a survivor who quickly learned how to steal a few coins from her aunt's purse and shift the blame on to her spiteful yet slow-witted cousins. She spent the money on cinema tickets and endured the intervening days by reliving the movies scene by scene, playing all the roles from honey-voiced slave girls to thundering sheiks with remarkable vocal dexterity.

Too plain and scrawny to pursue her dream of an acting career, she left school at fifteen to work in the millinery department of a leading London fashion house. While there, her snatched glimpses of the most celebrated women of the day spurred her ambition and she vowed – with her right hand laid reverentially on a bolt of ivory crêpe de Chine – that one day she too would command riches and respect.

Called upon one afternoon to deliver a hat to a well-known medium, Muriel was invited to make up the numbers at a séance. That afternoon, amidst the rattling tambourines, the groaning and clamouring and the flickering lamplight of Madame Azzari's drawing room she realized that the world of the paranormal was one in which, if she were blessed with imagination and a limber voice box, a girl as plain and uneducated as she could shine.

However, Muriel did not really fancy talking to the dead – all that ectoplasm could get very messy. Instead, she invented several exotic former lives and a gift for recalling them, jogging the memories of her previous incarnations with snippets of fact and fantasy gleaned from the *National Geographic* magazine and Hollywood movies. At her "demonstrations" in Madame Azzari's back room, Sophanisba, a Trojan dancing girl, Sargon, a Mesopotamian king, and the Amazonian queen Thalestris channelled their wisdom through her thin, painted lips and offered counsel to those seeking spiritual guidance. Usefully, all three of Esmé's former incarnations had made regular visits to the legendary island of Atlantis, a spot on the ancient globe they could describe at length without fear of contradiction.

Muriel soon left the fashion house, taking with her, purely as a memento, a golden hatpin in the shape of a ruby-eyed snake, mislaid by the Maharani of Jaipur. She changed her first name to Esmé and her second to Hiram (after the mystical mason who had built the temple of Solomon) and spent her mornings in second-hand bookstores gobbling up tales from the past to regurgitate as her own, quickly discovering that the truth about the ancient world was far more dramatic than anything she could invent.

During her researches she caught tantalizing glimpses of the true potential of the natural forces that mankind had once harnessed and revered and it was these fields of study that sustained her columns in *The Earth Mysterian*. However, the income generated from her articles was minimal compared to the money she made from her "psychic" work.

For all her professional success, Esmé searched endlessly for meaning in her life. The day she met a handsome stage hypnotist named Frankie Fontaine she believed she had found it. They danced that night until dawn, wrapped in each other's arms. Within a week they were married. As a wedding present, Esmé mortgaged her flat to pay off Frankie's creditors. The following day he took a ship to Buenos Aires, leaving Esmé with a pile of debts, bitterness in her heart and an old, vellum-bound Bible he had won at poker. The Bible had once belonged to a family called von Glottis and, according to the family tree on the flyleaf, the last of their line had died before the war. Loathe to let their noble name and title go to waste, Esmé took them for her own. That day she was reborn as Dame Esmé Hiram Glottis and soon, the only remaining traces of her former incarnation as Muriel Peebles were a love of hats and a taste for tinned tomato soup.

Esmé soothed her heartache by throwing herself into her work and for years the words flowed from her lips and fingertips as smoothly as the income from her best-selling books and prime-time show on the Mystic Minds TV channel poured into her bank account. But over the past few months younger seers and psychics had begun to undermine her position by agreeing to be investigated by

93

sceptical scientists with lie detectors and all manner of invasive technology. Esmé's refusal to submit to such public probings had resulted in plummeting book sales and the cancellation of her TV show.

She had been in despair, when a man called Ridian Winter had walked into her life and spun her a strange tale of other worlds, ancient stones and children of mingled blood, born to save the leys. Astonished and dismissive at first, she had studied him with the practised eye of a professional psychic, skilled at "cold reading" the nuances of her client's body language. Although she sensed he was holding something back, it appeared that at least some of his story was true. When he offered her a role in an audacious scheme to take control of the world's ley grid, she had agreed, deciding that she had little to lose and quite possibly everything to gain.

Her first task was to gain some editorial control of the *Earth Mysterian* magazine. Her second was to invent a previous incarnation called Kandass, a priestess of ancient Meroe who was to convince the children of mingled blood to embrace the power of darkness. Ridian gave her lines to learn in the strange guttural tongue of the Meroites, rehearsing her for hour upon hour until her pronunciation was perfect.

9

Kandass

D ame Esmé shook her head. "I'm sorry, Mr Forester, I applaud your vision but you just don't have the experience to run a magazine as prestigious as *The Earth Mysterian*."

The old man's face crumpled.

"However, I am prepared to make you an offer. I will double my current investment in exchange for an equal share of the editorial responsibility *and* the business. That way I can protect my own interests as well as those of the magazine."

"Noooo," hissed Wolfie, his ear pressed to the keyhole. "She's trying to take over the *EM*."

Tala reached for the door handle. "I'm going in."

"Hang on!" called Zi'ib, picking up his laptop and stumbling after her.

Caught off guard, Esmé turned sharply to see three scruffy children, one dark, one fair, one olive skinned. And those eyes! They were just as Ridian had described. Esmé shrank back, her mouth a crimson pucker. Could they really be of mingled blood?

"My dear lady," said Mr Forester. "There's no cause for alarm. This is Tala, Wolfie and Zi'ib, the young friends who are helping with the magazine. Now, why don't I make us all some tea?" He retired to the kitchen, eager for a moment to himself to consider Esmé's offer.

Tala glared at Esmé, perturbed by the strangely conflicting sensations this woman triggered in her star. She said fiercely, "If you care so much about the *EM* just lend Mr Forester the money. He doesn't need you telling him what to put in it."

"How dare you speak to me like that! You will kindly address me as *Dame* Esmé."

"Why should we?" said Zi'ib, "I've just checked the honours lists – you're no more of a dame than Elvis."

Esmé said loftily, "It's an ancient Prussian title, passed down through my late husband's family. Dame is an approximate anglicization of the German Altgraefin."

Zi'ib pointed to two extracts highlighted on his laptop. "It says here the von Glottises are lower nobility, so they never had titles, and here that the last of 'em got drowned in the Baltic Sea in 1933."

Esmé glanced at the screen and raised a painted eyebrow. "I see," she said slowly. "Those documents are in old German and . . . is that Russian? Fluent, are you?"

"We . . . um . . . do German and Russian at school," Zi'ib said quickly.

They possessed the mastery of tongues! Esmé stared into the depths of the boy's strange green eyes, sensing fear, sorrow and a weight of responsibility heavier than any child should bear. All lingering doubt about Ridian's strange tale disappeared. These really were the children of mingled blood born to be guardians of the leys! Awe threatened to overwhelm years of embittered self-interest. The battle was brief and brutal. Self-interest won. A steely flicker passed over Esmé's face.

Mr Forester backed through the door with a laden tea tray. "It's one of my own herbal brews, Dame Esmé, I hope that's all right. Try this delicious fudge, Wolfie's mother made it."

As he began to pour the tea, Esmé rolled back her eyes and in a rich rumbling voice cried out in the sacred tongue of the Meroite priests: "Hail to thee, O ye children of mingled blood born to be guardians of the forces of the earth."

An astonished sob rose in Tala's throat. She choked it down.

"I, Kandass, high priestess of the temples of Meroe swear to you that from the shadows of my grave I shall guide you down the path of true wisdom. And know ye this: the power of darkness is but the dark mirror of the power of light and each has its rightful place in the great mystery of the cosmos."

"Dame Esmé, are you all right?" said Mr Forester.

Esmé dabbed her face with the back of her hand, gratified by the looks of horror and disbelief on the children's faces.

"Just ignore me. Sometimes I struggle to control my former selves and the priestess Kandass is so terribly strong willed. . ." She smiled blandly. "Did she say anything . . . interesting?"

"I'm not sure," said Mr Forester. "It was in a language I didn't recognize."

"How curious. My past selves usually communicate in English. The trouble is, when I'm in deep trance I have no idea what they are saying."

Mr Forester frowned. "So how do you know what to put in your books?"

"I record the sessions and transcribe them afterwards." Disturbed by Elvis's penetrating stare she shifted round to block him from view. "While you were away your young friends and I had a most enlightening chat."

"I hoped you would get on," murmured Mr Forester. "All three of them have developed an interest in lost wisdom and they're stupendous dowsers. They work with a sensitivity I've never encountered before."

"Indeed, Mr Forester. I realized they were *special* the moment I saw them." She paused as if listening to a distant murmur. "I have the strongest feeling that they were all born near cosmic gateways."

"Extraordinary, Dame Esmé!" exclaimed Mr Forester.

"Tala was born at the foot of Mount Shasta, Wolfie, here in Thornham, and Zi'ib near the site of ancient Meroe in Sudan. I'm sure the leys drew them together for a purpose, but we've never been able to work out what it might be."

"How very . . . interesting. So, Zi'ib, my dear, where are your parents now?"

Seeing Zi'ib's pain at this question, Mr Forester said hurriedly, "Oh, his father is in Sudan at this very moment. More fudge?"

She helped herself to a piece. "Mmm, what is that unusual flavour?"

"Ah, it's the secret ingredient. Wolfie's mother grows it herself. She cultivates the cuttings in the airing cupboard!"

"I see. Now, have you made a decision about my offer?"

Mr Forester's eyebrows drooped. "Yes, Dame Esmé. Given the current state of the magazine's finances I have decided to accept. I'm sure that with a little, um, give and take on both sides, together we can take the *EM* to new heights."

"Excellent! My lawyer will be in touch."

Esmé chewed the fudge, testing the children with her eyes.

"Rather than preparing one of my usual *EM* columns for your first edition I think I'll use one of Kandass's far memories."

She glanced at her watch. "I mustn't miss my train."

She smiled sweetly at the children as Mr Forester helped

her with her coat. "It's been delightful to meet you. I'm sure we'll be seeing a lot of each other from now on."

"Indeed, Dame Esmé," said Mr Forester as she sailed down the steps, "and thank you again."

"How curious," he said, closing the door. "She sensed you were all born on cosmic gateways."

"She was just guessing," Wolfie said quickly.

"Unlikely," Mr Forester said thoughtfully. "And you know it was Einstein himself who said that the mysterious lies at the cradle of true science."

The children dashed back upstairs.

Tala cried shakily, "What are we going to do? She knows. She knows everything about us."

"Not necessarily," Wolfie said, trying to keep calm. "She says she's got no idea what's happening when she's in a trance. So even if she records what she spouts in Meroitic she won't understand it."

"I was sure she was a fake till she started burbling all that stuff," said Zi'ib.

"Do you think this . . . Kandass . . . I mean is it possible some dead priestess is really trying to communicate with us?"

The thought was both bizarre and troubling, but how else could Esmé have known who they were or spoken to them in the lost language of the Meroites?

"Maybe this Kandass is trying to help us cleanse the ley."

"It sounded to me like she thought dark energy was . . .

good. She said something about the power of darkness having its rightful place. It's blimmin' freaky," said Zi'ib. "I wish Dad was here."

Tala giggled nervously. "Did you see her piggy little eyes glinting?"

"And her stupid hat wobbling?" grinned Zi'ib.

"And her lips trembling like strips of raw liver?"

Wolfie stared into Zi'ib's face. "I've had a thought."

"What?"

"If you're descended from the guardian priestess Kandass. . ."

"Yeah."

"And Esmé really is her reincarnation. . ."

"Yeeahh?" said Zi'ib, guardedly.

"Then you and Esmé . . . are related! Come to think of it, I can see the family resemblance."

Tala rolled back her eyes like a demented ghoul and bore down on Zi'ib, cackling, "Come on, Zi'ib, give your Aunty Esmé a nice kissy."

It seemed like weeks since they had laughed and joked together, but all too soon their worries closed over them like choking smog.

Esmé boarded the train at Thornham Junction, trying to rejoice in the success of her mission, but she felt strangely uneasy. Far from having to engineer a meeting with those children, they had appeared from nowhere, even providing her with proof of their mastery of tongues to dispel her

101

doubts about Ridian's story. She had certainly rattled them, though, just like he wanted.

She sent a text to Ridian.

I think they bought it. Full report to follow. Can confirm that Zane Bakri has returned to Sudan.

Her carriage slowed beside a floodlit poster of a zigzag of cliffs jutting into a tranquil sea at sunset, before the train sped onwards into the dusk.

She gazed out at the pebble-dashed silhouettes of suburbia, imagining the rich dramas unfolding behind those doors and windows; dramas that a lonely spinster could only glimpse as a shadow on a curtain or a snatch of laughter drifting through a doorway. Esmé closed her eyes, and imagined herself embracing those children of mingled blood, offering to help them as Kandass had once helped the green-eyed wanderers from Lupus to hide the Stones of Knowledge.

"No!" she cried aloud.

The young couple in the opposite seats sniggered and snuggled closer. Esmé scowled at them, swatting away an image of her younger self wrapped in Frankie's arms. The scars on her wounded heart had hardened her against all sentiment. An opportunity like the one Ridian Winter was offering came only once in a lifetime, she smiled, or once in many lifetimes, and she, Dame Esmé Hiram Glottis, was not about to let it slip through her fingers.

Ridian smiled down at Esmé's text. How foolish these lesser Lupans were! All it had taken was a planted rumour and a couple of phone calls for Zane Bakri to run off in search of his missing wife like a mangy cur sniffing after a bone.

Even with Zane out of the way, Ridian still feared that those kids might heal the contaminated energies before he discovered how to use them to release the minds of the Manus Sacra from the void. He had learned to his cost that the positive energies in the leys often found the unlikeliest of people to aid the bloodlines of the guardians. Usually these so-called "righteous helpers" had no idea of the role they had played in turning the tides of fate. He must get Esmé to monitor every new person who came into the children's lives.

10
Mo

The demand for Brown's Traditional Fudge was growing fast. One new customer (Sarah thought it must be a coffee shop though she hadn't caught the name) had already phoned through two bulk orders that week and ordered a third for collection on Saturday lunchtime. She put its popularity down to the distinctive smokiness of the secret ingredient, the purple flowered Saravita. Unfortunately, the only place she had ever found it growing was in the cracks of the sweet-shop walls and now that the panther had eaten half the cuttings she was struggling to produce enough.

She had put Tala in charge of slicing the newly set fudge into squares. Tala took the job extremely seriously, cutting each cube with the precision of a master mason and, unlike Sarah, she didn't let anyone eat the scrapings left in the bottom of the trays. Instead she scooped them into little plastic bags, sealed them using a damp cloth and the tip of the iron, called them Fudge-bits – soon shortened to Fidgits – and sold them for 20p a bag.

Wolfie and Zi'ib, who had grudgingly agreed to spend Saturday morning helping her to meet the midday deadline, were now seriously regretting it. She had been bossing them about for hours, complaining they couldn't cut straight and slapping their hands whenever they absent-mindedly raised a square to their lips. They were all feeling grumpy and anxious.

Sarah was stacking shelves in the shop, refusing to give in to the ache in her head and wondering if the doctor would give her some stronger painkillers. She emptied a carton of crisp packets into the display rack and called to Wolfie to bring her another box of cheese and onion.

Muttering darkly about having to do *everything* round here, Wolfie climbed the wooden ladder in the storeroom and reached for the crisps. The shop bell jangled. Peeking through the curtained doorway to the shop he saw a tall handsome man in a coat of wheat-coloured leather. His chestnut hair, thinning very slightly at the temples, fell back from a high narrow forehead, revealing wide-set grey eyes and a slender nose with an odd little tilt at the end. The stranger crossed the floor in two fluid strides, clasped Sarah by the shoulders and pulled her to her feet. She jerked round. Wolfie leapt from the ladder, ready to rush to her aid. He stopped, utterly flummoxed when she broke into a smile. What was going on? His mum didn't know anyone who looked like that.

"M-Mo," stammered Sarah. "I can't believe it." She seemed pleased and embarrassed at the same time. Struggling to free her hands from the man's embrace she pushed her hair out of her eyes.

"What are you doing in Thornham?" she asked.

"I missed the old place."

Sarah pulled a face. "I don't think so. I saw that spread on you in the paper. *The enigmatic Englishman, New York's most influential gallery owner.*"

Mo laughed. "New York's been great but Lucy says it's no place to bring up a kid, and anyway the time was right to come home. I want to open a London gallery and a couple of my artists have got big exhibitions here this year. Jenna Falkirk – you remember her, she was in the year below us – she's creating the next installation at the Turbine Hall at Tate Modern and. . ." He trailed off, aware of Sarah's barely held smile.

Wolfie started to breathe again. This Mo was married with a kid, and anyway he'd stopped hugging Sarah quite so tightly and had pulled back to look at her.

Troubled to see his old friend looking so thin and drawn, Mo said softly, "You're not . . . ill, are you, Sarah?"

She shrugged herself free. "No, I'm fine, just tired."

Wolfie shrank into the shadows as Mo's eyes swept the shop, taking in the drab reality of Sarah's world. "Last time I saw you, you were taking a year out to look after your dad. What happened? You were tipped for great things, Sarah, all our tutors said so."

"Dad got worse and worse. I had my hands full looking after him and the shop, then I met Ron . . . and about a year later my son Wolfie came along." She paused. "Then Ron . . . left and Dad died. Suddenly I was on my own with a baby and I had to earn a living."

Wolfie knew the story well, but hearing his mother tell it to this wealthy stranger made him sweaty and uncomfortable.

"Why didn't you sell up?"

Sarah looked shocked. "I couldn't. This shop's been in our family for generations."

Wolfie barged through the door. Tala and Zi'ib, alerted by his alarm, trailed behind. "We've run out of cheese and onion," he said, breathing in the heady aroma of leather and expensive aftershave. The man looked up.

"Mo, meet Wolfie, Tala and Zi'ib," said Sarah. "This is Mo, an old friend from art school. Do you remember, Wolfie, I showed you an article about him in the paper?"

Wolfie frowned. It was coming back to him. "You're the one with the bathroom the size of a football pitch."

Mo smiled. "I think they took that shot with a wide-angled lens, but yes, our New York apartment is ridiculously oversized. I've got a daughter about your age; we must get the four of you together."

Wolfie threw him a scornful look. Why did adults say stuff like that? You never caught kids saying I know some

107

other old guy who's going a bit bald, so you're sure to want to hang out together.

"What's her name?" asked Sarah.

"Artemesia."

Wolfie and Tala exchanged glances.

"OK, it was Lucy's idea. I wanted to call her Jean after my mother. We call her Missy. She's a great kid. I'm sure you'd all get on really well."

No we wouldn't, thought Wolfie. Any daughter of Mo's would be a spoiled brat who had a butler to pick her nose for her.

"Hopefully I'll be spending a lot of time round here. I've just closed a deal with Jim Pullen."

"That sleazy bloke who owns the cash and carry?" exclaimed Sarah.

"That's him. He's sold me the old corset factory. It's going to make an amazing gallery. He messed me around for ages, claiming some big company was after it, but he fancies himself as an art lover so I swayed him with a promise of invitations to all the private views. Then he insisted on getting me over to his house to see his collection. The pictures were *awful*." He looked at Sarah. "All except one. Your painting of his kid staring at a stick insect trapped in a glass jar. He had no idea it was a thousand times better than any of the rubbish he'd paid a fortune for."

Sarah blushed. "I do a few pet portraits to pay the bills."

"When he said you were still living at the shop I came

108

straight round. This isn't just a social call, Sarah. I want to see the rest of your work. Where's your studio?"

"Don't be an idiot, Mo, I haven't got a studio. I work in the storeroom between serving customers."

"I see," Mo said, dismayed. "Well . . . anyway, I want to commission you to paint a portrait of Missy, a centrepiece for the first exhibition in my new gallery."

Sarah flushed. "I'd love to, but you mustn't feel. . ."

"I run a business, Sarah, not a charity. I'll send her over so you can make some preliminary sketches. Shall we say Wednesday, after school?" He kissed her cheek. "Meantime you look after yourself, get some rest."

He nodded to the children and was gone. Wolfie's mind boiled. He looked at his mother, tired and wan in her worn jeans and scuffed boots, her tumbled hair and the grey smudges beneath her eyes, trying to imagine what her life would be like if she hadn't met his dad, if she hadn't had him. Perhaps she'd have been a famous artist, living in a swanky New York loft, with a husband who looked like Mo and a daughter with a stupid name. He caught their reflections in the window: three scruffy kids and a tired-looking woman, outlined against the muddy green of the common. And he knew there never had been a choice for any of them. Thornham, this shop, their very existence had all been part of the mysterious purpose that had lain within the leys since time began. Whatever chance events had buffeted their lives, their fates had been sealed from birth, like those plastic baby mugs that always swung upright, however hard you hit them. A shutter of white cut across his thoughts as a van pulled up outside. A man with a clipboard threw open the door.

"Ten kilos of fudge to pick up." He handed Sarah an envelope of cash and held out his clipboard.

"Oh Lord, I forgot the time. Sign for me, will you, Wolfie?" She dashed to the kitchen, beckoning to Zi'ib and Tala to give her a hand.

Wolfie signed where the man was pointing. "Why do you want so much fudge?"

"I don't," said the man. "I just drive the van."

"So who's it for?" Wolfie skimmed the page looking for the delivery address. There wasn't one.

The man shrugged.

"Here you go," said Zi'ib, heaving a large cardboard box on to the counter.

Hoisting it on to his shoulder the man took his clipboard and left. As the door swung shut, a shrill scream touched Wolfie's nerves like a drill on a rotten tooth. He ran to the kitchen. Elvis was going wild in the yard, howling and battering the back door while Sarah was lunging at something in the larder with the broom, her face twisted in revulsion.

"What is it?" Wolfie yelled, rushing towards her. What he saw made him gag. The larder floor was a rippling carpet of black ants. "It's all right, Mum." He wrested the broom from her hand and swept a path through the heaving crush, horrified to see a stream of shiny black bodies come bubbling up through the cracks in the tiles. They were larger than any ants he had ever seen and their blunt, nodding heads and flailing legs made his flesh creep. A glance at the untouched trays of fudge on the lower shelves raised a warning in his star, quickly drowned by the roar of the vacuum cleaner. Tala was pushing past, thrusting the nozzle into the thick mass of insects, shouting to Zi'ib to grab something to cut off their escape. With a gritty whoosh the ants whirled up the metal tube. Armed with hoover, broom and baking tin the children battled on, until, at last, the ants were no more than an occasional crunch beneath their feet. Tala switched off the vacuum and let Elvis in. Hackles stiff, he ran to the larder and clawed the floor, growling softly.

Sarah nudged him aside and started sealing the cracks with Sellotape, shuddering as she worked. "Let's hope this holds till I can get Sid Poskitt in to fix the tiles." Shaking, she stood up, her hand to her mouth. "Ugh. The thought of those horrible things swarming under the house makes me feel sick." She reached for the bottle of tablets on the dresser and said wearily, "Could you get some ant killer? Take some cash from the till."

As they ran outside to get their bikes a tremor, not quite a noise, shivered on the wind.

"Do you think those ants were . . . you know . . . elementals?" Zi'ib said.

"I don't know, but normal ants don't ignore trays of fudge," Wolfie said, ringing his bell irritably at a fat black crow crouched in the road. He expected it to flap away. Instead it watched him coming with fearless beady black eyes and when, at the last minute, he swerved to avoid it, the creature barely blinked.

11

Restless Roads

"Sorry, mate, sold out," said the assistant in Frescos. "We've had a run on pesticides. Try the hardware shop on Dodds Hill."

"I'll check out the second-hand shop while we're there," panted Tala as they cycled up the hill. "See if there's something I can get Sarah for her birthday."

"Is she OK?" said Zi'ib.

"Why shouldn't she be?" snapped Wolfie.

"Those headaches."

Tala nodded. "And that Mo guy thought—"

"What does he know?" Wolfie was pedalling hard: *shut up, shut up*.

"I wondered if maybe—"

"Stop going on about it; she's just a bit tired," said Wolfie. His mum was never ill. Why wouldn't everyone just *shut up*!

They parked their bikes and had barely got their breath back before it was snatched away again by the bizarre display in Strowger's window. A moth-eaten leopard-skin rug, with its head and tail intact, had been tacked to a sheet of hardboard, crudely daubed to look like a jungle. Scattered all around it stood a dusty assortment of objects: a dog-eared book entitled *Man Eater*, a pair of binoculars, a shooting stick, a pith helmet and, arching over it all, a painted sign that read *STROWGER'S FOR ALL YOUR BEAST HUNTING NEEDS*.

Wolfie was transfixed by the stark outline of the splayed pelt. With its jaws frozen in a toothy snarl he had the feeling that any moment, it might leap back to life like a squashed cat in a cartoon. The drone in his head grew louder, rumbling like a bestial growl of resentment. Unable to bear it, he hurried off to the hardware store next door, calling, "Come on!" over his shoulder. Tala lingered for a while, picking over the scumbled mounds of engine parts, strange electrical goods, tea trolleys, books, one-armed bandits and gas masks spilling on to the pavement, and caught up with the boys on their way back.

As they pedalled home Wolfie said, "Can you hear a weird throbbing noise?"

Zi'ib nodded. "It's driving me crazy *and* it's clogging the signals in my star."

Wolfie strained to identify the restless sound. Sometimes it was no more than a broken trembling, at others it shook his whole body as if it came from the depths of his being.

114

No one said the words aloud but all three had a horrible suspicion that what they were picking up was the discordant hum of the dark energies, resonating through their limbs like a sounding board.

Sarah poked her head out of the outhouse as they crossed the yard. "Sid Poskitt's on his way," she called.

"What are you doing?" demanded Wolfie, glancing nervously into the gloomy interior.

"Moving this junk. I need somewhere to put the stuff from the larder."

"We'll do it," Wolfie said quickly.

He and Zi'ib hurried Sarah back to the kitchen, leaving Tala to slip into the squat stone shed and lift the lid of the dusty wooden cask stashed beneath the workbench. She whipped back a layer of sacking, revealing an obelisk of pinkish granite. She let go a long-held breath. The first Stone of Knowledge was safe. It was not much of a hiding place for something that had once held a portion of the secret of the Spheres but it was the best they could do.

She began making space on the workbench, stacking up the pieces of Sarah's broken plant pot, shunting along jars of wooden spoons and moving an old hotplate that Wolfie's grandmother had used for boiling up fudge. It should have been thrown out years ago. The smooth square top plate had tarnished with age, mice had nibbled the fabric covering from the wires and the green enamel base was blistered with rust spots. The boys came in laden with bags and boxes, ducking beneath the row of preserving pans hanging from the ceiling. Swinging round in the narrow space Tala knocked a bag of sugar out of Zi'ib's hands, dredging the hotplate with a thick dusting of white crystals.

"Idiot," she scowled.

"It was your fault," retorted Zi'ib. He straightened up, banging his head on one of the pans. A deep melodious note undulated through the gloom like a wave of bright water.

"Look at that," breathed Tala, pointing at the hotplate.

The sugar granules scattered across its flat surface were bouncing to the ripples of sound, shifting into an eight-armed star shape, delicate as a snowflake.

"That is totally weird," said Zi'ib. He stood back, amazed that sound could move matter. Taking a wooden spoon he tapped the pan again, raising the same note, this time with a sharper edge. Tentatively he hit the next pan. The sonorous clang reduced the eight sugary spokes on the hotplate to a cross. A small bucket of blackened metal with a crooked handle struck a swelling note that filled the outhouse, raising a single tapering needle through the bed of sugar and muting the noisome growl in their heads to a whimper.

"The darkness doesn't like it!" Wolfie exclaimed.

Zi'ib began to hammer the pan harder and harder as if he could beat the dark forces into submission. The deep rhythmic sound stirred the silted depths of his memory. He was in Sudan, a small child, woken from a bad dream by a strange rhythmic drumbeat drifting in from the desert. He ran to his mother's bed, and saw the harmless little snake that slept in the crack in the wall slither across the floor, following a silvery slant of moonlight towards the sound. His mother assured him that the noise was nothing, just superstitious women performing an age-old ceremony that was frowned on nowadays. It was called a Zar, she said, to drive out demons. For the rest of that night he had lain beside her, safe and content, listening to the haunting sounds of the pagan ritual, whose origins lay buried deep beneath the desert sands.

He cupped his hands around the bucket, muting the sound. Nothing could deaden his longing for his mother. He closed his eyes, silently praying that his father would find her. They cleaned up the sugar as best they could and headed back to the kitchen, where Sarah was sitting dejectedly at the table staring into a mug of tea.

"Don't worry about it, Mum, it's just a few insects," Wolfie said.

"It's not just that. It's this commission for Mo. How can I do it properly if I'm dashing in and out serving customers all day?"

"Use some of the money he's paying you to get some help."

"By the time I've settled our debts there'll be hardly any

left. Who'd want to work here when they can earn twice as much at Frescos?"

Esmé's written account of her trip to Thornham further confirmed Ridian's confidence that the negative forces were aiding his purpose. "The Chosen will prevail!" he muttered feverishly as he added her report to her file. His eyes fell on the name Frankie Fontaine. He sneered. Esmé's short-lived marriage to that swindler proved just how weak and susceptible these lesser mortals were, yet the notes his people had made on Fontaine made extremely interesting reading.

Dark-haired, blue-eyed, charming and entirely ruthless, Fontaine had started out as a gifted stage hypnotist able to manipulate his subjects like puppets at the snap of his long delicate fingers. Tiring of his modest earnings, he soon began to seek more lucrative outlets for his talents. He became a thief. He didn't break into people's houses but into their minds, developing a raft of psychological tricks that encouraged his victims to present him with large sums of money, while believing they were acting entirely of their own free will. But Fontaine grew greedy and eventually he went to prison. When he came out he set up a small private company selling his services to anyone willing to pay for them. He never asked questions and guaranteed complete discretion.

Ridian stared at the computer screen with the intensity of a chess player calculating his next move. Then he

118

picked up the phone and dialled the number of *Fontaine Solutions.*

Many mysterious tunes were resonating across the cosmos as the Sphere of Lupus wove and meshed and twined the threads of fate. Few could hear those melodies but down the centuries some of their distant chords had been reflected in the geometry of pattern and number.

"What are you doing?" said Wolfie. He and Zi'ib had come upstairs to find Tala gouging the attic floorboards with a screwdriver.

"Hiding Sarah's present."

Beside her lay a large willow-pattern plate and a battered old book.

"How much?" said Zi'ib.

"Three quid for both and I only had to leave a 50p deposit," she said proudly. "But the book's for us."

Zi'ib flipped open the cover. "*Anecdotes of the Manners and Customs of London* by James Peller Malcolm. 1810."

"I bought it so we could check for rituals to do with cleansing energies. Look on the back cover. There's some handwritten notes about a trip he made in 1811 to the 'outlying village of Thornham' to see the ceremony of raising the giants. Wolfie was right, though; all they do is traipse round the common chanting about St Michael."

A section of floorboard gave way beneath the

screwdriver. The papery smell of old dust made Tala sneeze. "There's loads of room. We could put Agnes's painting down here as well."

From behind his chest of drawers Wolfie pulled out a panel of strange symbols painted by his ancestor Agnes Brown. In the middle of a tangle of paths lay a grid of nine squares. In each square Agnes had painted images representing a number from 1 to 9, laid out so that each vertical and each horizontal row added up to fifteen.

This, they had discovered, was called a magic square.

By writing the numbers 1 to 9 along three rows and joining them up in the order they appeared in the magic square, the children had obtained an eight-point star shape, which had turned out to be a map of the ley lines at Thornham and set them on the path to finding the first Stone of Knowledge.*

As Wolfie tilted the panel the light caught the picture of twin crescent moons representing the number two in the top row of the grid.

If the taint is not cleansed within the waxing and waning of two moons, Zane had said.

Stifling a jab of panic, he said, "I was hoping Agnes had hidden some other message in here that could help us sort the black ley. But this stupid maze of pathways just keeps leading back to the magic square in the middle. I can't see how that's s'posed to help us with healing energy."

* See Appendix 2

Ridian Winter sat before his computer screen in his darkened flat in the Barbican. He had not slept for two days, but his mind still raced. Dreams of intellectual immortality had obsessed Lupan scholars for centuries. The theory was perfectly sound; since consciousness was merely a form of energy that could exist independently of the human brain there was no reason why, when severed cleanly from one body, it could not enter another. Although such downloading of consciousness had never been attempted before, Ridian clung to the belief that once he had recaptured the Sphere and reconnected the Link of Light, the minds of his Manus Sacra masters would show him how it could be done.

Two columns of names gleamed on his computer screen. One listed the members of the Manus Sacra in order of intellectual superiority, the other listed the human units suitable to house their conscious minds. The selection process was not easy. He had sat for hours like a ghoulish matchmaker attempting to pair minds with bodies. Stefan de Witt and Esmé Hiram Glottis were natural choices for a couple of lower ranking Manus Sacra minds, which was why he had felt free to lure them in with fragments of truth about his plans.

The greatest scholar of the Manus Sacra was Therion, former Keeper of Wisdom; then came Godfrey, former Master of the Exiles and one-time vicar of Thornham; and then Leonora, the exiled expert in the mysteries of the Spheres who had spent the final year of her sojourn on earth as the sub-librarian of Thornham library. These three sages had journeyed deep into the hidden realms of Wisdom to glimpse the deepest truths of existence. For them the choice had been obvious. He circled the names at the top of the list of vessels.

Wolfie Brown, Zi'ib Bakri, Tala Bean.

When the powerful intellects of Therion, Godfrey and Leonora were rehoused in the bodies of these unique children, the marriage of minds would surpass imagination.

And soon the Manus Sacra would rise invincible from the ashes of destruction, reborn through the power of dark energy. And at their head, Therion, Godfrey and Leonora, their three great leaders cloaked in the flesh of the only beings in the cosmos who had ever possessed the power to destroy them.

12

Raising the Giants

At precisely 7.30 on Monday evening, the committee of the Thornham Preservation Society filed out of St Michael's Church and on to the common, grasping lighted lanterns, the hawthorn twigs in their hats throwing strange horned shadows across the churchyard wall. Tala pushed through the gathering onlookers, making notes of everything she saw. "Look, there's Stinky," she said, pointing to the portly figure of their geography teacher.

"Who's that with him?" said Wolfie.

The firelight caught a flash of peachy skin and a sleek blonde bob beneath a black beret.

"Dunno, but she's never his girlfriend," Zi'ib said.

Mrs Poskitt's husband Sid tipped a load of dry wood on to the bonfire, his angular face made impish by the cigarette dangling from his lips and the battered trilby perched on his head. Poking a stick into the flames, he lit the four metal braziers set around the fire.

"What are they for?" asked Tala, as Mr Forester handed her a word sheet.

"Those four flames symbolize the two solstices and two equinoxes, the most potent points in the ancient calendar. Originally they'd have been true *bone-fires*, made from animal remains and pungent oils, all part of an ancient alchemy to prepare the minds of the participants for the ceremony. In any human interaction with earth energy the power of the will is always paramount."

Tala scribbled down his words.

"The committee refuse to accept that there was ever a stone circle here at all and when I suggested that tonight's ritual was designed to harness the earth energies needed to raise the giant *stones* to build that circle, they asked me to resign my membership! But with that wretched dark ley passing straight through the common, who knows what tonight's ceremony could stir up?"

The Tala darted a look at Wolfie that was equal parts excitement and foreboding.

Mr Forester looked round. "Isn't Sarah coming?"

"She's putting her feet up," Wolfie said quickly.

A woman with chestnut hair and coral-red lipstick came swiftly past, barking into a loudhailer.

"Welcome, everyone. I'm Fenella Haythorpe-Hardy, president of the Thornham Preservation Society. Despite some extremely outlandish theories being bandied around of late –" she cast a withering glance at Mr Forester "– we do not know the meaning or origin of the historic ritual of raising the giants. However, it is vital that we continue to preserve this scrap of living history, so thank you all for coming. Unfortunately the panic over the so-called panther has led to a rather disappointing turn out this year. Personally I have serious doubts about the existence of this creature. Images caught on mobile phones are notoriously deceptive."

"Ruddy cheek!" sounded the irate voice of Vera Poskitt.

"Mr Baxter, please proceed with the drumming."

As the churchwarden began to beat out a steady thrum on a snare drum, the Poskitts' poodle, Monty, bounded over to rub noses with Elvis, his tail waving like a woolly metronome.

"On the count of three," commanded Mrs Haythorpe-Hardy.

"One . . . two . . . three. . ."

> *Out of the earth the giants come,*
> *Out of the sea their sisters call,*
> *Out of the air the beating drum.*
> *Out of the sky the truth shall fall.*

The crowd murmured the lines nervously at first, some of those by the lychgate giggling, raising their eyebrows and shushing each other, yet gradually they began to sway in unison as the rise and fall of the words took on a force of its own, as haunting as the crash of waves on rocks. The discordant drone of the black ley swelled beneath the chant and something cruel and sly rattled the children's bones. A stagnant smell rose on the wind. Elvis and Monty leapt to the top of the rockery snarling into the darkness. Suddenly afraid, Wolfie stumbled backwards, pulling Zi'ib and Tala with him.

"Look out, there's the beast!" shouted Sid, running towards the flower beds. "I saw it, I swear I did."

Some of the giant raisers ran after him, their lanterns streaming light through the darkness. Others shrieked and cowered by the bonfire.

"Come now, everybody," cried Mrs Haythorpe-Hardy. "Mr Poskitt can't possibly have seen anything in the dark."

"It was right there by the rhododendrons," retorted Sid, "staring straight at me with great big yeller eyes."

After much feverish scurrying around, the disappointed giant raisers straggled back to the bonfire, Mr Pinkney and his chic companion bringing up the rear.

"This hysteria over the panther is just a collective delusion, fired by a mindless hunger for sensation," cried Mrs Haythorpe-Hardy.

"I'll give her collective delusion," muttered Sid.

The drumming and chanting resumed. Narrowing into a slithering chain, the crowd snaked behind Mrs Haythorpe-Hardy as she led them along the traditional route around the common, unaware that she was following an ancient processional pathway that had once been marked by an inner ring of standing stones. When the circuit had been completed she veered back to the bonfire and called the proceedings to a close. Sid lost his temper.

"I've told that woman time and again. We're s'posed to spread out now into eight groups and walk into the middle of the common. It's tradition. I should know. There were Poskitts, Baxters and Browns raising the Thornham giants for years before Mrs High and Mighty Hardy stuck her nose in."

"Really?" Wolfie said, intrigued.

"Course. And when your grandpa was organizing it we had proper flame torches, not these poxy lanterns. He was worried even back then that half the chant had got lost and now if we don't watch it, the whole thing'll go up the spout." He grabbed the fire extinguisher and stumped off to vent his annoyance on the bonfire.

Tala ran after him, pulling out James Malcolm's book. "Mr Poskitt, hang on. I think I might have found the missing verses."

Sid stopped squirting and turned to listen.

> *Out of the earth the serpents rise,*
> *Michael's foe and Michael's prize.*
> *Spears to kill and spears to heal,*
> *Spokes upon a starry wheel.*
>
> *Serpents sicken, time doth tell,*
> *Where shadows meet, the dark ones dwell.*

Pain and sorrow, fear and doubt,
Whetted spears shall cast them out.

A hushed silence had descended. Sid tipped his hat back, gripped by emotions he did not understand. "Very nice," he said huskily, "very nice, indeed. You let me have a copy of that and next year I'll make sure we do things properly."

Mr Forester reached for the book, his eyes shining with fierce excitement. "These stanzas noted down by Malcolm are perfect proof that tonight's ritual was all about manipulating earth energies."

"How do you make that out?" asked Sid.

"Snakes, serpents, dragons are all folkloric metaphors for the waves of natural energy vibrating through the ley lines. The Michael they mention is of course *Saint* Michael, Christian successor to Hermes and Mercury, who ruled the leys. Churches at major ley crossings are often dedicated to him."

"What's this got to do with raising giants?" demanded Sid.

"In a time beyond memory the megalith builders knew how to bring the vibrations of the ley energies to such a pitch they created an antigravitational effect which enabled them to raise giant stones. And once the stones were in place they reversed the process and returned the frequency to normal. In fact, there is a theory that the original magician's wand was in fact some kind of tuning device, capable of changing the vibrational speeds of mind, matter and energy and transmuting one into the other."

Sid grinned. "You're having me on."

"I never joke about such matters."

"Oh great," whispered Wolfie. "What we need is a blimmin' magic wand."

Tala dragged the boys towards one of the braziers and tilted the book towards the firelight.

"If serpents are symbols of the waves of energy in ley lines, this stuff about serpents sickening could be talking about the energies getting contaminated," she whispered.

Zi'ib squinted down at the words. "So these bits about spears to heal and whetted spears casting out pain and sorrow might mean using *spears* to heal the contaminated ley. But what's this Michael's foe and Michael's prize?"

A memory pinballed around Wolfie's head, hitting images of St Michael, a spear, a serpent. A broad grin spread across his face. "You know what? The stained-glass window of St Michael in the church shows him sticking a spear into a serpent, turning his foe into his prize!"

"So next stop St Michael's," breathed Tala.

Three sets of green eyes turned to look up at the church spire glimmering in the light of the waxing moon.

Sid came over and started riddling the brazier with a stick. "Pass us that shovel, would you, Mr F?" he called.

"By the way, Sid," said Mr Forester, handing him the

tool. "I wonder if you could have a look at a damp problem I've got in my new office."

"Where is it?"

"On the Crescent. Number forty-five."

"I'll nip round tomorrow. Anything to keep out of Mrs P's way. She's been driving me nuts since I retired, even comes down my allotment so she can nag, nag, nag." Sid made yapping jaws with his fingers, swiftly turning the movement into a cheery wave when he saw his wife striding across the grass.

"Sidney, why are you wearing that hat? I put it out for the jumble weeks ago."

Wolfie grinned. "I don't suppose you fancy doing a few shifts in the shop, do you, Sid? Mum's got tons of painting on at the moment."

"Anytime," replied Sid. He gave Tala a conspiratorial wink but she was gazing fixedly along the path of the dark ley reaching down to the shop.

"Cheer up, girl, it might never happen," he said.

Sarah, who had spent the evening dozing on the sofa, insisted on getting up and pouring everyone mugs of hot soup. She was congratulating Wolfie on enlisting Sid's help in the shop when the phone rang. Zi'ib waved the receiver at Tala. It was Dr Walker on the line, the coma specialist treating her father. With trembling hands she took the phone into the storeroom.

Wolfie and Zi'ib slipped upstairs. They added the words

Find spears and **Search St Michael's** to their list of action points and posted a message from Nikto Senki on the *EM* discussion board asking for information about using spears to heal dark energies.

"It's good news," Tala was telling Sarah as they came back down. "Dr Walker says Dad's heart is getting stronger every day and now and then he's responding to sound and light." She wiped her nose on her sleeve. "And she's just heard back from the company sponsoring her research. They say they're willing to go on paying for his treatment."

Beneath her smiles, Zi'ib and Wolfie could sense her fluttering fear that Jack Bean might never make a total recovery from his horrific weeks of incarceration in the Wilderness Between the Worlds.

Two coats of white emulsion had obliterated most of the faded roses on the wallpaper in the front room of number forty-five, but failed to hide the damp patch spreading like a strange organic growth beside the fireplace. Sid poked the spongy surface. "I'll see what I can do, Mr F, but this place is in a right state."

Outside he laid his hands on the mouldering brickwork, craning up at the building. "You'd be best off pulling the whole thing down and building a nice bungalow. Shame about the garden, though." Swinging his spade, he began to hack a pathway through the undergrowth towards a pair of moss-clad rooftops poking through the brambles. "Look at that greenhouse. Fix up lovely, that would. *And* a shed."

Scrambling over a mound of rubble he tugged open the door and cast an expert eye over the rusted tools. "Here, tell you what. I'll sort your damp for free if you let me have a go at this garden. I could have a veg patch over here, tomatoes in the greenhouse, deckchair and a nice little Primus in here for a brew. Paradise. And we needn't tell Vera a word about it."

"It certainly needs attention," agreed Mr Forester. "I'm sure the owner would be delighted to have a little order imposed on the chaos."

"Done!" said Sid, shaking him by the hand.

13

Knight Riders

Ridian suspected that the combination of wisdom flowing through those children's veins attuned them to subtleties of vibration which even the Manus Sacra struggled to fathom. After all it was Nessus, the wisest scholar of ancient Lupus, who had written, "He who grasps the mysteries of vibration, grasps the deadliest spear."

It was so frustrating that he couldn't communicate with the children directly. He could only hope that Esmé's campaign, combined with their extreme sensitivity to the discord throbbing from the black stream, would be enough to weaken their will to decontaminate the infected energies.

He clicked the computer and spent a long time rereading the posts from "Nikto Senki" on *The Earth Mysterian* website. Capturing Spheres, healing dark energies – they were plainly the work of those brats; who else would be focusing on those two particular topics? This query about using spears was extremely worrying. Who knew what answers they might receive from all those wretched wisdom seekers sharing information on the *EM* message boards? And who knew who any of those people calling themselves things like Stargazer and Stonescryer really were?

At length his face relaxed. Who knew indeed? And like a deft angler casting his hook, he began to type out a brief message of his own.

Vera Poskitt had spent most of Saturday burnishing the age-worn pews of St Michael's Church to a lustrous shine. She had just started on the pulpit when Wolfie turned up with Zi'ib and Tala, asking if he could sketch the de Monteneuf tombs.

She glanced at the three children: Wolfie sitting cross-legged between the tombs of Sir Guy and Sir Edgar, and the other two, who'd been staring up at that stained-glass window for a good half-hour. Why on earth they should be so interested in a picture of Saint Michael with his sword in one hand, a pair of scales in the other and a great ugly serpent twined round his feet she couldn't imagine. The late afternoon sun streamed through the windows as she bustled down the side aisle and handed Zi'ib the keys. "Mind your feet, pet, I've just polished that brass."

"Sorry." Zi'ib skipped clear of the gleaming effigy of Sir Edgar set into the floor.

"I'll be back in an hour to lock up," Vera said. Whipping out her duster, she flicked a speck of dirt from the head of the marble hound lying beneath Sir Edgar's feet, its lifted eyes fixed for eternity on the St Michael window. "That animal's the spitting image of your Elvis," she said to Wolfie. "Same bug eyes, same floppy ears, even got the same wiry build."

"Yeah, weird." Wolfie wondered what Vera would say if he told her a few of the other freaky *kinnections* that had linked the Browns and the de Monteneufs over the years. His eyes darted to the de Monteneuf crest carved above the tombs; it was a riven eight-point star, just like the star of a Lupan explorer broken in two.

Pulling on her coat, Vera stole an admiring peek at Wolfie's sketch. "You've got your mum's talent, no mistake, and a real eye for detail. Which is more than can be said for the joker who did the wording on that." She pointed to the plaque on the side of Sir Edgar's tomb. "Desecration, I call it. Puts my back up every time I dust it."

As she trotted away a vibration, as disturbing as a drawn-out note played on a untuned violin, strummed the children's senses, reminding them that the church lay directly in the path of the contaminated ley.

Waggling his fingers in his ears, Zi'ib said, "She's right, this plaque *is* a bit random." He frowned at the bewildering mix of upper and lower case letters, so oddly

135

spaced it was hard to tell where one word stopped and the next began. Why carve a garbled message so delicately? he wondered. And why go to the trouble of laying it out across a chequerboard of green and white marble and framing it with an ornate wreath of scrollwork? Some of the letters had even been edged with gilded squiggles.

"Hey, look at this," he breathed. The squiggles were tiny snakes, rippling L-shapes, pointing in all directions.

Tala tried to make sense of the letters. "Guy's s-y-g-n – is that an old-fashioned spelling of sign?"

"Maybe," said Zi'ib, running his eyes up and down the letters. "Or maybe it's a *sign* that this inscription is more than it seems."

Slowly Tala picked out the words. "Guy's sygn of fire burns like a thousand moons . . . de Monteneuf heirs inherit a knightly calling . . . a castle on Temple Stonham's sacred forest . . . here shall sweet wisdom's true adherents gather to begin a noble journey and follow the pilgrim pathways of the knights." She ran round to the matching panel on the other side.

"Behold Guy's noble line here interred where lies Thornham's divine church, established by this crusader from Normandy, here shadowy secrets lead to understanding . . . forearmed, a wise man halts at every marker square whose writing serpent—" The word leapt from the marble. She glanced at the stained-glass snake on the St Michael window and back to the carved words.

137

Behold	guy'S	nobl**E**	**I**Ine	he**R**e	in**T**erred	wh**E**re	**L**ies
t**H**orn hams	**D**ivine	ch**U**rch	**E**	**S**t	**A**blished by	**T**his	**C**rusa der
from **N**or man	d**Y**	h	**E**re	**S**h	**A**dowy	s**E**c	r**E**ts
lead	**T**o	**U**nder	**S**tanding	fo**R**e	arme**D**	**A**	wi**S**e man
h**A**lts at	**E**very	M**A**r	ke	**R**	square	wh**O**	**S**
E	wri	t**H**ing	**S**erpent	guide**S**	th	**E**	knight
Ri	**D**ers	f**O**r	**H**e who	**T**he grasps	serpent's	**F**iery stone
will tame the	ser**P**	**E**nt's	pow**E**rs		**H**ere	**W**	it**H**

". . . whose writhing serpent guides the knight riders . . . *for he who grasps the serpent's fiery stone will tame the serpent's powers herewith."*

Was there was method in this muddle of disjointed lettering? Did it hide a coded message for those who sought to tame the serpent energies?

"*A wise man halts at every marker square whose writhing serpent guides the knight riders,*" repeated Zi'ib. "It's telling us to focus on the squares marked with a snake."

"OK." Wolfie ripped a page from his sketch pad. "There's one capital letter in each marked square."

Tala's eyes slid across the inscription. "But if you pick out the capitals you just get a meaningless string of letters."

Wolfie frowned in concentration. "*And* some empty squares, but not enough for them to be word breaks."

"So, for some reason it was important to have –" Wolfie counted quickly, "– eight by eight . . . sixty-four squares."

And in the middle of that cold English church Zi'ib heard the jubilant cackle of his elderly neighbour in Sudan. The old man had taken an interest in this solemn, fatherless boy and taught him to play chess, bringing him along to compete with the village men after evening prayers and grinning with toothless delight whenever his pupil won. Suddenly Zi'ib's fingers were making stepped patterns across the grid. "It's a chessboard!" he breathed. "*Whose writing serpent guides the knight riders.* The snakes mark knight's chess moves from one capital letter to the next. Look. Each bend on a snake's body indicates one square and the direction of the move."

Following the snakes, Zi'ib made a knight's tour of the squares in both panels, calling out the capital letters in each one as he went. Wolfe jotted them down and Tala carefully grouped them into words. Finally she read them out, her voice echoing in the vaulted silence.

> *Knight of stone and knight of brass*
> *Lit by Michael's jewelled glass,*
> *Where sunset casts a ruby shade,*
> *There the seeds of hope are laid.*

"It's telling us to follow the light from the window!"

Above them the image of St Michael gleamed in the setting sun, the little lozenges of lead-rimmed glass throwing a kaleidoscope of colour from the floor brass of Sir Edgar to his carved marble tomb, bathing the effigy of his faithful hound in choppy rainbows of brilliance.

"Quick, before the sun sets. There's the knight of stone and knight of brass, so find the ruby shade."

The window threw multicoloured tints on to the tombs but the children had eyes only for the beams of crimson striking the corners of the floor slab surrounding the brass of Sir Edgar and spilling dabs of red on to the eyes, tail tip and central vertebrae of the marble likeness of his hound.

"*There the seeds of hope are laid.*" Tala dipped her fingers into the pools of red light on the dog's rounded eyeballs, exerting a little exploratory pressure with her thumbs.

Zi'ib's and Wolfie's stars registered a tiny shift in the stone. Holding his breath, Zi'ib laid his hands on the dog's ruby-lit backbone and tail while Wolfie crouched down, pressing his palms against the red splashes on the corners of the floor slab. "OK, push!" he ordered. With a grinding and whirring of ancient ratchets, the figure of Sir Edgar lifted clear of its bed of slate.

The hairs rose on the nape of Wolfie's neck. "Please let it be the hiding place for a spear!"

He gave the figure a tentative tap. Slowly the brass of Sir Edgar pivoted round on a metal spindle.

In the breathless silence, the door creaked open. A large crow fluttered into the church.

Ignoring it, the children stared down in puzzlement. Whatever it was, the strange object lying in the hollow compartment in the floor was definitely *not* a spear.

It reminded Wolfie of PC Mott's truncheon: a flattened cylinder of bluish stone, about twenty-five centimetres long, rounded at one end, slightly chamfered at the edges and riveted into a bronze casing with a handle shaped like a curving serpent.

Tala touched the stone. Its rough, sandpapery scrape set her teeth on edge.

"It's some kind of a . . . a . . . whetstone," she said, bemused. "My dad had a stone that felt a bit like this for sharpening his tools."

Slipping his fingers through the serpent handle, Wolfie raised the strange whetstone up, sensing the pride and skill of the craftsman who had infused this ancient tool with power and purpose. *"He who grasps the serpent's fiery stone will tame the serpent's powers,"* he said. "This is meant for us, for sharpening the spears to smite the dark energies." His spirits soared. Maybe cleansing this infected ley wasn't going to be so difficult after all, and as soon as they'd done it they could get on with bringing his dad home.

Zi'ib ran his penknife across the stone and in a welter of friction sparks the knife came alive in his hand, vibrating with an almost tangible power. Tala noticed some words etched into the dip where the whetstone had lain and began to call them out as if reading from an instruction manual.

> *When Michael's scales weigh dark and light,*
> *And hold the point 'twixt day and night*
> *Seize the hour to smite the dark*
> *And Michael's spears shall find their mark.*

They fixed their eyes on the pans of St Michael's scales, one a semicircle of white glass, the other a semicircle of deep blue, glowing in the fading sunset like the dark and light sides of a half moon.

"That first bit's telling us *when* to do it," said Zi'ib, bemused. "Though I don't see why the time should make any difference."

"Me neither," Wolfie said, wrapping the whetstone in his sweatshirt and slipping it into his rucksack. "And what does it mean anyway? Scales can't weigh light and dark."

The crow flitted down the aisle and perched on a pew, its jet-black eyes darting from one to the other before settling on Wolfie.

"We'll work it out," Tala said.

But how long is that going to take? thought Wolfie.

With a furious beat of wide black wings, the crow sailed towards him, swooping low. He ducked, gripped by a sudden panic. *If Tala's dad got better and Zane found Zi'ib's mum, they might both leave Thornham before they'd captured the Sphere. Then he'd never get his dad back.*

"Yuggh, that bird is gross. Get out, shoo!" yelled Tala. Whirling her coat, she chased the crow through the door.

Zi'ib returned the brass figure of Sir Edgar to its bed of slate and they set off home to hide the ancient whetstone beneath the attic floorboards.

Fired up by their find, Tala had dotted the chart with new Post-it notes scribbled with action points. Beneath the words **Find Wisdom of the Winds** she added:

Where?

How?

Find Spears

Where?

How?

Sharpen spears with whetstone

Spear dark ley

Time? When Michael's scales weigh dark and light
  and hold the point 'twixt day and night
Place?

Wolfie viewed the explosion of unanswered questions through a black fog of frustration. Hadn't he done enough for the positive energies? And what had they ever done for him except rob him of his father and steal away all the good times proper families had? All he wanted was his dad back. After ten years, was that too much to ask?

"Hey, there's a posting on the message board about Spheres," called Zi'ib. "From someone calling themselves Wisdomseeker." He spooled down and shivered. "Yuggh, creepy."

Wolfie and Tala read it over his shoulder.

Nikto Senki is obviously unaware that the simplest way to capture a Sphere is to draw it down using dark energy.

"He's a nutter," Zi'ib said.

A muffled feeling he didn't recognize stirred his star. He spun round. For a moment he and Wolfie stared at each other.

"Oh come on, what's the matter with you?" Zi'ib said. "Even if it's true. You heard what Dad said. If we bring a Sphere into a contaminated world we can't use it to open gateways."

"Actually, that's not what he said," muttered Wolfie. "He

144

said it would only respond to beings born of darkness, or who embraced darkness."

Zi'ib shrugged. "Same difference. Either way it'd be useless to us."

Tala tapped absently at her star, bemused by the strange fuzzy signals she was picking up. She was planning their next move. The whetstone had been hidden in the church – the site of one of the four entrances to the lost stone circle – so it seemed logical to search the other three entrance sites for spears. Zi'ib agreed. Wolfie just saw problems.

"We turned this place upside down when we were looking for the Stones of Knowledge and the pub's just been completely refurbished," he said gloomily.

"Something might still be buried in the gardens of the pub or number forty-five," insisted Tala.

"They are both huge. Even if we made up some excuse to dig around, where would we start?" said Wolfie.

"If you're going to be so negative, me and Zi'ib'll do it on our own," snapped Tala, and she flounced off to her room.

14

Missy

All the next day suffocating fingers of darkness probed the shop, smothering the children, leaving them depressed and short of breath, and magnifying their worries and resentments. After school, Tala got caught loitering in the garden of the Wish Hound pub, Zi'ib got told off by Sid for digging up his newly sown parsnip seeds and they both turned on Wolfie for not helping.

By five o'clock, when a black Bentley drew up outside the sweet shop, their frustrations had sprung open aspects of their personalities they barely knew existed. A girl jumped out of the back seat, her long auburn hair swinging in the wind. She wore a black jumper, a short denim skirt, black tights and flat black pumps. Her face was heart shaped, her brows curved and her skin the colour of cream. Across her tip-tilt nose lay a scatter of pale freckles. She read the peeling sign above the shop window and her little pout of a mouth parted to reveal a row of even, gleaming teeth. She clenched her fists with excitement. From one wrist dangled a loop of gold ribbon attached to a white cardboard box and from the other hung a loop of pink ribbon attached to . . .

All three children stared, incredulous. "It's a blimmin' tortoise," breathed Wolfie.

The girl saw him and smiled. He didn't smile back. He didn't want her here, reminding Sarah of her posh art-school friends and how her life might have turned out if she hadn't met his dad.

Suddenly aware of his grubby jeans and torn sweatshirt Zi'ib backed away. "Come on, Tala. We've got spears to find."

"Oh, thanks," hissed Wolfe. "What happened to the ties that bind through darkness unto death?"

"Death . . . no probs."

"See ya."

Turning to run, Zi'ib and Tala bumped into Sarah, coming through from the storeroom. She swept them firmly forwards as the girl pushed open the door.

"Hello, Artemesia. I'm Sarah. This is Wolfie, Zi'ib and Tala."

"Call me Missy. Artemesia is such a dumb name. Wow, this is great, I've heard loads about Thornham but I've never been here before."

"Why are you dragging that tortoise around?" Tala demanded.

"Dad said Sarah might want to paint me with a pet. Johnny knows a guy who breeds tortoises so he went and picked me one out."

"Who's Johnny?"

"Johnny Yu, our driver." The tortoise paddled the air as she turned to wave at the car.

A man in a peaked cap lifted his hand in salute as the car slipped smoothly down the crescent.

Missy held up the white box. "I brought you a cake."

"Did Johnny pick that out too?" said Tala.

"How kind," Sarah said, quickly. "Why don't you take Missy into the kitchen? I'll just shut the shop."

Missy followed Zi'ib and Tala. Sarah reached for the top bolt, swayed and stumbled back. Wolfie caught her arm.

"Ooh, I'm a bit . . . dizzy," she said, blinking hard.

"Go on, Mum, I'll lock up."

When Missy saw the fire blazing in the grate and all the tea things laid out, she dropped the cake box and wheeled round in delight, sending the tortoise slipping from its ribbon. She screamed. Tala leapt forward and caught the quivering reptile in mid-air. He lay in her cupped hands, his under-shell a deep creamy colour dotted with five black spots like the dots on a die, his little legs waving helplessly. Gently, she turned him over.

"Bonbon, are you OK?" cried Missy.

"Bonbon?" snorted Tala.

"Cute, isn't it? It's 'cos he looks like a chocolate truffle."

Tala would rather have stuck the poker in her eye than admit it, but the little tortoise's rich brown upper shell, ringed with bumpy squares, *did* look a bit like a dome of chocolate.

"He's not a piece of candy," she said crossly.

Missy blushed and lifted Bonbon out of Tala's hands. "I never had a pet before. I didn't want him to escape. Guess I didn't think."

She kicked off her shoes and lay back on the sofa, curling like a cat among the cushions, with Bonbon on her lap. Her hair gleamed in the firelight, the worn leather framing her delicate face in flame-warmed browns and sharp black shadow.

Sarah tilted her head. "l might paint you like that; you look as if you belong there."

Tala scowled.

Sarah screwed up her eyes. "But it needs a splash of colour. . ."

A muffled bark interrupted her thoughts.

"Who shut Elvis out?" snapped Wolfie.

"I did," admitted Sarah. "I thought Missy might be scared of dogs."

"Don't worry, she *loves* animals." Tala threw open the door, noting with satisfaction that Elvis was covered in mud. Lashing his tail, he bounded across the kitchen, and hurled himself at Missy. She cringed into the cushions, waiting to be smothered in a blanket of fetid fur, but was astonished when he laid his head on her knee and looked up at her with adoring amber eyes. Bonbon, now recovered from his aerobatics, peeped his wrinkled head out, quite unperturbed when his beaky mouth encountered a large wet snout. For a held breath the girl, the dog and the tortoise seemed to slip out of time, as if reflected in a mirror hanging in another age. Missy put out tentative fingers to stroke Elvis's head. "He likes me."

Tala yanked Elvis's collar. "He must be sickening for something. Probably needs worming."

"He's all right, leave him," said Sarah. "He can stay in the picture if he'll keep still."

Mr Forester came through the back door, tired and preoccupied.

"Come and meet Missy," said Sarah. "She's the daughter of an old friend of mine."

"Hi," said Missy.

"Delighted, my dear," murmured Mr Forester. "Zi'ib, there have been a couple of messages on the discussion board from a user calling himself Wisdomseeker, claiming he could capture a Sphere using dark energies." The old man's usually gentle eyes blazed sternly. "Could you delete them, please, and tell him it's the editorial policy of the *EM* to reject such postings. Anyone who thinks they can meddle with dark forces is either a fiend or a fool."

"No probs," said Zi'ib.

Wolfie turned sharply, knocking his sketch pad off the arm of the sofa.

Missy picked it up and started leafing through it. "These are cool; who did them?"

"Me," said Wolfie.

"You should show them to my dad."

Wolfie ground his teeth.

"So, er, have you inherited Mo's talent?" asked Sarah. "He was a brilliant painter when we were at art school."

"No. I'm going to be an architect," Missy replied with airy certainty. "I'm helping with the design of Dad's new gallery. It'll be great. Whenever I'm done over there I can come and hang out with you guys."

"That'd be lovely," said Sarah. She glared at Wolfie, imploring him to wipe the scowl off his face. "How about some of that cake?"

He ripped open the box. A gasp jolted from his throat. The cake was a round chocolate sponge, smooth, expensive and unadorned except for a simple pattern stencilled on the top in a dusting of icing sugar. Tala and Zi'ib leaned over to see what was wrong. The shape in the sugar was an eight-point star divided in two.

"Why did you choose *this* cake?" Wolfie demanded.

Missy came over to look into the box, nervously clenching her fists. "Don't you like chocolate?"

"I meant the decoration."

She relaxed. "The Patisserie Madeleine always puts the riven star on stuff they make for us."

"Why?"

"It's the logo for Dad's business."

151

Sarah sliced into the sponge. "You must have seen the de Monteneuf crest before. It's on the tombs in the church."

Tala gagged. "You're Artemesia *de Monteneuf*?"

Missy nodded and took a piece of cake. "Dad's family lived round here yonks ago. They had some old house that burned down, so they moved out."

Mr Forester's dejection had melted like snow in the sun. "My goodness, Missy, I'm going to be featuring the history of the de Monteneufs in my magazine."

"Why?" said Missy, letting Elvis lick the crumbs from her fingers.

"For a series on Thornham's mystic history. Your ancestor Sir Guy, the one who built Thornham Hall, he was one of the Knights Templar."

Missy frowned. "Who were they?"

"Protectors of the sacred paths and pilgrim routes during and after the crusades. By keeping the streams of pilgrims moving, they ensured there was a constant stream of focused consciousness regenerating the energies flowing along the ley lines."

"Ley lines?"

"Paths of natural energy that criss-cross the earth." He smiled. "You may even have inherited your interest in architecture from him."

"Really?"

"Oh yes. Templars were great builders. They hid all sorts of arcane knowledge in the fabric of their buildings.

152

There's a legend that Sir Guy built a vault beneath his manor house that opened into another dimension."

"Wow," said Missy, "I'll tell Dad. He loves that kind of stuff."

The old man looked at Wolfie. "Didn't you find some ancient connection between the Browns and the de Monteneufs when you did that local history project last year?"

Wolfie stuffed an enormous lump of cake into his mouth so he wouldn't have to answer. Mr Forester pulled a tufty eyebrow. "That's right. One of the de Monteneufs gave your ancestor the land to build this house. Agnes Brown, wasn't it?"

"Ban't bebember," Wolfie mumbled.

"Ah well," sighed Mr Forester. "How charming that time's circling course has revived the 'kinnection' between two such ancient Thornham families."

"What's a *kinnection*?" demanded Missy.

"A fateful link brought about by the energies in the ley lines."

"Wow," she said again.

Ridian Winter was working feverishly on his plans to revive the power of the Manus Sacra, but the silence from his broken star was eating at his soul. Everything depended on capturing the Sphere and using it to restore the Link of Light. Once he could communicate with those wondrous minds they would tell him how to use the black stream to set them free. Yet for all the calm confidence he had displayed to Stefan de Witt, his plans for getting hold of the Sphere were little more than threadbare hopes.

None of the crumbling stone energy receptors on this benighted planet were in good enough condition to serve his needs. And so, like some barbaric necromancer groping after truth, he would have to cobble together a makeshift point of magnetic force, powerful enough to draw the Sphere down from the Wilderness Between the Worlds. He tried to steady his nerves, holding to the knowledge that vibration and rotation lay at the heart of all things. And all things, from the smallest particle to the greatest planet, moved in constant circles. All he had to do was create the perfect combination of matter and negative energy and transmute its vibrations to the right frequency at the exact moment when the orbiting particles of the Sphere were in perfect synchrony with the movement of the earth. That time was drawing near. The Chosen would be avenged.

PART TWO
The Devil's Dancers

15

Still Waters

"How's the investigation into the revival of the leys going? Shall I go through the file of all the writers who've sent in material?" Wolfie asked as he and Tala took their places at the horseshoe of wobbly metal tables set up in the sitting room of number forty-five.

"It's all right, Esmé's looking after it," said Mr Forester.

Wolfie blanched as Esmé came in from the hall. "I wondered if you would do an illustration for my next column." She handed him a couple of sheets of paper handwritten in purple ink, her sharp little eyes drilling searchingly into his. "Read it carefully. I think you'll find it very . . . interesting."

She glanced round. "Where's your friend Zi'ib?"

"He's coming in a minute," said Tala.

"My taxi is here, I must hurry," Esmé said. Adjusting her hat, she set off down the front steps, passing Sid on his way in with his tools.

Tala glared after her, annoyed that Esmé acted as if she owned the place and bewildered that Mr Forester didn't seem to mind.

"Why do you put up with her?"

"At first, I had no choice," said Mr Forester. "But she is an astute businesswoman and to be honest it's rather a relief to share the burden of running the *EM* with someone with such a profound knowledge of ancient wisdom."

Tala noticed a copy of Esmé's book, *My Travels in Atlantis*, lying on the desk. "Can I borrow this?" she asked, hoping it might hold a clue to its unfathomable author.

"Looks to me like there's a leaky pipe in your brickwork, Mr F," announced Sid. "I'll have to dig out your plaster to have a look."

"That's fine, Sid. Wolfie, a chap called Senki has posted a couple of extremely interesting comments on the message board about his research into Spheres and cleansing dark leys. Just the sort of topics the magazine needs to be covering. Can you email him and see if he'd be interested in writing an article for me on a subject of his choice? Readers will respond better to his postings if they see some longer pieces from him."

"Erm . . . OK," Wolfie said.

"And get him to send me a photo," added Mr Forester.

"Photo?" gulped Wolfie.

"I'm going to include byline shots of all the contributors. I'm told it encourages reader loyalty."

"Don't worry," whispered Tala, "I'll write his article and if we pretend he's some weirdo reclusive artist who hates being photographed, you can draw him a self-portrait."

As Sid hacked at the wall, Wolfie looked down at Esmé's column. Entitled "Strangers at the Temple Gate: A Far Memory Recalled by Kandass, High Priestess of Ancient Meroe", the piece described Kandass's meeting with three green-eyed wanderers from another world, known to the ancients as the Lands of the Wolf.

Terrified that she had written about the prophesy of their birth, he skimmed the words, his panic steadying when he saw there was no mention of the children of mingled blood. He reached the final paragraph:

The wise wanderers from the Lands of the Wolf talked of the threads of force that bind the worlds of men and the sacred Spheres that govern their flow.

And I asked them, "O wise ones, tell me how I might draw such a Sphere into my temple."

Wolfie went rigid. Was this it? Was he about to read the secret that would allow him to capture a Sphere and bring his father back from Lupus?

His heart pounded more loudly than the smash of Sid's hammer.

And the wise ones answered, "To draw down a Sphere on a thread of light, O priestess, would take a lifetime. To draw down a Sphere on a thread of darkness would take less than the waxing of a single moon."

He felt sick. That was pretty much what Wisdomseeker had said. Swallowing hard, he went on reading.

"And would the darkness not infect its powers?" I cried. And they bowed low and said, "O priestess, thou knowest that the powers of darkness are but the sable sisters of the powers of light, no more to be reviled than thine own reflection in a pool of darkened water."

He felt himself falling into a pit of hope and uncertainty. Could that be true?

"Is something wrong?" Mr Forester asked, looking up.

"This, er, stuff Esmé wrote about using dark energy to capture a Sphere."

"Oh yes. She claims she merely transcribed the words Kandass put in her mouth. Though I suspect she may have put it in to spice things up a bit. However, given the extreme sensitivity of the subject and the *EM*'s declared stance on the matter, she has agreed to delete that section."

When no one was looking Wolfie quickly emailed Wisdomseeker from Nikto Senki's account.

Isn't it dangerous to mess around with dark energy?

Although Ridian Winter felt absurdly out of place on Esmé's chintz-covered sofa, her flat was a useful venue for their secret meetings. He read Wolfie's email on his Blackberry and sent a response. **Only the ignorant and the foolish fear darkness**.

160

"One of them is succumbing," he told Esmé. "I wonder which it is? One is all it will take to break the power of their combined wisdom, but we must keep up the pressure on all of them and stay vigilant. The positive energies will almost certainly be trying to throw helpers in their path.

Each time Ridian looked her way Esmé caught something black and bitter in his eyes that deadened her soul, confirming her suspicion that she was caught up in something vast and terrifying that could have dire consequences for the whole cosmos. Exhilaration swept her fear away. She cared for no one in this world and no one cared for her. For the first time in her whole life she was part of something grand and exalted. Finally her existence had meaning.

Zi'ib came rushing in holding a long, plastic-handled object with what looked like a tilted silver halo on the end. He waved it over Sid's tool bag, setting off a loud bleeping.

"What's that?" Tala said.

"A metal detector. I got it in Strowgers for a fiver! Come on, let's give it a try!"

"You mind my veg!" Sid called as they dashed outside.

"It's brilliant," said Zi'ib. "If there's a spear buried here it'll tell us exactly where it is."

He went first, striding up and down, sweeping the detector in wide arcs. Tala ran behind carrying Sid's spade, shrieking with excitement when the beeps led them to a handful of rusty nails, four bottle tops and an old penny.

Wolfie leaned against the wall of the house. Watching them. Not seeing them. His head was full of thoughts of the Sphere, of dark energy, of his dad, as brittle and confused as the branches of the old thorn tree twisting above him against the sky.

"Come on, Wolfie, have a go!" called Zi'ib. "It's like dowsing, only it's battery operated!"

"No, you're all right."

Zi'ib thrust the detector at him. Instantly it started beeping. Zi'ib swung the search coil left. Beep. Right. Beep, beep.

Tala plunged the spade into the soil by Wolfie's feet, hitting something hard just beneath the surface. Zi'ib took over, slicing away the turf from a pocked iron manhole cover the size of a bicycle tyre with a large ring bolted into a dip in the middle.

"Probably drains," Wolfie said, intrigued all the same.

With Zi'ib levering the edge with the spade and Wolfie heaving on the metal ring, they hefted the cover aside. A clear sharp smell pricked their nostrils. Zi'ib peered into a hole beneath lined with tiered slabs of mossy stone like a tiny amphitheatre, leading down to a bubbling spring of rust-coloured water fringed with pale, sun-starved ferns.

Tala ran to fetch Sid and Mr Forester, shouting, "Hey, we've found a well!"

"You be careful," cautioned Sid, rushing over to pull Zi'ib back from the edge. He smiled. "Looks like they've found the source of your damp, Mr F."

Mr Forester pointed to the side road running past the garden. "Rag Tree Road! There had to be a healing well round here somewhere." He patted the thorn tree. "And this must be the old rag tree itself."

"Rag tree?" queried Tala.

"When the sick came to drink the healing waters they'd tie a rag to the tree as an offering."

"Water can't heal you."

"It can if it's full of minerals. Look how red it is, brimming with iron."

Sid scratched his forehead with his thumb. "Best I could do is divert the water and fill the whole thing with concrete."

"Oh no!" cried Mr Forester, appalled. "I'm sure the damp will dry out of its own accord now the healing waters have let us know they're here. They're a force for good, you see, positive energy to counteract the dark stream."

Sid kicked a stone into the well. It dropped with an echoey plop. "Death trap, that is."

"Why don't you build a little wall around it, so no one can fall in?" suggested Mr Forester.

"You're the guv'nor." Sid's face brightened. "I could use that rubble lying round the greenhouse, save me taking it down the dump. If you kids give me a hand carting it over I'll make a start first thing."

Elvis bounded around barking while everyone started clanging lumps of rubble into Sid's wheelbarrow.

"Clean 'em off first," chided Sid.

Zi'ib showed Wolfie a piece of stone he'd just rubbed clean. "What's a nitch?"

Wolfie flicked away a nub of mud. "Not nitch, *snitch*."

"There's writing all over 'em," Sid said, peering into the wheelbarrow.

"Creepy. This one says devil's doorway," said Tala.

Sid picked out a large wedge-shaped block. "This one's a keystone. Looks like we've got the remains of an old arch."

"Then it was probably set into a wall above the well," said Mr Forester. "It would be fascinating to know what the inscription said."

Soon everyone was scraping stones and handing them to Zi'ib, who moved them around like giant jigsaw pieces, using a chiselled wave of decoration along the inner edge of the arch to guide which blocks went where.

"Now, what have we got?" said Mr Forester, fumbling for his glasses.

"This bit says, *The itch, the snitch, rheumatic and the gout.* . ." intoned Sid in his poshest voice. ". . .*if the devil puts them in you, let these waters take them out.*"

"It rhymes. That helps," said Zi'ib, pairing up rhyming words. "Here we go: *life strife, dance lance, fear.* . ." His hand froze. ". . .*spear,*" he finished softly. Quiet hope sped his fingers as he dropped the final pieces into place.

When the arch was complete, Tala fetched her notebook and copied out the words as Zi'ib read out the rest of the rhyme.

If the Devil does his dancing on the roads that lead
  to life
Take a needle from these waters to relieve the world
  of strife.
If the Devil's doorway opens and his demons join
  the Dance
Then seek across the oceans for a spur and spear
  and lance.
For the Devil he is clever and the Devil he is sly
And the roads grow sorely restless when the Devil
  passes by
But you'll not hurt him with your weapons till your
  will's a whetted spear
For the will's the only weapon that the Devil's
  Dancers fear.

"What's that all about?" said Sid.

Mr Forester read it through two or three times, pulling his eyebrow. "I'm not certain, but these references to devils and demons dancing could possibly be trace memories of malign vibrations given off by dark energy."

Tala brooded over this explanation, underlining words in her notebook. After a bit she said, "So *relieving* the world of strife – could that be *cleansing* the dark energy?"

Mr Forester reread the poem and smiled at her admiringly. "Well, yes, I suppose it could. How insightful."

"So how do you 'take a needle from these waters'?" asked Zi'ib.

Mr Forester shook his head. "I have no idea."

Sid cocked his ear. "Phone's ringing, Mr F."

Zi'ib ran inside and grabbed the receiver. It was Zane, shouting to make himself heard over intermittent bursts of static.

"Any news about Mum?"

"Not yet. I'm still in Khartoum waiting for a flight to Chad. I called the shop; Sarah said you were helping with the magazine. How's that going?"

"Erm . . . OK."

"Any sign of Ridian Winter?"

"No, nothing."

"Any headway against the dark ley?"

"Some, but it's slow going. We've definitely got to find spears, but we don't know where or how."

Zane's voice grew urgent. "You must hurry; the taint will be strengthening and spreading fast. Look around you, Zi'ib. The good energies will be desperate to show you the way."

"OK, Dad, we're doing our best."

"Zi'ib. . ."

"Yes, Dad."

"The dark energies aren't getting to any of you, are they – you know, tempting you with any funny ideas?"

"No way, Dad. We're on this one hundred per cent. But there's this weird psychic woman, Dame Esmé, who went into a trance and started burbling in Meroitic, claiming she was Kandass, a priestess of ancient Meroe. She knew who we were, but when Esmé woke up said she said she didn't have a clue what Kandass had said."

He felt the jump of Zane's star. "The workings of the leys are subtle and strange, Zi'ib. Transference of disembodied consciousness is theoretically possible, but to my knowledge has never been achieved. This woman may have been sent by the positive energies to help you or by the negative ones to hamper you. You must use your own wisdom to judge. Be wary."

Zi'ib glanced over his shoulder. "Shall I put you on speaker? Mr Forester and the others are coming."

"Sure. I'm staying with Professor Salah for a couple of days. He's been showing me the artefacts you found in the desert, very impressive."

"How is the professor?" called Mr Forester. "Do send him my regards."

"He's fine, Remus. More than fine, actually. Some big company are giving him a huge grant to finish the excavations at Meroe and build an on-site study centre."

"What? So they can sink a couple of oil wells in the ruins?" exclaimed Tala.

"He insists they're not like that – they're into renewable energy, and preserving the planet's ancient heritage. Zemogen, I think they're called."

A flake of recognition floated up through a mire of memories in Tala's mind and sank again before she could catch it.

"That's the outfit taking all the advertising in the *EM*,"

said Mr Forester. "And they've offered their new London headquarters as a venue for SILK's big earth energies conference."

There was a long crackly pause before Zane said, "If you get a chance, try and find out a bit more about them."

"OK," said Zi'ib.

"Look, I've got to go. I'm meeting with the commissioner of police. I'll call you in a couple of days."

"Bye, Dad."

"OK, Google. Find me Zemogen." Zi'ib scanned the laptop screen. At random he clicked a press release from the previous year. Beneath an elegant silver Z and the slogan *Zemogen: natural energy for you and your world,* the release read: *Zemogen International has acquired the disused power station at Battersea on the South Bank of the River Thames for conversion into their new headquarters.*

"This building is a temple of power, a cultural landmark equal to St Paul's Cathedral or Stonehenge," said Zemogen's Head of Special Projects, Stefan de Witt. "To demolish what is left of this iconic building would be totally out of keeping with the ethos of Zemogen. The office complex proposed for the accompanying site will be leased to companies with aims complementary to Zemogen's own."

Mr Forester nodded approvingly. "You know, modern power stations are frequently found on natural power nodes. There's an interesting theory that the landscape has memory that continues to influence future generations, even when the type of energy generated on these ancient sites changes radically."

"I'm sure I've heard of Zemogen before," Tala said, frowning.

"Me too," said Zi'ib.

"That's the skill of these global corporations," said Mr Forester. "They slip their branding into the very warp and weft of our existence."

Zi'ib spooled down to a photograph showing Stefan de Witt with his twin brother, Zemogen's chairman Johann. Behind them a huge glassy bubble glistened between the chimneys of the power station.

The original roof was removed by the previous owners. We have mitigated this vandalism by covering the exposed areas with a transparent eco dome made from crystex, a silicone-based material developed and manufactured by Zemogen Industries that replicates all the properties of natural quartz crystal.

"You'd never think those two guys were twins," Tala giggled, pointing to the mousey, balding Stefan and the dark, handsome Johann.

"Hey, we'd better go," said Zi'ib. "We said we'd help Sarah with another big fudge order."

"Any chance you could pop back tomorrow afternoon? I'd really appreciate some help before we go to press on Monday."

"Yeah, 'course," said Zi'ib, as they gathered up their things and rushed away.

"That metal detector is brilliant," Tala said. "We'd never have found this rhyme without it." She was pinning the words to their chart.

"What do you think *you'll not hurt him with your weapons till your <u>WILL</u>'s a whetted spear* means?" said Zi'ib.

"Probably that your brain's got to be giving off strong positive vibrations before you can have any impact on negative forces. So if your will to heal the contaminated ley is weak, you've got to toughen it up, just like sharpening a blunt blade into a deadly one."

Wolfie flinched. His own will to cleanse the dark ley was weakening fast. Yet even as he admitted the shameful truth to himself and felt the pull of positive energy plucking at his conscience, in his mind's eye he saw the quivering radiance of a Sphere descending to earth on a thread of dark energy and imagined it unlocking the gateway that would bring his father home.

Tala was raking the metal detector over the mess in the room, laughing every time it beeped. "Let's take it to the pub tomorrow. We'll say we're doing a school project on archaeology. You're quiet," she said, glancing at Wolfie, who was now poring over the copy of Esmé's article.

He looked up guiltily. "This stuff Esmé wrote about it taking a lifetime to capture a Sphere using positive energy, but no time if you use dark energy. Do you think it's true?"

Tala frowned. "Even if it is, there's no point if it would

contaminate the Sphere. She'll say anything to get attention. You should read her book. It's full of murder and intrigue."

Zi'ib said, "Dad said the negative *or* the positive energies could have sent her and we should use our wisdom to judge. Trouble is my star has gone so weird I can't work out what it's telling me about anything." He glared at the laptop screen. "Blimmin' cheek, look at this. Now Wisdomseeker's been banned from the discussion board he's sending stuff to Senki's private inbox."

Wolfie's belly tightened. "What's he say?"

"*He who embraces dark energies holds the keys to untold power.*"

"You heard what Mr Forester said. He's either up to no good or really stupid." With a couple of exasperated jabs Zi'ib deleted the message.

Sarah looked up from a steaming vat of melting sugar, her cheeks two burning spots of pink in her thin face.

Wolfie took the wooden spoon from her hand. "Sit down, Mum, forget the fudge."

She slumped into a chair. "I wish I could, but they want fifteen kilos this time, all by tomorrow."

Elvis crept close and nuzzled her knee.

"That's ridiculous; who are these people?"

"Whoever they are, they'll have to make do with twelve. I haven't got enough Saravita to make any more."

"I bet they're selling it on for a huge profit," Tala said.

"As long as they pay me, they can do what they like with it."

"Maybe they're trying to work out the recipe," said Zi'ib.

Sarah smiled wanly. "What good's the recipe without the Saravita?"

Zi'ib handed her a crumpled form. "Can you sign this? I've got to run in a school sports event."

Sarah read it through. "I wish I could come and watch you, Zi'ib, but Wiltshire's miles away."

"Don't worry, I'm only going because Mr Pegg's making me."

Wolfie looked at his pale and exhausted mother and thought how great it would be if his dad were there to look after her.

When Zi'ib and Tala were outside scanning the yard with the metal detector, Wolfie sat in his room finishing Nikto Senki's self-portrait, stealing constant glances at the picture of his father on the mantelpiece. Zi'ib and Tala came stomping upstairs.

"We didn't find anything," complained Zi'ib. He tossed down the metal detector and threw himself on his bunk.

Wolfie held up a pen and ink drawing of a thoughtful face with a wide brow, high cheekbones, a slightly crooked nose and dark spiky hair. "Meet Nikto Senki."

"I'll just check his emails," grinned Zi'ib, opening Senki's mailbox. There were two new messages. The first was from a South African anthropologist called Dr Karin Angstrom.

I have been studying some newly discovered rock art in a remote area of the Drakensberg, depicting snakes and demonic beasts which I am convinced portray a landscape infected by negative earth energies. As you can see from the attached photographs, the images show human shamans standing in the path of a dark ley (represented by a black snake) and impeding the flow of bad energies by absorbing some of their malignity (represented by a coiled snake symbol on the forehead of the shaman). Further images of these shamans depict sickness and usually death. Some, however, are seen to shed the coiled snake symbol and resume their normal rituals. I interpret these tableaux to mean that the shamans carried the contamination inside them until either it destroyed them or the ley itself was cleansed.

I assume there was something in the particular make-up of these shamans that made them peculiarly susceptible to the energies, since the other human figures in the scenes are left unmarked. Unfortunately none of the tableaux showing the actual cleansing rituals have survived.

"Typical," said Tala. "Stick a printout on the board anyway."

"Oh no, Wisdomseeker's at it again," groaned Zi'ib,

173

opening the next message. He put on a mock spooky voice. *"The forces of light and the forces of darkness are but twin faces of the same cosmic power.* What's the matter with him?"

"Tell him to get lost," said Tala.

"Yeah," Wolfie said and added quickly: "Tell him to stick his wisdom where no one'll want to seek it."

For much of that night he lay awake pondering Wisdomseeker's words, wondering if a world flooded with dark energy would be such a terrible place if his dad was living in it, looking after Sarah, looking after him.

Stealthily he climbed down from the top bunk, checked to see that Zi'ib was asleep and sent a reply to Wisdomseeker's private mailbox.

> *Can we meet up somewhere? I need to know exactly how to use the dark forces to capture a Sphere.*

Wisdomseeker's response came quickly.

> *Be patient. When the time is right I will tell you everything you want to know.*

Wolfie sprang back from the computer and turned to see Elvis's glowing eyes staring at him reproachfully out of the darkness.

16

Power Points

"Just shout if you need help," Sarah told Sid the next morning, dragging a box of Easter eggs into the shop.

Sid hefted the box on to the counter. "There won't be much I can't handle. You look all in."

"Just a headache, but I . . . I wondered if you could cover for me all day on Tuesday." She noticed the kitchen door was slightly ajar and dropped her voice to a whisper. "I don't want the children to know, specially not Wolfie. I've got a hospital appointment. Just a scan and some tests, but you know how these things can drag on."

"I'll stay as long as you want. Why don't you go up now and have a lie-down."

"I can't, Sid, I've got someone coming for a portrait sitting in half an hour."

"So lie down for half an hour. Do you good."

As Sarah stumbled gratefully upstairs, Tala pulled back from the door, a familiar pain squeezing her heart. Her mum, her dad, now Sarah. Bad stuff happened to everyone she cared about. She waited a moment, sweaty and upset, before blundering through to get the big brass scales from the shop and dumping them on the kitchen table. Wolfie and Zi'ib were getting ready to box up the week's fudge orders and frowned at her, wanting to know what was wrong. They got no response and the ferocity of her glare silenced their questions.

At ten o'clock the Bentley drew up outside. Sid nipped upstairs to knock on Sarah's door and was back behind the counter in time to receive one of Missy's almost perfect smiles as she swept past, clutching Bonbon's box. She flopped on the sofa, tipped the tortoise on to her lap and ruffled Elvis's head, watching intrigued as Wolfie, Tala and Zi'ib got on with cutting, weighing and boxing the piled-up trays of fudge.

"You guys must come over to my place," she said. "Johnny would pick you up and bring you back. We could see a movie or there's a great new diner I want to try." Misreading the horror on their faces, she gabbled nervously. "Don't worry, I'll pay. I've got loads of my allowance left."

"What planet is *she* from?" whispered Wolfie.

Sarah came in, pinning up her hair.

"Is it OK if I listen to music?" Missy rammed in an

earbud. "The sound quality on this thing is amazing. Dad got it in Japan."

"Yeah, how about some music?" said Tala. She dumped down a box of fudge and switched on the radio, filling the air with the tinny whine of a local station. "The sound quality on this thing is rubbish, Sarah got it in a jumble sale."

Blushing, Missy slipped the earbud into her pocket. Sarah made a few valiant attempts to get them all chatting but the effort proved too much. After an hour she sat back, rubbing her neck. "Let's stop for today. Johnny will be here any minute." She smiled at Missy. "You must be getting a bit stiff."

"Must be tough lolling about on the sofa," huffed Wolfie.

"There's a bloke come to pick up some fudge," called Sid.

Wolfie and Zi'ib scooped up the packed boxes and followed Sarah into the shop.

"Why are you being so mean to that poor girl?" she hissed. "She can't help it if her dad's rich."

"So get him to buy her a brain," muttered Wolfie.

This time it was a different delivery man who handed Sarah an envelope of money.

"I'll sign for it," said Wolfie, taking the clipboard. "There's no address. Where's it going?"

"Sorry, mate. Client confidentiality."

Wolfie's curiosity turned to suspicion. Who was this

mystery customer? Why were they so determined to keep their identity secret? He handed the clipboard back and spotted Johnny easing the Bentley into the space behind the van. He ran to the kitchen. "Hey, Missy, why don't you take us for a drive, right now?"

"Sure," Missy said, popping Bonbon back into his box. "We can go for lunch somewhere."

"No. I fancy a bit of sightseeing." Grabbing her coat, Wolfie hustled her through the door.

"Hurry up," he called over his shoulder to Zi'ib and Tala.

"Have you gone mad?" growled Tala.

"Shut up, just come on."

"Get lost."

He beckoned to Zi'ib, who shook his head. "We're s'posed to be helping Mr Forester this afternoon *and going out with the metal detector*," he said meaningfully.

Wolfie dragged Missy on to the pavement just as the van was pulling out. Johnny Yu held open the door as they dived into the back and slid along the soft leather seat.

"Where to?" he said, getting into the front.

"Follow that van . . . please," said Wolfie. Swamped by the cocooning comfort of the Bentley, he sat forward with his hands on his knees, fearful of dirtying the creamy leather or smudging the walnut veneer.

Missy giggled. "What's going on?"

"I want to know who's buying up Mum's fudge. She thinks it's a coffee shop, but I think it's someone trying to steal the recipe 'cos they won't say who they are and they pay cash so she can't trace them."

"We can't have that," Johnny said, hitting the accelerator.

At Clapham Common, Wolfie panicked, convinced they were following the wrong van. He caught Johnny's young, handsome face in the rear-view mirror.

"Relax," Johnny said.

Wolfie could not relax, not with Tala's fury churning his star and making him feel guilty. Well, she'd better get used to it. He wasn't going to do anything to help cleanse the dark forces until he'd talked to Wisdomseeker. And anyway, tracking down this mystery about the fudge was important too. His suspicion that he was on the trail of something a lot more sinister than culinary espionage grew stronger as the fluted chimneys of Battersea Power Station appeared on the horizon, silhouetted against the grey South London skies. The white van sped past Battersea Park and pulled up in front of a set of tall iron gates.

"This sure ain't no coffee shop," Johnny said in a mock gangster voice.

A security guard came out to inspect the driver's pass.

"Oh, noooo," groaned Wolfie.

Johnny tossed a comb into his lap.

"Smarten up," he commanded. "OK, Missy, go for the Douglas Harrington." He inched the car forward.

Wolfie tugged the comb through his tangled hair. "Douglas who?"

"Shh. Keep quiet." She fluffed her fringe and took a little notebook from her bag. Johnny lowered the windows.

"Good afternoon. I'm here to pick up Lord Harrington."

The guard cast a bored glance over his clipboard. "Not according to this."

Johnny leaned his elbow out of the window. "That new private secretary's as daft as they come, but there'll be hell to pay if His Lordship doesn't find his car ready and waiting. I've got his granddaughter and her friend in the back – he's taking them to some big charity do."

Wolfie shrank back as Missy gazed up at the security guard.

"It's an auction to raise money for orphans. I'm introducing the whole event. I've got my speech ready and everything." She clutched the notebook to her chest. "If we're late Gramps will go mad." A single tear rolled down her cheek.

"All right, all right," said the guard, slapping a green sticker on the windscreen. "Which company is he visiting?"

Johnny's shoulders stiffened. "I've got it written down," he said, flipping open the glove compartment.

Wolfie ran his tongue over his dry lips. "I think it's called Zemogen."

Missy flashed him a look of surprise as the security guard buzzed open the gates.

"Thanks, mate," said Johnny. "Do I follow where that van went?"

"No, he's going to the labs, you want to keep right for the Zemogen HQ and park up in the visitor's car park."

Johnny nodded and steered the Bentley through the gates.

"Brilliant," grinned Wolfie. "You've done that before, haven't you?"

"Oh, yes," laughed Johnny. "We usually do Lady Pilkington-Howard but I thought we'd give His Lordship an outing today."

Missy giggled. "Johnny's saving to go to drama school, so we act stuff out to help him practise." She bit her lip. "Dad would go bonkers if he knew, specially the stuff about orphans. He gets all serious about charity work."

Wolfie's body jolted. The Bentley was passing through powerful lines of force as Johnny followed the curving track around the power station.

Behind the mesh fencing, JCBs churned wide furrows in the dark clay while men in hard hats dotted the scaffolding. A shaft of sunlight hit the eco dome rising between the towering chimney stacks, causing it to shimmer like the meniscus on a gigantic water drop.

"That dome's really cool. Maybe Dad could put one on his new gallery," said Missy.

Wolfie wasn't listening. He was tuning in to the arteries of energy coursing towards the power station. What was this place? The forces here had a feeling of purpose so utterly different from those at Thornham. He knew it was not a gateway but some other sort of exchange point; a pulsing nerve centre on the living curve of the earth.

They came to a fork. In the distance they spied the van parked beside some prefabricated huts. A man in a white coat was signing for the delivery while another unloaded the fudge.

"Hop out. I'll go and park," said Johnny. "Call me if there's a problem."

Keeping close to the fence, they crept forward and bolted into the muddy gap behind the huts.

"Give us a leg-up," whispered Wolfie.

Linking her fingers, Missy staggered beneath the pressure of his filthy trainer. He grabbed the window sill and peered through the glass.

"Empty," he mouthed, jumping down.

Edging along a stack of railway sleepers, they peeped through the slatted blinds of the next hut. Beneath strips of glowing neon, men and women sat at slate-topped benches, their white coats bright against the dark surface. Some were hunched over microscopes; others, surrounded by flasks and specimen jars, inspected steaming pipettes of fluorescent liquid, or tended beakers of bubbling gloop balanced over hissing jets of flame. Those nearest the window were tweezering tiny fragments of matter on to slides. Despite the new and expensive-looking equipment there was something makeshift about the bundles of extension leads snaking across the floor, the skewed wallcharts swinging from blobs of Blu-tack and the crude strips of duct tape holding up the ventilator that gave the whole set-up a temporary, put-together-in-a-hurry sort of feel.

Crouching low, Wolfie lugged an empty packing case towards the far window, testing the flimsy wood with his hands before climbing up and squinting through the slats to get a better view of the wallcharts. Amidst the printouts and timetables hung a diagram of a plant with a head of eight-petalled star-shaped flowers growing from a fat round seed.

"Oi, you kids, come 'ere," yelled a voice.

"Run!" gasped Wolfie, jumping down. To his astonishment Missy stood her ground, pushing a couple of buttons on her mobile while smiling sweetly at the angry-looking man striding towards them.

"Come on!" Wolfie hissed.

"I'm Beatrice Harrington, Lord Harrington's granddaughter," lisped Missy. "I'm so sorry. We were touring the company and got lost. We were just looking for the rest of the group. Please don't worry about escorting us back to the main building. Gramps' driver will pick us up. Look, here he is now."

The Bentley swung into sight. Johnny leapt out, nodding deferentially at the man.

"Allow me to apologize on Lord Harrington's behalf." He turned sternly to Missy. "He was very worried about you, Miss Beatrice. Next time, please make sure that you stay with the group."

Hearts pounding, they jumped in. Johnny backed the

Bentley expertly down the track and rocketed towards the gates, murmuring a gratified "Yes!" when they opened electronically at his approach. Saluting his thanks to the security guard, he hit the accelerator and veered smoothly on to Chelsea Bridge. Wolfie let out a roar that was relief, laughter and disbelief all mixed up. "You two deserve Oscars!"

"So what *were* they doing with that fudge?" Johnny said.

"Analysing it," Missy said, wide-eyed with excitement.

"You'd better tell your mum to cancel their order," Johnny said, glancing at Wolfie in the mirror. "By the way, how did you know the company was called Zemogen?"

"Just a hunch," Wolfie replied, staring back at the great fluted chimneys.

The barman at the Wish Hound had been a bit suspicious when Tala and Zi'ib turned up that lunchtime armed with a spade and a metal detector, asking to search the beer garden, but they looked so serious he gave in, teasing them that he wanted a cut of any treasure they found. They returned half an hour later looking totally fed up and dumped £9.57 in muddy coins on the counter. They didn't even cheer up when he swept the money into a plastic beer mug and said they could keep it. *Honestly!* What did they *think* they were going to find under a load of manky old picnic tables, some priceless museum piece?

"It feels weird without Wolfie," Zi'ib said as they trudged home. "Like we'll never win out against the dark energies unless all three of us are working together."

"Then if we fail it will be all his fault," snapped Tala.

17

The de Monteneuf Tower

"Where to?" asked Johnny.

Missy glanced shyly at Wolfie. "If you come to the apartment I could show you Dad's pictures."

He was about to refuse, but the stormy waves of Tala's fury churning his star put him right off the idea of going home. He had enough problems on his mind. Why were Zemogen after the Saravita? Would decontaminating the ley destroy his one real chance of bringing his dad home? Why was Wisdomseeker making him wait? Why, why, why had he been born a guardian? He gazed out at the streets of London, trying to ignore the restless pulse of the positive energies calling to his conscience through the turmoil in his star. Johnny turned off the Embankment into a maze of expensively converted warehouses whose narrow alleyways offered grudging glimpses of the river. He dropped them outside the de Monteneuf Tower, a soaring block of blue-tinted glass and pale stone, before disappearing down a ramp into an underground garage.

Beneath a sky the colour of cold ashes the grinding roar of the city throbbed thick and savage. The street sign caught Wolfie's eye – Lambspring Passage – and he thought how strange these old London street names were. A uniformed concierge saluted as he followed Missy through a marble-floored lobby to the lifts. Missy keyed a number into the wall pad. The doors slid shut. Wolfie reached unsteadily for the mirrored wall. Darkness pressed his eyes. His star wailed a warning.

"What's wrong?" said Missy.

"Bit . . . queasy."

"You're as bad as Mom. She says this building's got a bad vibe."

The doors purred open. An immense, seemingly endless white entrance hall hung with enormous abstract paintings stretched towards a world beyond of spacious rooms and corridors. Yet what struck him was the melancholy seeping through the walls, as if something really bad had happened here . . . or was about to happen.

"Won't your mum mind me coming round?" Wolfie asked.

"She won't know. She uses the apartment downstairs for writing in so she won't get disturbed."

"*What*? You could hide a herd of elephants in this apartment without anyone ever noticing."

Missy said hurriedly, "It's not like Dad had to *buy* it for her – he owns the block." She blushed. "He inherited it; well, the land. . ." She gave up. The de Monteneufs were stinking rich, why pretend?

"Don't you get . . . lonely here on your own?" He had almost said *frightened* but that would have sounded weird.

"Oh, no. Johnny's around most of the time and the housekeeper lives in. And sometimes, if Mom's working, Dad takes me to a gallery or the movies. I see loads more of them than if I'd gone to stupid boarding school." She pulled a face. "Mom had got me the uniform and everything. She went crazy when I refused to go."

"So what school *do* you go to?"

"St Winifred's. I hate it. But at least I get to live at home." She led him into a wide airy room, furnished with delicate antique sofas set around a single Persian rug, its patterning softly faded with age. The walls were hung with paintings and tapestries. Portraits of a haughty-looking man in a ruffled collar and a doe-eyed woman with pearls in her hair stared across the room, as if watching the extraordinary panorama of Bankside visible through the sliding glass doors. Wolfie couldn't imagine anyone flopping down in here to watch television, especially as the de Monteneufs didn't seem to have one.

"Where's your . . . stuff?"

"Mom doesn't '*do*' clutter." Missy added quickly, "But *my* room's a real mess."

A wave of something burdensome seemed to wash

through the building. Suddenly the room was a great white mouth pegged with spindly teeth closing in to swallow Wolfie's strength. He shivered.

Missy set down Bonbon's box. "Sit down, I'll get you some water."

He perched gingerly on the edge of a narrow, unyielding sofa, staring at the huge tapestry of a forest on the opposite wall, waiting for the room to feel normal again. Missy brought him a beaker chinking with ice. "I love that tapestry. Every time you look at it you see something different."

Wolfie went closer, dazed by the thousands of tightly packed pixels of thread combining to create a mystical woodland. Every inch of subtly shaded wool-work told a tiny tale: a crimson bird drinking from a stream; a white stag running through the foliage; rabbits, weasels, even a turtle scuttling for shelter. And there in a shadowy thicket, a wider patch of pure black, relieved only by two yellowy flecks fashioned from a strange metallic yarn. He screwed up his eyes, trying to make sense of the dark outline: an almost triangular head, a long sloping back, a thick pendulous tail. He pressed his arm against his mouth. A large cat-like beast was lurking in the shadows of this medieval forest, sinuous and evil eyed, drawing him in. He tore his eyes away, fastening them on the pure white of the stag, trying to fight the pull of the panther. Dark light, good bad, positive negative, the battle between them was everywhere.

He blinked hard. The pure white animal was not a stag. It looked more like a unicorn with a single stump of broken horn in the centre of its forehead, and far from running away it was caught in a thicket of thorns, weeping tears of blood.

"You need some air," Missy said and Wolfie was glad when she dragged him through the glass doors and down to a wide terrace, laid out with carefully tended shrubs and miniature trees in tubs. Stumbling to the parapet, he grasped the railing. Directly opposite stood the brick-clad bulk of the Bankside Power Station, now the Tate Modern art gallery, its solitary chimney a narrow brown digit pointing like a pylon to the sky. He felt a throb of the same subtle purpose he had sensed at the Battersea Power Station. He dropped his eyes to the chimney's long wavery reflection reaching out across the broad brown river, as if marking a hidden pathway that linked it to the de Monteneuf Tower.

Missy let Bonbon loose on a shallow trough grassed over to make a tiny lawn and opened the box of lettuce. With a grunt of disgust she flung it away. Wolfie recoiled. The box was crawling with black slugs. Remarkably unfazed, Missy fetched a dustpan and brush. "It's been happening lots lately, slugs, spiders — Mom will freak if she finds out."

Something sickly swilled in Wolfie's stomach. Were the slugs elementals? What was with the tapestry and the dizziness? Why was the outline of the Tate Modern dragging at his gaze? Was he going crazy? His body felt like a battleground but where was the enemy? He could no longer trust his instincts to tell him. He heard Missy's footsteps go and come.

"Thought so."

He forced his eyes open. She was waving a glossy magazine open at an article about Battersea Power Station.

"It's the same guy!"

"Who is?"

"Giles Gilbert Scott. He designed the Bankside Power Station *and* the one at Battersea."

The terrace was spinning. Wolfie closed his eyes. Had the architect been responding to some primal link between the two locations?

"That's what I want to do," Missy was saying, "build stuff that makes you tingle when you look at it."

Wolfie watched the darkening skyline, wishing he could think straight, wishing the others had come, wishing he could ignore Tala's anger pounding his star.

"Mom says soda settles your stomach." Tala pushed a can into his fingers and stood beside him while he sipped and shivered. "Maybe it *is* this building. Don't tell Mom, she'll make us move and Dad and me like it here. Come and see this."

She led him round to a narrower terrace on the other side that looked out over the unruly sprawl of the city; a living mosaic of towers, domes, lanes, office blocks and churches.

"That's Ludgate Hill. Dad says it's the oldest part of London."

This side of the apartment felt calmer. Wolfie leant against the wall, trying to snatch back his breath. Missy looked down, nervously clenching and unclenching her fists before blurting, "Why was it such a big deal when you found out I was a de Monteneuf?"

"It . . . wasn't."

Splashes of rain spattered their faces. Missy didn't move. "I'm not blind. You, Tala *and* Zi'ib, you all looked . . . kind of angry, like I was intruding on some big secret."

Wolfie felt bad. "We were just surprised 'cos of that story Mr Forester mentioned. We found it in an old chronicle. My ancestor Agnes was some kind of herbalist and she cured your ancestor who was dying of fever. He rewarded her with a piece of land and her husband Costantino built the shop on it, from the remains of an old stone circle that used to stand on Thornham Common. Then Agnes and Costantino got accused of witchcraft and someone poisoned them. When they died the de Monteneufs took in their baby son Stanley and looked after him till he was ready to inherit the shop."

"Which de Monteneufs?"

"Sir Edgar and his wife."

She gazed at him intently, rain sliding down her face. "Then there's something you should see."

Wolfie followed her down a long, light corridor, hung with abstract paintings similar if not identical to ones he had seen in his mum's art books. He longed to linger and look at them properly but Missy had disappeared around a corner. He caught up with her as she opened the door to Simon de Monteneuf's study, a large, lived-in room lit by the greenish glow from the computer on the antique desk. One wall was fitted floor to ceiling with wide, shallow drawers. Sliding one open, Missy lifted out two flat packages wrapped in black tissue and laid them on the desk. Carefully, she unwrapped the first one. It was a portrait of a young nobleman, staring up at them through heavy-lidded grey eyes. He had a pale complexion, a narrow nose tilted at the tip and auburn hair cut high over his ears in a short blunt fringe. He wore a padded, tight-waisted jacket of orangey red and in the background gleamed his coat of arms: a golden star riven in two, encircled by a ring of thorns set above the motto *Trust in Truth*. A stack of headed paper beside the printer bore the same emblem. Originally a heraldic crest and now a business logo, it occurred to Wolfie that the riven star had symbolized the power and wealth of the de Monteneuf family for nearly a thousand years.

"It's Sir Edgar," said Missy, breaking into his thoughts.

"He looks like you."

"Thanks a bunch."

Wolfie grinned. "Must be the haircut."

Missy giggled nervously, unused to being teased. "There's another one that's probably by the same artist, called *Portrait of a Boy*, but Dad doesn't think the kid's a de Monteneuf. If he was he'd have been named and he'd be wearing fancy clothes. I was wondering if maybe it could be . . . Agnes's son."

Wolfie tensed as she slipped the tissue from the second painting. It was not the face of the solemn-eyed toddler in a brown linen cap that held him or the strange symbols dotted across the scene. It was the background. The child was sitting in a small walled garden in front of a low stone building, similar in shape to the old outhouse in Wolfie's back yard. The drab setting was relieved by the spreading bushes of bright berries, the curious shrubs laid out in the dark earth and the clusters of purple Saravita spilling from cracks in the stonework and the boy's pudgy fist.

"It's him," Wolfie said quietly.

"How do you know?"

"Because Agnes was an artist as well as a herbalist and she's painted her son in the walled garden where she grew her herbs. It's our back yard and what's left of that building is our outhouse."

"Herbalist . . . is that like an alchemist?"

"S'pose. Why?"

"These symbols, Dad says they're alchemical signs for elements. This circle with the arrow sticking out of it is iron and this double triangle thing is arsenic, so the painting's kind of like a chart telling you which plants contain which elements."

Wolfie eyed the little circle with a dot in the middle above the purple Saravita.

"What's that the sign for?"

"Gold, but don't get your hopes up, the plant isn't real."

"What do you mean?"

"The petals of the flowers make a star with eight points, just like the family crest, so Dad asked this famous botanist to get him some and she said it didn't exist, which was weird because all the other plants in the picture do." She smiled. "But next time I'm round your house I'll have to check out your yard, just in case."

Wolfie thought very carefully. How much could he tell her about the Saravita without unravelling the secret of his Lupan heritage?

"Look," he said, "if you must know, that plant's the secret ingredient in Mum's fudge. But you mustn't tell anyone 'cos I think that's what Zemogen are after."

Missy brought her hands to her mouth in excitement. "I swear I won't."

Outside, heavy rain was falling from the cloud-darkened sky. She switched on the desk lamp. They leaned into the pool of light, transfixed by the faces of their ancestors. The man and the boy stared back across the centuries; two Browns and two de Monteneufs separated by half a millennium. Missy shifted her elbows, dislodging a sheet of paper with a silver Z on the letterhead. She moved the letter into the light. Her tip-tilt nose twitched with bemusement.

"You know that company that tried to outbid Dad for the corset factory?"

Wolfie nodded.

"It was Zemogen. And now they're offering him twice what he paid for it."

By the time Johnny dropped Wolfie at the back gate it was nearly ten. Still loathe to face Tala and Zi'ib, he lingered in the yard like a stranger, watching them through the kitchen window. They were sitting on the sofa leafing through Esmé's book, stopping every so often to laugh at something they'd found.

"Sargon, sounds like something off a bad video game," Zi'ib was saying.

"Oh no, he was a real king. Esmé says so in the introduction. . ."

Something moved in the gloom. Wolfie turned his head, searching nervously for the panther. Another flutter of movement. He swung round, afraid, and caught his own reflection staring up at him from the greasy depths of a puddle.

The powers of darkness are . . . no more to be reviled than thine own reflection in a pool of darkened water.

Feeling angry and excluded, he cowered by the back door, listening to Tala reading something out in a stupid gruff voice.

"*. . .and when I saw the sickness and mayhem, the weeping women and the angry youths I cried out to my warriors, 'I, Sargon, command you to silence the roar of the dread fiend that prowls the city. Smite its tail and cankered heart! Pierce*

196

the hump of its writhing back and wound its head and throat
that I might have peace in my kingdom. . ."

He threw open the back door.

Zi'ib stopped laughing. Tala turned away, tight lipped.

"What's so funny?" Wolfie demanded.

"*My Travels in Atlantis*. It's rubbish," Zi'ib said.

"Where's Mum?"

"Gone to bed. Your shepherd's pie's in the oven.

"It's OK, I . . . had something."

"I s'pose some maid cooked it," snapped Tala.

"We . . . went to a restaurant."

She glowered at him.

"You could have come too," Wolfie said fiercely.

"*If* you remember, we had to take the metal detector out
to *search for spears*. We didn't have time to jerk around
with miss *ooh look at these cute little poor people, I'll get*
Johnny to pick me one out to play with." She turned and
flung herself out of the kitchen.

Incensed, Wolfie ran upstairs and wrenched open her
door. "I didn't go off with her for fun. I needed to know
who was buying all Mum's fudge. I got Johnny to follow
the van."

"Good old Johnny. What *would* we do without him? You
should have been with *us* but you don't care about
cleansing the dark ley *or* helping Mr Forester or even
getting *your* dad and *my* mom back from Lupus, you don't
even care about *Sarah*, you'd rather spend your time
joyriding!"

"Don't you dare say that!"

Zi'ib came rushing in and shut the door. "Shut up. You'll wake Sarah up."

Wolfie wanted to explain about the tapestry and the paintings and the weird atmosphere in Missy's apartment so they could work out what it meant together, like they always did. Anger stopped the words. "I wasn't joyriding," he growled.

"So what *were* you doing?"

"Following that delivery van. It went to Battersea, to the Zemogen HQ. We sneaked round the back of their labs and saw them analysing the fudge."

Tala sniffed, her mouth quivering at the corners. "So what? No one can copy the recipe without the Saravita."

An image of the laboratory flashed through his head. Suddenly the poster and the tweezers and test tubes and all those people analysing fragments of fudge made sense. "They're not after the recipe!" His cry bounced off the bedroom walls. "They're trying to clone the Saravita!"

Tala paused but her fury had an unstoppable momentum of its own. "Don't be stupid."

"Then why was there a diagram of a Saravita plant on the wall?"

"I don't *care* what Zemogen's up to."

"Well you should because they know there's something special about the Saravita. Maybe they've even sussed out it's from another world. And there's something else. It was Zemogen who were trying to outbid Missy's dad for

198

the corset factory *and* they're still trying to get it off him."

Wolfie felt Tala's anger brim over and spill through his veins, splashing and burning like molten metal.

"Who cares about Missy's dad and his stupid factory?" she shrieked.

"This isn't about Missy's dad, it's about *us* if you'd just shut up for five seconds and listen," shouted Wolfie.

"He's right," said Zi'ib, stepping between them. "There's something weird about this Zemogen company. They've got posters all over the place, they're advertising in *The Earth Mysterian*, funding Professor Salah's excavation, sneaking after the Saravita, trying to buy the corset factory, hosting the SILK conference. They're everywhere we go."

Tala wrenched the door handle. "Then we'd better get pickier about *where* we go and a heck of a lot pickier who we go there *with*." She stormed downstairs.

The light came on in Sarah's bedroom. Wolfie put his head round the door, surprised to see Elvis blocking the way.

"Shall I take him out?"

"Let him stay. I think he's a bit poorly as well. He's been moping around for days."

"Can I get you anything?"

"No thanks, love. What's the matter with Tala?"

"Nothing, you know what she's like." He sat on the end of her bed. "Mum, listen, you've got to stop supplying that bulk order with fudge."

199

"Why?"

"I saw the van delivering it to the labs of this company called Zemogen."

"They probably sell it in their canteen."

"No, Mum, I think they were analysing it."

"Don't be silly. And anyway, I don't mind what they do with it. They pay really well, cash on delivery. You know how much we need the money."

For the whole of that Sunday, Wolfie and Tala moved around the house trapped in black bubbles of self-righteousness that sealed in their fury and sealed out the light of reason.

18
The Track

It was Monday morning and Zi'ib sat alone at the back of the school coach, keeping watch on Marcus and Wayne, sure they were planning something nasty. He couldn't take it, not on top of the worry about his mum and dad, the fight against time to purify the black ley and this thing with Tala and Wolfie tearing him apart. There was so much jealousy and resentment raging through his star he wanted to rip it from his throat. Everything had been fine till that stupid Missy poked her nose in. He squeezed his forehead. No it hadn't. Everyone's tempers had been tinder dry for days. He longed to burn off his stress on the running track but he couldn't even do that in case he won. Winning would only start people talking about his miraculous recovery from the gunshot wound that had brought him to

England and the last thing he needed was anyone noticing he was "different".

His hands twitched as if something had tweaked a nerve. The coach was passing through a strong river of power. He stretched out his fingers, tuning his senses to the current flowing through his bones. Mr Pinkney's voice shattered his focus. "Look to your right, everybody. Stonehenge, the most famous stone circle in the world, once known as 'The Giant's Dance'."

The tumbled circlet of giant stones nestling on the downs was a bold reminder of the way the world once was, when megaliths were as common as electricity pylons are now and stone circles were as necessary as power stations. The energies flowing from this time-worn henge coursed strong and smooth all the way to King Alfred's Academy. Zi'ib stared out at the car park, excited. Was it a sign? Had the leys brought him here for a reason? Mr Pegg began handing out purple armbands. "Wear these at all times to identify which school you're from. Unless your parents signed a release form to take you home, we'll meet you back here after the prize-giving. Now, good luck, everybody. Don't let your behaviour on or off the playing fields let Blackstone down."

In the hall, Zi'ib joined a mass of children in identical navy tracksuits queuing for orange juice and croissants. From every wall hung banners emblazoned with the Labs for Life logo. He had to blink hard to erase the imprint of the fiery yellow lightning bolts from his eyeballs. Mr

Butterworth, the headmaster of King Alfred's, climbed on to the stage and gave a short welcome speech before introducing Hadley Hunter, a representative from Labs for Life.

An elegant blonde woman in a suit, who looked vaguely familiar, took the microphone. "At Labs for Life we believe that achieving personal goals is as important as winning medals. All we want is for you to focus on doing your very best. . ."

Blah, blah, blah. Mr Pinkney squeezed past him, rapt with attention. Of course! Hadley Hunter had been at the raising of the giants with Stinky.

An army of coaches led the competitors out to the sports fields. In the middle of the grounds, glinting in the sunlight, stood a huge stone statue of a runner breasting the finishing line, arms upheld in triumph. Zi'ib felt his star twitch. There was a statue just like that on the pictures of the track Labs for Life were going to install at Blackstone. He was staring at the statue so hard he bumped into a plump ginger-haired boy. The boy grinned, said his name was Alex, and launched into a tirade of grumbling about Labs for Life.

"I dunno why our school got picked. We're all useless at sport and we're gonna get slaughtered by that lot from St Saviour's." He pointed to a group of tall athletic types engaged in some kind of leg stretching routine and rolled his eyes when a lean Australian coach called Les lined them up for another pep talk. "When you're running, I want you to forget about winning and losing and focus on your feet as they strike the ground. Think yourself into the movement of your muscles and feel the power you expend flowing in your wake. It's not a one-way thing: imagine the track as something vibrant and dynamic offering up its own vitality in exchange for yours. With every step think *me and the track, me and the track, me and the track*."

"What a load of cobblers," whispered Alex.

Zi'ib grinned but noticed some of the other boys hanging on Les's every word. When, in the first heat, a tall blond boy from St Saviour's elbowed him aside before springing ahead, Zi'ib fought the temptation to overtake him.

"You in the purple armband, you're holding back," called Les. "Put some welly into it! Keep focused – me and the track, me and the track, me and the track."

OK, OK, I get it. What is wrong with these people?

At lunchtime Alex came limping towards him, red-faced and panting.

"You should take it easy," Zi'ib said.

"I know, but that stupid *me and the track* thing . . . makes your legs go on . . . even when you're about to collapse." He flopped on to the ground, fighting to catch his breath. "Some . . . kid said to tell you . . . the Blackstone coach is picking up . . . from the overflow car park . . . by the back gate."

Zi'ib fetched them both drinks and sandwiches from the canteen. They ate outside, watching the supporters arrive. Marcus's dad drew up in a red sports car and his mum got out wearing a tight skirt and a big pink hat that wobbled in the wind.

"Don't you hate it when your parents turn up for school stuff?" Alex said.

An image of his mum and dad laughing and waving as they crossed the car park knocked the air from Zi'ib's lungs, but he managed an almost careless, "Yeah."

Before the finals, Zi'ib sprinkled dirt into his trainers. The air bristled as he joined the row of determined boys at the starting line, some already mouthing, "Me and the track." *Weirdos*. The gun cracked. Zi'ib pushed gently off the blocks. He catapulted forward. Les's trackside cry of "Me and the track!" was overriding the messages from his brain forcing him on until he was neck and neck with the boy from St Saviour's. Just when he could have sprinted to victory, Zi'ib concentrated on the grit digging into his feet and managed to pull back, crossing the finishing line third.

He staggered away to join Alex, who was sitting slumped against the statue. Although the day was cool, the stone appeared to be giving off a shimmering heat haze. He ran his hand through the wavering air. His star went wild. It wasn't heat. It was energy. And the stone wasn't giving it off, it was drawing it in. Zi'ib knew he was the only person on the whole track who could see it.

At six o'clock they were summoned to the hall for the buffet and prize-giving. Zi'ib was biting into a burger when the head coach came up behind him. "Zi'ib, isn't it?

You've got real potential. I couldn't believe it when I heard about your leg injury. Your focus is all over the place but we can sort that out. I'll be keeping my eye on you."

Zi'ib mumbled nervously and hurried off to find Alex. The Harrisons cheered loudly when Marcus went up to receive the bronze for the high jump. As soon as it was over everyone began to surge towards their coaches.

Zi'ib found the overflow car park and watched coach after coach pull away as he searched for the Blackstone bus. Alex must have got the message wrong. He ran to the other car park. It was empty.

"What's your school?" called one of the marshals.

"Blackstone."

"They've gone."

"They can't have."

"Must've thought your parents were picking you up."

"No, we had to fill in a form. They wouldn't leave without me."

"Well, they have."

A red sports car roared past. Pressed against the tiny back window Zi'ib saw the faces of Marcus and Wayne contorted with laughter. He was furious yet impressed. They must have doctored his form and fed that message to Alex.

"Come on, let's have a word with Mr Butterworth," said the marshal.

The headmaster was in the hall chatting to Hadley Hunter as she packed up her banners.

"Oh dear, there's always one," he said, when he heard what had happened. He consulted his contacts list. "I can try phoning Mr Pegg, but with all these problems with mobile connections. . ." He dialled and got a hiss of static. "Thought so." He sighed. "I suppose I'll have to take you home with me and put you on a train in the morning." He shook his head, inviting Hadley to share his exasperation, then broke into a smile. "Hang on. Aren't you going back to London, Miss Hunter?"

"Well, yes. . ."

"You couldn't take this one with you, could you?"

"I suppose I *could*," Hadley replied without enthusiasm.

"There we are then, problem solved," said the headmaster.

Hadley turned her deep brown eyes on Zi'ib. "You can help me load the car." She pushed the box of banners into his arms, dropping her car keys on top. "It's the white Range Rover by the fence. I'll be with you in a minute."

Relieved at his escape from a night with the Butterworths, Zi'ib hurried to the car park, stowed the box in the boot and climbed into the front. Hadley was taking her time so he started flipping through a brochure lying on the dashboard. It was all about Labs for Life, expensively bound with the fiery lightning logo gleaming on the front. Inside there were profiles of the participating schools, fixture lists and a lot of cliché-packed praise for the scheme sponsors from some government minister: *These beacons of industrial excellence with a presence on every high street are empowering our future.*

He shut his knees to catch a slip of paper that dropped from the pages. It was a printer's invoice. The date, November 14th, snagged his attention. It was his birthday, the birthday he shared with Tala and Wolfie. Hadley opened the door and slid into the driver's seat.

"That's the proof of the brochure we'll be sending out to all the schools," she said, slipping off her high heels. "It came out well, didn't it?"

"Yeah, great," Zi'ib said, putting it back.

"Keep it. Send us some feedback on today's event. The email address is in there."

"OK." Zi'ib stuffed it into his rucksack.

To his relief she didn't want to chat, preferring to play loud pumping music for most of the way. The traffic was bad and it was nearly ten o'clock by the time they reached Thornham. When he gave her directions to the sweet shop she didn't mention that she knew the area. But then, why would anyone want to admit they'd been hanging out with Stinky?

*

To: ridianwinter@hotmail.com
From: esme@pastlife.com
As you predicted, Forester says there is some upset between the children.

Ridian smiled.

208

He also says Sarah Brown is sick and it could be serious.
There's a gardener/handyman type hanging around but
no one of any significance. However, Forester has
requested SILK to find geomancers to cleanse the
Thornham ley. Please advise how I should avert this.

Ridian typed *No action* and pressed send. A couple of
dabblers from SILK would stand no chance against the
taint of the nether void.

19

The Firebrand

For the first time in ages Wolfie was alone. No Zi'ib tapping away at his laptop, no Tala pinning notes on the noticeboard, just him and the dark misshapen idea stirring inside him. It was an idea so ugly that he thrust it away, but it kept slithering back to gnaw at his resistance, fill his ears with furtive whisperings and prod his limbs until he found himself prising up the loose floorboard and unwrapping the whetstone from his old sweatshirt. He slipped it into a carrier bag. As he crept downstairs, all was darkness except for a thin strip of light beneath Tala's door. It didn't take long to bury the whetstone deep in the flower bed by the outhouse, or to slip a couple of spoons beneath the surface soil to confuse any attempts to find it with the metal detector. It was only as he skulked back to the attic and tried to bundle up

Sarah's rolling pin in the sweatshirt to disguise what he'd done that his hands began to shake. The back door slammed. Zi'ib was back. He broke into a sweat, shoved the floorboard back, switched off the light and swung himself up into his bunk.

Zi'ib came upstairs and lay in the moonlight, staring at the photo of his parents and plotting hideous revenge against Marcus and Wayne. Something was teasing his thoughts like an annoying little itch he was desperate to scratch yet couldn't quite locate. The trapdoor creaked open. Tala scrambled into the attic, carrying Esmé's book.

"Couldn't sleep," she hissed. "I've been reading this again, trying to work out if Esmé's for real. I dunno about Sophanisba, but Queen Thalestris and King Sargon definitely existed, I checked. It looks like Esmé nicked his 'memories' from some old clay tablets—"

"Can't you two keep quiet?" grunted Wolfie.

"But, guess what?" went on Tala, ignoring him. "That stuff about Sargon fighting a dread fiend attacking his city; I think it might have been a coded myth about fighting dark energies."

Zi'ib sat up.

"Don't get excited, there's nothing about spears. He just sends his men off to smite it."

"Shut up," moaned Wolfie.

Tala scowled up at the top bunk. "How did it go today?"

"Weird." He told her about the "me and the track" mantra and the waves of energy pouring into the stone statue.

211

"Maybe next time we should come and watch and check out what's going on."

"Great." Switching on his torch, he skimmed the Labs for Life brochure looking for the fixtures list. The mental itch flared up, and began to burn. Frowning, he shook the brochure, flung it on the bed and started rummaging in his rucksack.

"What are you looking for?" said Tala.

"This." Zi'ib held up the printer's invoice. "Look at the date."

"November 14th. Our birthday. Maybe it's an omen that you're going to win the running cup."

"It's not an omen. It's a warning."

"What do you mean?"

Zi'ib pointed to the list of participating schools. "Mr Pegg said he and Stinky worked on the Labs for Life application over the Christmas holidays, right?"

"Yeah."

"So how come Labs for Life already knew which schools were going to be selected when they printed these brochures in November?"

Wolfie waggled his fingers over the side of his bunk. "Give it here."

Tala held the brochure tight.

"Give it *here*."

Zi'ib felt their anger pressing in on him, hot and black and thick.

Wolfie sprang out of his bunk, grabbing the flimsy

pages with both hands. Tala clung on, suddenly a wild thing with savage eyes, and he was brutish, his face contorted with uncontrollable anger. Swept up in a tide of fury, they wrenched and snarled like jackals fighting over carrion.

Elvis came bounding upstairs and crouched growling by the trapdoor, the hair rigid along his back. In a burst of fear Zi'ib shouted, "Stop it!" Grasping their wrists he yanked them apart as if breaking an electrical circuit, ripping the brochure.

Wolfie glowered at Tala. "Now look what you've done!"

"You should have let go!"

Choked by the force of their feelings, Zi'ib lashed out, "Give it a rest, both of you." He gave Wolfie a shove. "You've been acting like a sulky kid for days." He turned on Tala. "And you're just jealous of Missy 'cos she's rich and pretty and—"

"What's going on?" It was Sarah calling from the landing.

"Sorry, Mum. Pillow fight."

"Go to sleep." Her door clicked shut.

They slumped in the moonlight.

"What's got into us?" said Tala, frightened by the feelings still simmering inside her.

"Dark energy," Zi'ib said flatly. "Don't you get it? The vibrations are messing with our heads as well as with our stars. The more time we spend fighting each other, the less time we spend looking for the spears."

A leaden lump hardened in Wolfie's stomach as he closed his conscience to the fading cry of the positive energies. He was doing this for his dad, and when he bought Kara home as well, Tala would understand. Instinctively he put his hand out to Elvis. The great dog backed away.

Sleep seemed an impossibility. Painfully wide awake, Tala pressed her face to the window. The moon was full, hanging in the sky like a silver coin. Less than six weeks left to cleanse the dark ley. She pinned the torn Labs for Life brochure on to the noticeboard.

"What are you doing?" Wolfie said.

"Reminding us not to let the dark energies get to us again."

She stared at the glossy pamphlet. The rip at the top had severed the fiery lightning bolt logo, creating a Z of flame. As she smoothed it flat, a sickly dart of recognition pinioned her heart. She ran to her room. Within minutes she was back holding out the business card given to her by the doctor treating her father. Below the words Dulcie Walker, MD, gleamed a tiny flaming Z, identical to the one on the torn section of the cover.

"Email her for me," she gasped, her hands shaking too much to do it herself. "Ask her what it stands for."

It was early morning in California and twenty minutes later Dulcie Walker returned from her ward round and fired off a reply.

Hi Tala,

That fiery little Z is the logo of Zemogen International's development arm. They bought out my original sponsors, Vasco Pharmaceuticals, a couple of years ago and now they're funding all my research. Their head of development is particularly interested in the experimental treatments I'm using on your dad.

You will be pleased to know his blood work is almost normal and there have been some definite limb movements.

Dulcie Walker

A terrifying certainty flooded every cell of Tala's body. She leant across the keyboard and googled *Zemogen, Head of Development*. And there it was, twelve letters that consumed her with alternate waves of fear and rage. Ridian Winter. That's why the name Zemogen had sounded familiar! She had googled Ridian weeks before, when she first discovered he had stolen her guardian's identity. Zemogen International had appeared in the long list of his directorships and consultancies, but at the time the name Zemogen had barely brushed her consciousness.

All three children felt trapped in a maze that turned ever inward, always leading back to Ridian and the Manus Sacra. Zi'ib was the first to shake off his shock. Within minutes his fingers were clattering across his laptop, confirming that Zemogen was the major sponsor of Labs for Life and either owned or had a major holding in all the other sponsor companies: Greenlight Fuels, Vasco Pharmaceuticals and Sacher Communications.

"We don't know that Ridian's got anything to do with Labs for Life, though," Tala said.

Zi'ib said, "Oh come on, that thing with the statue and the energies is dead fishy. He's got to be behind it."

Struck by a sudden thought, he took down the Labs for Life brochure and opened the interactive ley line map he had been developing for the *EM*. He began methodically plotting the location of every school in the scheme. He worked on through the small hours, and when Wolfie and Tala got back from delivering the papers they found him asleep at the keyboard, askew like a discarded marionette.

Tala shook his shoulder. "What did you find?"

His eyes jerked open. "Nearly half of the schools are on ley lines."

"That's not enough to count for anything."

"No, but the rest are positioned in straight lines that connect those smaller leys to three major ones running towards London. It looks like Zemogen is planning to make new energy paths that join up all the leys in Britain and divert them straight to their London HQ at Battersea. They're going to make it the hub of the whole energy grid."

"How?"

"You know those processional ways and pilgrim paths Mr Forester's always going on about, how people with a purpose, walking them again and again, affected the energies?"

216

Tala nodded.

"That weird 'me and the track' thing, that wasn't about improving our running speeds. Labs for Life were using the power of our concentration to create new energy paths." The chilling truth hit him. "That's what those stone statues are for. They're there to channel the flow, just like ancient standing stones." He ran the cursor over the map. "If they put something like that in all the outlets of the companies they're backing as well as in the Labs for Life schools, they'd just need to get hold of a few key megalithic sites, to have every major ley in Britain covered.

"Ridian must have taken years setting this up. Getting Zemogen to buy into the other companies, planning the Labs for Life scheme and probably doing loads of other stuff we'll never know about. Don't you see? He was getting everything ready for the Manus Sacra leaders to arrive with the Sphere of Lupus and take over the ley grid. And I bet no one else at Zemogen's got a clue there's any sinister connection between his schemes."

"Yeah, and for some reason he's got the Zemogen labs to try and clone the Saravita," frowned Wolfie. He was remembering the powerful earth currents converging on Battersea Power Station and the glimmering curve of the crystex roof. "That dome on Zemogen's HQ. It's a replica of the crystal dome on the chamber of Lupus. Ridian must have had it built specially. It's where he was going to house the Sphere!"

Zi'ib shivered, frightened and at the same time thrilled by the scale of the Manus Sacra's ambition.

"You've got to hand it to those creeps," he said, "but how were they going to take over Zemogen?"

Tala's eyes flashed. "Think about it. If we hadn't stopped them they would have got hold of all the power in the Stones of Knowledge *and* the secret of the Spheres and the Sphere of Lupus itself and right now they'd be using the leys to control the tides of fate. They could make anything they want happen."

Wolfie glanced at the torn cover of the Labs for Life brochure, the sharply angled rush of flame; a potent symbol of the merciless conquest planned by the Manus Sacra. "The day they took over Zemogen I bet they were going to get rid of that boring silver Z and rebrand everything they controlled with this flame logo." He grimaced. "Oh blimey. That's why they've been buying up all that advertising space. Imagine waking up one morning and finding that flaming Z plastered everywhere like the flag of some conquering invader."

Images of Therion danced in their heads, vivid as a scene from a war film: that creep Godfrey Peasemarsh and the vile Leonora Grindle staring down at the world from their Battersea HQ, empowered not by an army but by their hold over the leys.

Zi'ib said slowly, "Ridian's never going to let all that planning go to waste."

"What choice has he got?" replied Wolfie. "He's stuffed

218

without the Sphere. Even if he managed to get hold of it, he'd never share control of the ley grid with anyone except the Manus Sacra. And thanks to us and Elvis they've all been sucked into the nether void."

"Exactly," Tala said. "So can we please concentrate on cleansing the dark energies. Tonight I want to go through all the back copies of *The Earth Mysterian* for stuff about ritual weapons."

"Yeah," agreed Zi'ib. "If we managed to scupper the Manus Sacra's plans for world domination, surely we can track down a few old spears."

A cold rush swept through Wolfie's bones as he thought of the whetsone lying buried in the yard.

The aerial shot on the screen began as a tiny nugget of green embedded in the centre of a smeary patchwork of grey brown blobs. Slowly, Stefan de Witt zoomed in. Buildings, streets and the fuzzy detail of roofs, garages and gardens began to crystallize. When the ring of Greyfriars Crescent was a stark black circle speckled with tiny cars centre of frame, the image froze. As if touched by a fairy wand, a ripple of computer-generated magic spread from the middle of the common, sweeping back the layers of time until the landscape returned to bare primal sward, with the slope of Dodd's Hill rising to the north. And then, as if alive, vast stones sprang from the turf; an inner and an outer ring of glistening granite monoliths.

"So, Ridian, that's what it would have looked like originally," Stefan said. "And this is the overlay."

He clicked the mouse. Slowly the buildings of Thornham began to flow back into place, stopping abruptly when they reached the outer edges of the mound. St Michael's Church, the shabby villas of Greyfriars Crescent, the Wish Hound pub and Brown's Sweet Shop were gone, replaced by the soaring monoliths of freshly hewn granite, creating an immense stone circle in the centre of a star-shaped layout of pathways rising through the fabric of the town. The pathways followed the pattern of the ley lines, some picking up on existing roads and alleys, others slicing through the current sites of tower blocks, shops and houses.

Ridian nodded approval. "Good graphics."

"Hadley Hunter's done a great job mapping the energy flows, but I'm not so sure about Pinkney's judgement."

"He has his uses, or he will do when the receptors are up and running in Blackstone school."

"There's still a problem with a couple of key Thornham properties," Stefan said. "Obviously, Zemogen owns the pub now. You own number forty-five Greyfriars Crescent, but de Monteneuf's refused our latest offer on the corset factory here on the north-east point of the star of leys, and to rub our noses in it he's even ordered one of Zemogen's crystex domes to go on the roof. Shall I tell him he can't have one?"

Ridian smiled. "Let him have it. It'll make him think there are no hard feelings."

"And that Brown woman at the sweet shop sent the estate agent packing again even though he was offering her double the market value."

Ridian tapped his fingers together. Long term, he wasn't worried about the factory and the shop; they would fall instantly into Manus Sacra hands when Wolfie Brown and Simon de Monteneuf became vessels for Manus Sacra minds. But for the next few weeks he didn't want de Monteneuf dropping by Thornham to see his factory and bumping into those kids. The mystical wisdom of that family had weakened over the centuries but they had a long and disturbing history of service to the bloodlines of the guardians.

A small fire at de Monteneuf's gallery in New York should provide a crude but effective distraction from his interests in Thornham.

20

The Only Weapon

They were exhausted, but after school Tala insisted they went straight round to number forty-five. She sped through the gate, spied a small behatted figure standing by the window and skidded to a halt.

"Quick, back up. We'll come back later."

"I don't get that woman," grumbled Zi'ib as they made off down the crescent. "She knows there's no money in the *EM* so what's she—" He swerved, shocked at the sight of the shop, shuttered and unlit so early in the day. Dread burned Wolfie's veins as they neared the bleak frontage.

There was a note on the mantelpiece.

I've closed up early and gone to bed. Can you make yourselves beans on toast and feed Elvis? Sx

Wolfie threw it in the bin. "It's that flu bug. Loads of people have got it."

Tala's secret gushed out, sour as vomit. "It's not flu. I heard Sarah talking to Sid. She went to the hospital for tests."

Wolfie struggled to breathe. "Why didn't you tell me?"

"Or me?" cried Zi'ib.

"She told Sid she didn't want us to know."

"She's *my* mother, I had a right to know!" cried Wolfie.

A deep sob shook Tala's frame. "I'm sorry . . . OK? I thought if I kept quiet about it, tried not even to think about it, I could . . . stop it being true."

Wolfie charged upstairs. Pushing open Sarah's door, he stepped over Elvis and thought how small his mum looked curled beneath the covers. She opened her eyes.

"Why didn't you tell me you went to the hospital?" he choked.

She eased herself up on her pillows. "I didn't want to worry you."

"What's wrong with you?"

"They don't know. I need more tests."

"How . . . how long have you been ill?"

"The headaches started the day you saw the panther." She forced a grim smile. "You'd almost think they had something to do with those dark energies Remus is always talking about."

Wolfie let out a piteous moan. Sarah held out her arms. He ran to her and she wrapped him in a hug. It gave him no comfort. All he could feel was the thinness of her arms and a weight of darkness throbbing through her skin.

If the positive energies wanted his attention, they had it now.

Terrified and gasping with guilt he left Sarah to sleep, snatched the noticeboard from the attic and ran to the kitchen. He waved the message from Karin Angstrom, the anthropologist who had been studying cave paintings of a contaminated landscape. "It's Mum," he sobbed. "She's absorbing the dark energy like those shamans in the rock art! That's why the black stream stops at the shop." In a strangled croak he read out Karin Angstrom's words. ". . .*they carried the taint inside until either it destroyed them or the ley itself was cleansed.*" Hot tears brimmed from his eyes. "It's my fault, it's all my fault."

"Course it's. . ." began Zi'ib. His star burst into life and the sudden force of Wolfie's shame ripping through his veins quelled his protest. He swallowed hard. "What have you done?"

The confession clung to Wolfie's tongue but he spat it out. "I've been trying to meet up with Wisdomseeker. . ."

"What? He's some slimy weirdo."

"He was going to tell me how to use dark energy to capture a Sphere. I thought it was the only way I'd ever get Dad back." A sound that was barely human gurgled through his throat. "I couldn't stop you searching for the spears so I . . . I hid the whetstone."

Tala backed away from him, her voice a thin horrified

wall. "Are you insane? Didn't you care about contaminating the Sphere and maybe the whole world?"

Wolfie could only speak in ragged gasps. "It was like there was something inside me shutting off everything except the need to protect the darkness. But if you'd told me about Mum—"

"Don't you dare blame me! Every moment we've lost because of you has made the dark energy stronger and Sarah sicker!"

Wolfie buried his burning face in his hands, swamped by waves of misery. *What if it was too late?*

Zi'ib said, "Leave him, Tala. It could have been you or me."

Tala stamped her foot. "No!" She flung an accusing finger at Wolfie. "I want my mom back more than anything in the world but I would never *ever* have done what he did."

Zi'ib said quietly, "It happened to Dad."

"What did?"

"He was tempted once to embrace the power of dark energy. He told me. I think that's partly why he went away even though he was still so sick. He was afraid it might happen again. It could happen to anyone."

Tala fell silent, rocked by the realization that for all their wisdom and heroism their Lupan parents were flawed and vulnerable.

Wolfie ran outside and dug up the whetstone, clawing frantically at the earth with his bare hands. Indifferent to

225

pride or dignity, he laid it on the kitchen table and stood there wiping his snotty tears with bloody, mud-stained fists.

"Sarah will be all right," said Zi'ib. His voice wobbled. "We'll cleanse the ley and *make* her all right."

"Yeah," Tala said vehemently. "We've got the whetstone." She looked at Wolfie, a deep clear glance that bridged the gulf that had opened between them. "And now we've got the will again. That's our most important weapon."

Zi'ib gave Wolfie's shoulder a hard squeeze and unpinned the verses they had decoded from Sir Edgar de Monteneuf's tomb.

> *When Michael's scales weigh dark and light,*
> *And hold the point 'twixt day and night*
> *Seize the hour to smite the dark*
> *And Michael's spears shall find their mark.*

"We just need to find the right spears and work out exactly where and when to use them," he said.

Tala nodded, deciding not to mention her worries about the missing Wisdom of the Wind. "First we'd better check how far the contamination has spread."

As she ran to fetch the map and pendulum a clear bright warmth crackled through their stars. Wolfie felt something nuzzle his leg. It was Elvis. He knelt down and buried his face in his thick rough fur.

*

226

Out and back, out and back the crystal pendulum swung over the map, tracing the gloomy flow of corrupted energy, further and further into the heart of London. The crystal hovered briefly on the South Bank before pushing on across the watery bulwark of the Thames and coming to a sharp halt. Sickened to see how far the taint had spread, Wolfie peered at the street name. As if stepping through thin ice, he experienced a moment of disbelief before plunging into an icy lake of clarity. This was Lambspring Passage and there, at the foot of the de Monteneuf Tower, yawed the fetid mouth of the dark ley. *That was why the building had affected him so badly*. He blurted out everything about Missy's apartment, the panther and the unicorn in the tapestry and the leaden desolation that had engulfed him when he was there. Tala listened but said nothing, never letting her concentration waver from the pendulum. "The movement feels different," she said. "It's trying to tell us something else, but I don't know what."

"Here." Zi'ib grasped the silver chain. The crystal swung back and forth along the dead straight ley line from Thornham to Lambspring Passage and up to Ludgate Hill, cutting through a little road whose name Tala had to squint to make out. Her voice was shrill, excited. "Look! *Knightrider* Street! Like on the plaque on Sir Edgar's tomb – *A wise man halts at every marker square whose writhing serpent guides the knight rider*. That's got to be a *kinnection*." The pendulum swung onwards, not stopping until it had reached beyond St Paul's Cathedral to the outer edges of Paternoster Square.

"OK. We'll check out the whole area, tomorrow straight after school," said Wolfie. "Missy said it's the oldest part of London *and* it's right on the path of the infected ley. There's got to be something there that'll help us."

When his turn came to take the pendulum it took a long time before Wolfie was calm enough to let the crystal have its way. When it did, its movements were swift, decisive and totally unexpected. It hovered briefly over Tate Modern before veering south-west across the Thames to Battersea Power Station. There it paused before swinging back to the site of the de Monteneuf Tower. Again and again the crystal swung between these three primal powerpoints, defining a triangle of ancient energy lines, long and narrow as the blade of a spear, etched deep into the face of the earth.

"What does it mean?" whispered Tala.

Wolfie screwed up his eyes, blotting out everything except the sway of the pendulum. "I don't know what it *means*," he said at last, "but it *feels* like I'm listening to an old, old man trying to tell me something important he's remembering from when he was very young."

21

Paternoster Square

Each time the train rumbled past a Zemogen poster, Wolfie looked away, refusing to think about anything except annihilating the infected energies and making Sarah well. He leaned over to Tala and Zi'ib. "Remember, look for *anything* that might be a spear and *anything* that points to a particular date or time."

They got out at City station. Grasping his map, Wolfie marched towards Paternoster Square, pausing briefly to allow Zi'ib to buy a guidebook from a newsstand.

"Hey, look," Tala said, as they passed the gilded figure of justice crowning the dome of the Old Bailey courthouse. "She's got a sword and scales, same as St Michael."

Wolfie swivelled round to gaze up at the statue, wondering what ancient landscape memory had projected these symbols through time to appear in the path of their search.

Zi'ib was picking out nuggets of fact from the guidebook. "There used to be a Roman temple where St Paul's Cathedral is now and they think the site has been used for ritual purposes since the Bronze Age."

Wolfie felt certain that this ancient place, overlooked by a sword and scales, must hold the secrets they sought. "Go on, what else?"

Zi'ib shut the book and shrugged. "Boring stuff."

Wolfie tugged the guide from his hands. "Much of the area around St Paul's was destroyed in the Great Fire of London in 1666 and by the end of World War Two, huge swathes of the old city were reduced to ruin."

Could the clues they longed for have survived the Great Fire and the Luftwaffe? He trudged on down a narrow cut, past sushi restaurants and jewellers' shops into Paternoster Square. It was worse than he had feared – a modern pedestrian precinct enclosed by pristine office blocks and wine bars spilling over with weary stockbrokers whose voices echoed dully across polished planes of stone and glass. And then a peal of bells rang out. The children looked up to see the great dome of St Paul's Cathedral floating creamy white and silver grey against the city sky and for a moment the newness of the square came alive with the ghosts of London's past, mellowing the barren buildings with dirty, noisy memories of gossip shared, battles fought and goods bartered on this ancient patch of ground.

They walked across the piazza, tuning their senses to the path of the ley, scouting for a sign, a symbol, anything. Gradually, as Wolfie pushed through the layers of thought and action that had left their spectral imprints on this sacred hill, he grew conscious of a purpose in this place that no bombs or fires or zealous planning departments could erode. He kept walking until his way was blocked by a wall of polished white stone. His eyes travelled up the windowless flank of a solid angular building and came to rest on a strange image: a narrowed figure of eight. The loops were formed from hundreds of little stripes chiselled into the stone, scored at intervals by longer lines. They were labelled by the months of the year. His breathing stopped. At the top a gleaming steel bracket jutted from the stone.

Zi'ib scrabbled through the guidebook. "That building is the New London Stock Exchange. The carving is something called an analemma. It's a sort of sundial that tells you when it's noon and when it's the . . . equinox."

When Michael's scales weigh dark and light, And hold the point 'twixt day and night. Of course! Equi-nox. Latin for equal night. The two times in the year when the lengths of day and night are the same.

Wolfie's legs went rubbery with relief. He stared at the analemma: a clever timing device whose only moving parts were the earth, gripped by certainty that a similar equinoctial marker had stood in that spot in another age, engraved on a structure that in its day had been even more of a powerhouse than London's Stock Exchange.

Tala was thumbing through her diary. He seized it from her. "When's the next one?"

"March 20th. I just checked, so you can stop reading that, it's private." She made a grab for the diary but he dodged her, flicking frenziedly. "I'm not reading it, I'm counting the days." He stopped, uncertain whether to be pleased or horrified. "Three weeks to the spring equinox." He noticed the little moon symbols in the diary. The equinox fell on the last day of the waxing moon.

Three weeks to find the spears. Three weeks to save Sarah. Three weeks before the grip of the negative forces grew too strong to reverse.

"Come on. Now we've got to find Knightrider Street."

Constantly alert for signs from the positive forces, they followed the path of the ley back towards the river. The guidebook said Knightrider Street was named after the medieval knights who used to ride through it on their way to the tournaments in Smithfield. Now it was just a narrow lane lined with modern restaurants and offices.

Tala walked the pavement, testing the energies until she felt a scarring beneath her feet. "There was a stone here once, an important one. Maybe it's where the knights gathered."

"The positive energies keep pointing us back to knights. Knight riders, knight's moves in chess, heirs to a knightly calling," Wolfie said.

"Mr Forester keeps on about the Knights Templar who protected the ley paths," said Zi'ib. "So maybe it's the secrets of the Knights Templar that will lead us to the spears."

The question now was ... where to start looking for them.

22

The Relaunch

"Sid will be here at half eight to open up," Wolfie said. "Is there anything else you need before we go?"

Sarah smiled at the three tired, red-eyed children gathered round her bed. "No, thanks. I feel bad enough that you're having to sort *and* deliver the papers on your own." She was leaning back on her pillows with *The Times*, and the untouched breakfast tray they had brought up earlier balanced on her lap.

"Can't you try and eat something?" Wolfie said. "You've got to get your strength up for the *EM* party tonight."

"Mr Forester will be *really* disappointed if you don't make it," added Tala.

"OK," Sarah said absently. She tapped the folded

newspaper. "Have you seen this? There's been a fire at Mo's New York gallery."

"Blimey," Wolfie said. "Anyone hurt?"

"No, thank goodness. But he lost an etching he'd just bought in a private house sale that was waiting to be authenticated. He'll be devastated." She pointed to the photo of it in the paper. "It says here it might be an unknown sister work to Rembrandt's famous etching of Faust in the British Museum. Even if it wasn't a Rembrandt, it was obviously by an extremely gifted artist. Look at the amazing detail."

The etching was of a wizened figure, bent over a small flame that threw a soft patch of light into a vaulted crypt overflowing with globes, scales, crucibles, flasks and all the curious paraphernalia of an alchemist's workshop. The old man's quiet concentration as he tipped a dusting of powder into a phial of bubbling liquid reminded Wolfie of the scientists he had seen at work in the Zemogen lab. Some of the books and scrolls scattered at the alchemist's feet bore notations in the glyphs and pictograms of ancient languages; there was even a clay tablet imprinted with tiny wedge-shaped characters. To the children, whose broken stars empowered them with the Mastery of Tongues, the meanings were clear. Each script repeated one or more of the words stone, gold, earth, water, sound, as if the old man had been dipping into the lost past to gather the ingredients for a magical brew.

There was not a spear in sight, or as far as they could see, anything to do with Knights Templar or the equinox, but their stars sang out so loudly that Zi'ib asked if he could keep the cutting and before they went to school he pinned it to their noticeboard.

By six o'clock that evening the sitting room of number forty-five was looking, if not luxurious, at least clean and festive. Tala had hidden the rickety desks beneath paper tablecloths and set them with vases of flowers and copies of *The Earth Mysterian* arranged in fan shapes. Zi'ib got ready to take coats, Sid put himself in charge of the drinks and Wolfie and Tala stood by with trays of snacks.

"Erm, Mr Forester," said Wolfie. "Can we come round tomorrow and go through your research for the feature on the Knights Templar – and maybe help you dig up more stuff for it?"

"Of course, that would be a great help. Now let me know if Nikto Senki turns up, I'm dying to meet him," replied Mr Forester, opening the door to the first trickle of luminaries from the worlds of archeo-astronomy, ley hunting and alternative history.

A group of dowsers who had visited the common on their way to the party arrived, vying with each other to describe the terrible effect the black stream had had on their sensitivities. When pressed by Wolfie, however, none could offer any practical suggestions as to how to cleanse such pernicious vibrations.

He moved on through the crowd, wondering nervously if one of these smiling chatty people was the perfidious Wisdomseeker.

An earnest-looking woman called Rhianna, who claimed to be an "aromancer", stopped Mr Forester as he passed and presented him with some stubby little bundles of withered herbs. She said they were "sage smudge sticks" used as energy purifiers by shamans worldwide. Lighting one, she wafted the smoke up and down the hall. To Tala's surprise, the sharp, pungent smoke really did seem to dent the darkness in her head.

"I'll look after them," she said, slipping a couple into her pocket as she headed for the kitchen.

At nine o'clock, Dame Esmé made a grand entrance, dressed in a black silk dress with a cream lace collar set off with a velvet cap trimmed with crimson feathers. An outfit, which, in Sid's opinion, made her look like a "turkey what's had a nasty shock".

She worked the room, dispensing smiles and nods as she navigated her way towards Wolfie. "I was very impressed by your illustration for my article," she said.

He backed away. She fixed him with her shrewd little eyes, her voice low. "Of course, Remus was quite right to remove that final paragraph about dark energy. Not for the eyes of innocents. However, truly enlightened adepts of wisdom might find that darkness is merely—"

"Leave me alone," growled Wolfie. "I'm not interested in anything you or Kandass has got to say about dark energy."

Frowning, she turned her back on him. "Remus! Where is Wolfie's mother? I'm dying to meet the person responsible for that delicious fudge."

"She's over there, talking to the man in the tartan trousers, but I think she's about to go."

Dame Esmé sailed across the room. "Sarah Brown?"

"Yes, hello."

"I'm Dame Esmé Hiram Glottis."

"How do you do? This is Ffarley Snodgrass, he's a publisher."

"Delighted," said Ffarley, thrusting out his hand. "I'm a great fan of your work on proto-Assyrian sacerdotal pathways."

"I'm flattered," said Dame Esmé, her eyes fixed on Sarah.

"It's lovely to meet you," said Sarah, "but I'm just leaving."

Esmé laid her hand on Sarah's arm. "Don't go yet, my dear." She tightened her grip, steering her away from the door. "I hear you paint. Animals, isn't it?"

"Um, mostly."

"Do tell me more. I'm thinking of having a portrait done of my cat, she's a Persian, quite exquisite."

"I've got a lot on at the moment."

"I'm in no hurry."

Sid approached with a bottle of wine. "Fancy a top up, ladies?"

"No thanks, Sid, I'm going now," Sarah said.

Esmé let out a strangled cry. The buzz of conversation stilled. Heads turned and those nearby saw her clench her teeth and draw back her thin red lips as if in pain. Her glass slipped from her hand, smashing to the floor. She clutched her throat as if trying to stifle the deep vibrant voice gurgling up from deep within.

"O Sarah, daughter of Stanley," she cried, "keeper of a sacred gateway to the stars. I, Kandass, greet you from the grave. "

Sarah shrank back. "Can you keep an eye on her, Sid? I've got to go."

"No probs," said Sid. He patted Esmé's shoulder. "My old gran used to get like this when she'd been at the cooking sherry."

Esmé shrugged him off and snatched Sarah's arm, holding it in a blood-stopping grip. "You and I are bearers of the same precious burden," she cried. "It falls to you to care for the flesh of the prophesied ones and to me to guide their spiritual path!"

"I'm sorry, I don't know what you are talking about," Sarah said, struggling to free herself.

"Aid me, Sarah. I am sent to help them yet they refuse to heed my words. . ." Dame Esmé's lip quivered.

"Please let go, I have to get home."

The bewildered guests looked on agog as Esmé, holding grimly to Sarah's arm, switched to an outpouring of ancient Meroitic.

"O ye children of mingled blood. You yearn to capture a

sacred Sphere, yet you seek to destroy the very threads of darkness that would draw it to your world."

"I can't take any more of this. I'm going to test her," said Tala. She rifled through memories of the time they had spent among the Meroitic ruins looking for clues to the Stones of Knowledge, searching for something the real priestess Kandass would have known. Slipping through the crowd, she planted herself in front of Esmé, hands on her hips, and said, "OK, *Kandass*, if you really are a priestess of ancient Meroe, tell us the name of the Lion God who has a temple at Naqa."

A fascinated silence descended as the guests waited for Kandass's reply. Barely missing a beat, Esmé raised her hand as if in supplication to an entity drifting away towards the tray of cheese balls. "No, Kandass, don't leave me," she quavered. "A child, a dear innocent child wishes to question you. She meant no disrespect . . . forgive her. . ."

The clock struck ten.

"She is gone," Esmé moaned.

Releasing Sarah's arm, she flopped down into a chair like a rag doll emptied of sawdust. The buzz of conversation resumed, many guests tittering at "Kandass's" failure to respond to Tala's question.

Sarah made a hasty escape. Calling to Tala to fetch the boys, she hurried down the front steps and caught Elvis and Monty slinking out of the greenhouse. It might have been the wind but she was sure the dogs nosed the door shut before loping across the newly dug soil to the driveway.

"That was pretty suspicious," whispered Tala as they searched for their coats.

"Maybe. But if she wasn't getting the information from Kandass, how could she know about us?" said Zi'ib. "The only people in the whole world who know who we are and that we're after a Sphere are Dad and—" He paused, the evidence driving his brain towards one chilling conclusion. "Ridian Winter."

"That's it!" cried Wolfie. "Ridian must have told her. He knows Dad and Kara are on Lupus, because it was him and the Manus Sacra who put them there. It's not rocket science to suss out that we want to get hold of a Sphere so we can bring them back."

"Then it must be Ridian who taught her those bits of Meroitic," said Zi'ib.

"But why?" said Tala.

Wolfie blushed, remembering how Kandass's hints about the power of dark energy and the messages from Wisdomseeker had caught him like pincer and drawn him in.

The truth rushed at him like a great wave, horrifying and inescapable. "Ridian is Wisdomseeker." He wanted to throw up. "For some reason he wants to stop us cleansing the dark ley. And he was using Esmé to help him."

The battle against Ridian and the battle against the dark energies were one and the same!

241

Cold dread gripped them. What did Ridian want the dark energy *for*?

They heard Sarah calling and ran to her.

"That nightmare Esmé woman is up to something," she said. "I just wish I knew what it was."

"Yeah, she's trouble," said Zi'ib. "Fom now on we're keeping right out of her way."

Elvis limped towards them, his back paw dangling loosely. Bending to see what was wrong, Tala found blood trickling between the pads. Wolfie swept the gravel with his shoe and dislodged a glinting, golden spike sticking up through the stones. He pulled it free. It was a long, gilded hatpin shaped like a snake with glittering red eyes. "I bet that hurt," he said. As he stroked Elvis's head a dark van sped past, its engines roaring.

"What's his hurry?" said Tala, taking Sarah's arm. A throb of warning stirred their stars as they neared the shop, but nothing prepared them for what they found inside. The kitchen was a wreck. Drawers turned out, cupboards ransacked, furniture tipped over. Even the grandfather clock had been wrenched open. Wolfie ran to the stairs.

"Stay here," Sarah cried. "They might still be up there. I'll ring the police."

Her portrait of Missy lay face down on the floor. Zi'ib propped it back on the easel. The background was smudged and flecked with dog hairs but the figures of

Missy, Elvis and Bonbon had survived relatively unscathed.

One of the officers who arrived was Constable Mott. The other, a woman with a soft Jamaican accent, checked the shop while Mott searched the upper floors.

"All clear up here," he shouted from the landing. "But your airing cupboard's a mess. I don't know what they thought they'd find in there."

"Mum. The Saravita!"

"Don't worry," Sarah said calmly. "The cuttings weren't doing very well in the airing cupboard so Sid took them up to his greenhouse."

The children grew twitchy, anxious to see if the first Stone of Knowledge was still in the outhouse.

Mott's distrustful eyes swept the kitchen. "Funny they left your telly and didn't touch anything in the shop, not even the cigarettes."

"They must have been disturbed," said the policewoman, handing Sarah a slip of paper. "You'll need this crime number for your insurers. They'll want a list of everything that's missing."

Wolfie stuck the slip of paper to the larder door with the snake hatpin, sure from the look on his mother's face that she had forgotten to keep up the payments. "You go to bed, Mum, we'll clear up in the morning."

As soon as the police had gone, the children ran to the outhouse and switched on the light. Like mourners at a funeral they stared down at the old wooden cask lying empty on its side among the broken shards of Sarah's planter. The granite obelisk, the first Stone of Knowledge, had gone.

They ran to the common. A street light burned beside the bus stop, intensifying the gaping darkness beneath the old stone bench where its central support had once stood. The second Stone of Knowledge was missing too.

"Ridian again. It has to be," Zi'ib said, plonking himself down on the bench. "Apart from us and Zane he's the only person in this world who knows the Stones of Knowledge even exist."

Tala spun round. "That's what Esmé's performance was all about. He got her to keep Sarah at the party to give the burglars time to ransack the shop."

Wolfie rapped the knuckles of both hands against his head. "He's got two out of three Stones of Knowledge and he tried cloning and nicking the Saravita so he'd have all of them. But what's the point? The rest of the Manus Sacra have all been destroyed. We know they were sucked down into the nether void. So who is he doing this *for*? We keep going round and round in circles and it always, always comes back to that!"

Once home they tried to clear their brains of everything but the bare facts and wrote up a new batch of notes for their noticeboard. One by one Tala stuck them in a circle, linking them with arrows.

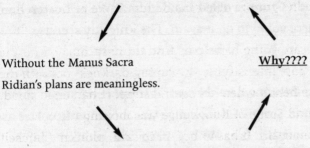

The Manus Sacra have been
consigned to the nether void.

Without the Manus Sacra
Ridian's plans are meaningless.

Why????

But Ridian is trying to protect the dark energy
and get hold of the Stones of Knowledge
and continue his plans to use Zemogen to take
over the ley grid.

Tala stood back. "When you have eliminated the impossible, whatever remains, however improbable, must be the truth. . ." she said.

"What are you on about?" Wolfie said.

"That's how Sherlock Holmes cracked his cases."

Wolfie studied the board, carefully assessing each fact before moving along the trail of evidence. A raw panic overtook him. Mentally he reshuffled the information, searching wildly for alternatives to the horrifying conclusion he had just reached. He found none. With terrifying clarity the facts pointed to one improbable, bizarre and sickening truth. Ridian thought he could get the Manus Sacra *out* of the nether void. And he needed the dark energy and the Stones of Knowledge to do it.

A flood of fury swelled inside him. "We've beaten him once. We're going to do it again. The knightly secrets of the Templars are going to help us find those spears."

Blasted child! How dare she humiliate me! Esmé stared at her reflection in the gilded looking-glass above her fireplace as she took off her hat. With a pang she realized that her favourite gold hatpin was missing. A beautiful thing: she had coveted it from the moment she had spotted it adorning the head of the Maharani of Jaipur all those years ago. It was only much later that she had discovered it to be a valuable antique, designed to fasten the cloak of a Mogul noble.

Her mobile buzzed. She stiffened when she saw Ridian's name flashing on the screen.

His voice was icy. "We only got two stones out of three. It's not enough. There were no plants in the airing cupboard."

"It's not my fault," snapped Esmé. "That's where Forester said Sarah kept the cuttings."

"The dog wasn't there either."

"How was I to know they'd bring the wretched animal to the party?"

A burst of static severed the connection. But Esmé had never had any intention of telling Ridian how badly her own evening had gone. If his plans were unravelling, she preferred to let others take the blame.

*

Ridian threw down his mobile. How difficult could it be to get hold of one tiny plant? All he needed was a single fresh specimen with the tiny stone-like seed. Cloned, stolen, he didn't care. Time was running out. According to his calculations, 17.32 on March 20th, the vernal equinox, was the only moment when the tilt of the earth and the resonance of the negative energies could create a magnetic pull powerful enough to draw the Sphere to earth. And if, when that time arrived, he wasn't prepared, he would remain cut off from the minds of his masters for another year, forced to go on fawning to imbeciles like Stefan de Witt and that hag Hiram Glottis. How ironic, then, that the moment of the vernal equinox, when day and night are equal, yet poised to tip over on to the side of light, was the only point in the year when those severely polluted waves of energy could be transformed into a stream of positive power.

At his instruction, the crystex dome above the Zemogen conference hall had been designed to open like the lids of an insect's eye. To create a force powerful enough to draw the Sphere down through that gap he needed to pass a charge of negative energy through a mass of pure matter at the precise moment of the equinox. It made no difference whether that original matter had manifested out of light or darkness.

Obtaining the contaminated energy would be no problem. He had already posed as an engineer and entered the basement of the de Monteneuf Tower, drilled down through the floor and inserted an angled row of powerful white crystals mined from Alaska, deep beneath the broken crust of concrete. When activated by the moment of the equinox, the crystals would create a barrier that would divert the dark energy along an age-old power line connecting the ancient ritual site beneath the de Monteneuf Tower to its counterpart beneath the Zemogen HQ.

The problem was obtaining the pure matter. On this primitive planet, matter as pure as Lupan gold, as pure as the sacred Stones of Knowledge or as pure as the elemental life forms that manifested from the forces in the leys was rare indeed. Unfortunately, the "panther" was barely formed and it would be a while before it became corporeal enough for his purpose. The dog Elvis, fully realized from positive energy long ago, was a wise and elusive beast that had so far evaded capture. Then, of course, there were the half stars hanging at the throats of those half-bred brats. But Lupan stars could only be surrendered willingly by their rightful bearers or removed after death. He needed the children alive and he knew they would never give up their stars willingly. The problems spun round his head, colliding to create a single solution: one simple means of getting hold of Elvis *and* cheating those kids into handing over at least part of their stars as a ransom. What's more, he knew just the man for the job: Frankie Fontaine.

23

Girls Together

That Saturday there was no fudge to box up because Sarah had been far too unwell to make any, so the children got on with clearing up the mess left by the burglars. Mr Forester came round to help and by 9.30 when Sarah came slowly downstairs in her old dressing gown, the kitchen was almost back to normal.

"I suppose I should be pleased they didn't take much," she said, opening her post. She glanced at an embossed card and let it drop on to the table. "Mo's invited us all to the opening of Jenna Falkirk's installation at the Tate."

"Cool," said Wolfie.

Sarah looked at him with dark-shadowed eyes. "Jenna was in the year below me at art school and she's won one of the most prestigious commissions in Britain. I can't even get one little painting right."

"Don't worry, my dear," said Mr Forester, "you'll soon repair the damage."

"It's not the damage that's worrying me. It's the whole composition; there's something missing."

Tala busied herself with the kettle while Wolfie and Zi'ib gathered round the the portrait of Missy. Sarah had captured that ethereal, looking-glass moment when the strange combination of girl, dog and tortoise had seemed to stare out from another age, but she was right, there was definitely something missing.

Tala passed her a mug of tea. "You're an amazing painter. Whatever it is that picture needs, you'll find it."

Sarah swallowed her tablets, sipped her tea and said gently, "Your jeans are halfway up your ankles and that jumper's had it. You need to go shopping."

Tala blushed. "This stuff's fine."

It was true that she had grown out of all her clothes. It was also true that she had no money replace them.

Mr Forester thrust an envelope into her hand and passed two more to Zi'ib and Wolfie. "Please accept my apologies for the delay. I've only just got round to doing my accounts."

"What's this?" Wolfie asked, pulling out twenty-five pounds.

"Pay day. I'm sorry it's not more. You've all worked so hard on the magazine. However, the way subscriptions are picking up, it should be more next time."

Sarah took a bundle of notes from her pocket. "And I

owe you for all the help you've been giving me." She handed them each another twenty-five pounds. She frowned at Tala. "Zane left me a bit extra for emergencies, and I think the state of your jeans definitely counts as one." She gave her another twenty-five pounds.

Tala looked down at the money. Seventy-five pounds. A fortune. "Thanks," she said, her eyes smarting. Sarah laid a hand on her tangled hair. The gentle pressure loosened Tala's tears.

"That posh bird's here," called Sid. They heard the shop bell jangle and Missy's giggling voice.

Wolfie looked nervously at Zi'ib and then at Tala. No one had told them she was coming.

"Hi Tala." Missy skipped in, twirling a new designer handbag. "This is going to be great."

"What is?"

"Shopping."

Tala paled.

Sarah said, "I forgot all about Missy's sitting and by the time I rang her to cancel they'd left. So Johnny is going to take both of you into town."

"I can't. We promised to help Mr Forester research his feature on the Knights Templar."

"Wolfie and Zi'ib can do that without you, can't they, Remus? Spending a bit of time with a girl your own age will do you good."

Wolfie shot his mother a suspicious look. It wasn't like her to interfere. Sarah was already shuffling towards the stairs. Passing Tala on the way, she gave her a little push. "Go on, get your coat."

Moving like a condemned prisoner approaching the gallows, Tala followed Missy to the Bentley. Johnny opened the passenger door and gave her a wink. Bristling with annoyance, she buckled her seat belt.

"First stop, Gerard's," announced Missy.

"Who's Gerard?"

"Mom's hairdresser. He's a genius. He said one of his trainees will do your hair for free."

"Oh." Tala's eyes brimmed. The last time she had had her hair cut her dad had trimmed it with the kitchen scissors, pruning it like an unruly sapling.

They passed the corset factory with its new crystex dome glinting through a cage of scaffolding. All the way to Mayfair, Missy babbled excitedly about Mo's plans for a café and a bookshop and a studio for an artist-in-residence in the gallery complex, only stopping when Johnny dropped them outside a marble-fronted salon full of elegant women reading glossy magazines. Tala shrank back as a plump man with very white teeth and a golden tan came rushing towards them, arms outstretched.

"Missy! Enchanting as ever. I've arranged for Roxanne to do your hair."

"Hi, Gerard, this is my friend Tala."

Tala flinched – whether from Missy's use of the word friend or Gerard's tanned fingers reaching out to grab a hunk of her hair, she was not sure.

"This is a disaster!" he said, pushing back her straggly fringe. "Look at the wonderful eyes hiding under that mess." He snapped his fingers at the receptionist. "This one I will do myself."

The waiting clients gasped, as if they had caught royalty taking in washing. Tala ducked from his grasp. There was no way she was going to spend all her money on a haircut. "Missy said one of your trainees would do it for free."

Gerard's eyes flickered with amusement. "I wouldn't dream of charging you. I rarely get the opportunity to work miracles."

Before she could resist, Gerard had whisked her away to the inner sanctum of the salon and, as he washed, brushed, snipped and combed the ugly snarls from her hair, she closed her eyes and felt her thoughts loosening from a dark tangle. Only when Gerard laid down his dryer did she dare to look in the mirror. Her hair was smooth and shiny, pouring like dark water on to her shoulders and framing her face in soft wisps.

"Thank you," she whispered.

Gerard gave a her a little bow. "My pleasure."

Missy came bounding over and he smiled approvingly at her cascade of soft auburn waves. "Tell Sir Simon I'll happily donate a free haircut for his next charity fundraiser," he said as he escorted them to the door.

Tala felt clear-headed, calm and somehow taller as she ran towards the waiting Bentley, her hair floating in the wind.

"You look great," Johnny said.

Tala blushed.

"Told you. Gerard's a genius," Missy said. "Let's go to Covent Garden."

"Who's Sir Simon?" Tala asked.

Missy pulled a face. "Dad. He's Sir Simon de Monteneuf, though he hates being called anything but Mo."

"He's a knight, right?" Tala murmured, as if thinking aloud.

"Yeah, how weird is that?"

"And way back your family were . . . Knights Templar."

"Yeah, whatever they are."

Tala stared at Missy, powerless against the stream of *kinnections* to the noble de Monteneufs that came rushing and bouncing into her head: the mysterious vault built by Sir Guy that had sucked the Manus Sacra into oblivion; Sir Edgar, who had befriended Wolfie's ancestor Agnes and protected her orphaned son; the cryptic messages about knights on his tomb that had led them to the whetstone. And now here she was with Missy, heiress of the de Monteneufs, whose home lay right on the path of the contaminated ley.

De Monteneuf heirs inherit a knightly calling.

It wasn't knightly *secrets* that would help them find the spears. It was *Missy!* She was the heiress to the de Monteneuf family's knightly calling. And that calling was to aid the bloodlines of the guardians. Tala gazed at Missy, frightened to think how close she had come to shutting her out of their lives.

*

Missy gloried in the bustle of Covent Garden's covered market, peering in shop windows while Tala dawdled behind, doubtful that this de Monteneuf heiress could help them find anything except overpriced designer shoes. While Tala waited outside a dress shop she overheard a young couple chatting in Japanese about a dance troupe due to perform by the piazza. She followed them to where the dancers, dressed all in white, were twirling like dolls to the amplified strains of a string quartet. Across the circle of spectators the Japanese man took out a professional-looking camera, handed the woman his equipment bag and began to follow the dancers, pressing the shutter again and again. The music quickened; the crowd began to clap.

"I'll distract her, you get the bag."

"Meet me in the alley."

Two men, speaking in a language Tala understood but could not identify, squeezed through the crowd to sandwich the Japanese woman, smiling, nodding and encouraging her to clap along to the music.

Tala's warning cry of, "Your bag! They're after your bag!" was swallowed up by the music and the roar of English voices filling the market. She took a huge breath and yelled the words in Japanese. The photographer twisted round. The woman was turning in panic, grabbing at the severed strap hanging from her shoulder.

"The man in the blue anorak!" Tala shouted, pointing to the thief, who was slipping away with the bag stuffed into a holdall.

Lunging through the crowd, the photographer wrestled back the bag. In a flash the thief had melted into the crush. By the time the man looked round for Tala, she had gone to find Missy.

"Aren't you getting anything?" Missy asked.

"I can't afford this stuff."

Missy reddened. "Let's go to Oxford Street. There's always somewhere there having a sale."

Johnny dropped them outside a shop with *Closing down!* daubed across the window. Tala pounced on the racks of half-price items. With money in her pocket and all these bargains to choose from she almost began to enjoy herself.

"This would look great on you," said Missy, holding up a white jumper.

"Artemesia de Monteneuf!" hissed a sour voice. It belonged to a rangy girl with eyelids shiny with make-up. Even the way she tilted her head had a smug insolence about it. "I had *everyone* over for a sleepover last night." She paused to let Missy register her exclusion. "We couldn't believe it when Sophie saw *you* in *here*."

Moving in unison like a shoal of fish, a posse of girls fanned out behind her. Missy's cheeks burned. "Georgina," she murmured, edging round to block Tala from view.

Georgina seized the bargain jumper and twirled it in the air. Her retinue sneered dutifully, all except for a curly-haired girl at the back who gave Missy a pained smile and a little wave. Georgina pushed Missy aside and stared pointedly at the inches of ankle visible beneath Tala's jeans before letting her caustic gaze drift to her face. "Who's this?"

Choking back spasms of fury, Tala met Georgina's cold blue eyes. As bullies went, she made Marcus and Wayne look almost human.

"I said, who's this?"

"Tala," Missy said. "She's staying with a really important artist who's a friend of my dad's."

Tala tuned in swiftly to the language of this alien world ruled by the monstrous Georgina. It was a language of subtle derision, punctuated by studied facial expressions and barely perceptible movements of the hips and head. She knew instantly that however well she might tip her chin and spit back some damning retort, nothing she could say would have any effect. The key to this language was power. And she had none.

Bored with this scruffy little nobody, Georgina turned on Missy, who shrank away, misery and loneliness etched across her perfect features.

Suddenly Tala spied the Japanese couple from Covent Garden looking into the shop window.

Without a word she ducked beneath the bargain rail and ran out to them, returning minutes later to find Missy backed into a corner, red-faced yet defiant.

"I'm really sorry, Akito," Tala said, loudly. "These are the best I could find."

Georgina and her entourage turned to stare first at Tala, then at the elegant Japanese photographer standing next to her, framing them in his lens. Taking out a notepad and pen, his girlfriend nodded to Tala and said in halting English, "We are ready."

"OK, Yumi, the one with long auburn hair is Missy de Monteneuf," announced Tala. "As you can see, she's perfect: fantastic hair, great skin, loads of personality."

The woman made a note. "Georgina, the lanky one next to her wearing too much make-up, obviously hasn't got the bones for it: piggy eyes . . . no character in her features." She motioned the astonished Georgina aside. "I wondered about the girl behind her. Sophie, is it? Come into the light." Dazed by the camera, a thin brunette stepped forward. Tala sucked her breath. "Oops . . . sorry, I hadn't noticed that *chin*."

"What's this about?" demanded Georgina.

"We're scouting for extras for a movie set in a boarding school. They've hired me to find girls with the kind of style and personality that will appeal to kids of our age." One by one she beckoned Georgina's acolytes forward, before apologizing to Yumi for their flawed appearance and personalities. Only when she came to the curly-haired girl did she show any mercy.

"Name?"

"Ella," mumbled the girl, "but I don't want to be in a film, I'm not. . ."

"Shame," said Tala, "You've got real potential." She

pushed past Georgina. "I'd better go change. It's a drag having to dress like this but it's the quickest way to test whether the girls we find are stuck-up snobs." Quickly, she steered the Japanese couple across the shop. Georgina stomped out into Oxford Street with Sophie dancing attendance. The other girls had broken ranks and were leaving in huddled groups, casting wistful glances at the photographer. Missy came running over.

"Was that OK?" asked Yumi.

"Awesome," breathed Missy. "How can I ever thank you?"

"It was our pleasure," said Akito. The couple bowed and left the shop.

"Who were they?" Missy asked, barely able to believe what had just happened.

Tala shrugged. "Long story." Still riding high on nervous energy, she ran up and down, selecting a pair of jeans, two jumpers and, after a moment's deliberation, a short denim skirt not unlike Missy's, some thick black tights and a pair of black pumps.

"What you just did was brilliant," Missy said in the queue for the till.

"It's easy doing stuff like that for other people. Not so easy when it's you the bullies are after."

"Who'd dare bully you?"

"There's these kids at Blackstone who've got it in for all of us, specially Zi'ib." Tala told her all about Marcus Harrison and Wayne Snaith. "What really upsets him is when they call him Charity Boy."

"Why Charity Boy?"

"He got injured in Sudan and it was this charity, INFASIC, that brought him to England to get his leg treated."

"I've heard of INFASIC," Missy said thoughtfully. "Dad's involved with their fundraising."

"Yeah, well, Marcus and Wayne think the kids they help are all scroungers who should go back where they came from."

"So how are you going to get this Marcus and Wayne back?"

Tala shrugged. "Dunno. They're creeps but they're not thick. I can't see them falling for anything we come up with."

Missy said nothing; she was too busy making a note in the memo pad of her phone.

24

Lo-pan

Missy dumped her packages in the back of the Bentley. "I'm starving. Let's eat."

Tala squeezed her empty purse. "I'll have something when I get home."

"No," Johnny said. "My treat – we'll have Chinese in my favourite restaurant."

Missy looked surprised. "OK."

He parked in a side street and they walked into Chinatown, past restaurant windows hung with red paper lanterns, racks of wind-dried duck and discs of frilly-edged squid. Nimble-fingered street sellers twisted wisps of dragon's beard candy and tweezed steaming noodles into paper cups. It seemed that everyone in these bright narrow streets not engaged in the serious business of selling or preparing food was intent on the even more serious business of eating it.

Johnny turned out of the bustle of Gerard Street and slipped into a grimy alleyway fringed by neon-lit openings spilling strange gaudy fruits on to the cobbles.

"Hey, where are we going?" demanded Missy, disappointed that they would not be lunching in one of the plush, red-lanterned restaurants on the main thoroughfare.

Johnny waved them through a scuffed, muddy door. Above the lintel, a flickering globe illuminated the word Lo-pan, hand painted in Chinese characters. Tala's star thrummed to the levels of meaning filtering through her brain: Lo meant net, a net that holds everything; and pan, a dish that gives access to the universal mysteries. And together they hinted at heaven and earth and the fields of force that hold them together and a compass that might guide you through them. Alert and excited at the significance of the sign, she followed Johnny up a narrow staircase into a small, dimly lit room crammed with diners, all Chinese, eating at plain wooden tables. A dainty woman barely taller than Tala, wearing a red silk dress, came towards them, chastising Johnny in Mandarin for arriving unannounced. "I would have cooked something special."

She was probably in her late fifties, lively and commanding, with expressive eyes and jet-black hair piled into a glossy bun.

"I thought I'd surprise you, Aunt Flo," replied Johnny in English. He made the introductions and the woman greeted Missy and Tala. "You are welcome. You are my nephew's guests."

Missy plucked Johnny's sleeve. "How come you've never brought me here before?"

"There's always some glitzy new place you want to try."

Missy looked put out and asked the waiter for a menu. He laughed, calling across the room in Mandarin. "Anyone got a menu?"

The diners grinned and chuckled. Sweaty-faced cooks gathered at the kitchen door to share the joke. Missy frowned. "What's so funny?"

"There is no menu. Flo decides what you eat."

Flo brought bowls of aromatic soup, tiny crisp dumplings and mysterious dishes full of finely chopped meats and vegetables and came to sit beside them, telling them which sauces to try with which dish, and how to stuff lettuce leaves with exquisitely spiced fillings and twist them into tight little parcels.

While they ate, Flo told them stories about Johnny's childhood, which made him blush, announcing that when he got his big break he was going to be a famous movie star. A waiter brought tea. Tiny flowers floated on the pale liquid, served in little white cups. Tala took a sip and asked the question that had been swirling around her mind ever since they had arrived.

"Why is your restaurant called the Lo-pan?"

Surprised by her perfect pronunciation, Flo asked, "Do you know what it means?"

Tala shrank from lying to this woman. "A sort of compass."

Flo disappeared through a door marked private and returned carrying a large red leather box, embossed with golden dragons, turtles and tigers, held shut by a fluted metal clasp. Flo laid it on the table and raised the lid. "This is a lo-pan."

Inside lay a disc of yellow lacquered wood, mounted on a square of red lacquered wood. The disc was divided into concentric rings, like a slice through the trunk of an ancient tree, each circle inked with tiny characters in black and red. A mariner's compass, about ten centimetres in diameter, had been set into a little well in the centre, divided into four by an axis cross of tightly stretched red string. It was a beautiful thing. As Tala reached out to touch it a charge of energy shot up her arm. The compass needle swung wildly, whizzing one way and then the other. Quickly she plunged her tingling fingers between her knees.

"My grandfather would have been impressed by your natural affinity with energies," Flo said in her gentle voice. "He was a geomancer, you see. He made this lo-pan and bequeathed it to me along with some of the secrets of his craft, though I will never attain his level of understanding."

"What did he use it for?" Tala asked.

"To analyse the position of places and buildings in the landscape and measure the intangible energies, the chi that runs through them. He studied the ancient art of feng shui with a master for many years."

Tala's heart beat fast as she absorbed the meaning of feng shui – wind and water. *This was why the leys had brought her here.*

"He was thirsty for knowledge," went on Flo, "and he travelled across many continents searching for wisdom concerning the energies of the earth. Look." She tilted the lo-pan to show Tala the disc of opalescent crystal affixed to its underside. "When he brought this piece of crystal back from Alaska, there were many who mocked him, for no traditional lo-pan has a crystal base, but he just smiled and nodded and puffed on his pipe and told them to consult another geomancer if they were not happy with his methods. They always came back to him in the end."

"Why? What did he do for them?"

"He calculated propitious locations for new buildings and propitious dates for undertaking important tasks, but mainly he cleared bad energies from the landscape."

There was a heartbeat pause before Tala said, "How did he do that?"

"With a form of earth acupuncture. Placing needles in the ground to change the pulse of the energies. His skill lay in knowing exactly where and when to place them."

Tala could hardly breathe. "What sort of needles?"

"Traditionally they would be metal, but again my grandfather made his own. The materials he used and the way he placed them were determined by the problem he was seeking to solve. Sometimes he used no needles at all, taming the negative chi with nothing but his will and the guidance of the lo-pan."

The wisdom Tala sought was here, elusive as flashes of light on water. She panicked. How could she ever unlock the longed-for mysteries that Flo's grandfather had taken a lifetime to amass?

"We could do with something like that in our apartment," Missy was saying. "Mom says it's got a bad vibe. Even Wolfie felt sick when he came round."

"Oh, I don't do much work with energies now, I'm so busy here."

Missy's expression grew suddenly pleading. "If you made the apartment feel better, maybe Mom would spend more time there. She got so fed up with it, Dad took her to Switzerland, then they went straight to New York because there was a fire at the gallery so I haven't seen them for ages."

Flo felt a surge of pity for this lonely child who Johnny had told her so much about. She smiled. "Of course, Missy. I would be happy to try. I will ask Johnny to drop me round so I can take some measurements and assess the problem. When I have done the calculations and found a propitious day I will let you know. But first you must tell me about the apartment and the people who live in it." She jotted down Missy's answers in a notebook, making little noises in her throat.

In the light from the table lantern, Tala studied the

markings in the circles of the lo-pan, her eye taken by the clusters of dots in the second ring. They represented the numbers one to nine, arranged so that the one was opposite the nine, the eight opposite the two, the three opposite the seven and the four opposite the six.

"Where's the five?" she asked.

Flo broke off her questioning. "The five is omitted so that the opposing numbers all add up to ten. If it were there in the middle, the numbers would add up to fifteen, a number that has its own powerful associations. It is the total number of days in a complete waxing or waning of the moon."

The chatter in the tiny restaurant rose to a roar in Tala's head. She thought of the two moons whose waxing and waning framed the window of hope for cleansing the taint of the nether void, and of Agnes's painting with its grid of images representing these same numbers, embedded in a tangle of paths.

"It's like a magic square," she whispered.

"It *is* a magic square, the Lo shu magic square." Flo laid her neat fingers on the table. "Let me tell you a story. In the ancient time of China, there was a huge flood and the people offered sacrifices to the god of the Lo river to calm his anger. The river god would not accept their sacrifices and every time these gifts were laid at the water's edge a turtle with a curious pattern of dots on its shell would appear and walk around them. And then one day, a child noticed that the dots represented the numbers one to nine set out in a three-by-three grid in which every row including the diagonals added up to fifteen."

"What did it mean?" said Tala.

"It was a sign telling the people to look in the right place and to understand what they saw. When the people realized the meaning of this sign, the river god accepted the sacrifice and the flood abated."

"What's understanding stuff got to do with spots on a turtle?" Missy asked.

"I have always interpreted this story to mean that knowledge can be gathered by the eye but wisdom must be gleaned by the heart. So often the answers we seek lie right in front of us and yet we do not recognize them."

Tala looked at Missy, heiress to the knightly calling of the de Monteneufs, and nodded. "I . . . I've seen this square before," she said. "But it wasn't anything to do with Chinese wisdom, it was . . . kind of to do with ley lines."

"Towards the end of his life my grandfather studied the theories surrounding ley lines. Some echoed our own concepts of dragon lines of chi in the landscape, some conflicted with them. But he used to say that all seekers of lost wisdom are studying a few threads, at best a fragment, of the vast and intricately woven fabric that is the cosmos. Only if we were able to see the whole sweep of the design could we ever unpick the truths from the falsehoods and understand how all those separate threads interconnect. But in those places where many wisdoms meet we can be sure to find a glimpse of perfect truth."

Flo smiled at this knowledge-hungry child and went on, "One such truth accepted by the enlightened all over the world is that only by looking up to contemplate the heavens and down to examine the natural forces of the earth can we come to understand darkness and light, negative and positive, yin and yang."

Missy said, "I had a T-shirt with that black and white tadpole yin and yang thing on it. But I never knew what it meant."

"It symbolizes the cosmos in flux. The never-ending interplay of opposing forces constantly giving rise one to the other in an endless cycle of birth and destruction. The white dot on the black and the black dot on the white represent the seeds of one forever sown in the other. The three-by-three magic square is a powerful symbol of that polarity and it's found in many ancient cultures." Flo tore a page from her notebook and drew the square.

4	9	2
3	5	7
8	1	6

"The odd numbers are yang and the even ones yin. If you join the yang ones together you get an upright cross that represents heaven and the four yin ones in the corners represent the earth and the five in the middle is the cosmic axis at the centre of the world."

Tala pressed a hand to the fluttering leap at her throat.

"The Mayan Indians of Mexico, the Hausa of Nigeria, the ancient Babylonians and the alchemists of Arabia all venerated this square for its mystical significance. Its interpretations are infinite and its power limitless. They are crucial to the work I will be doing to heal the energies in Missy's apartment."

Shaky with excitement, Tala gazed down at the magic square. "Can I come and watch?" she asked. "And maybe bring some friends of . . . mi . . . *ours* along as well?" Out of the corner of her eye she caught Missy nervously clenching her fists.

Flo frowned. "I don't usually work with an audience."

"*Oh, please*," begged Missy.

Flo looked from Missy's fair, dimpled eagerness to Tala's dark, brooding desperation and knew she could not refuse.

"All right. I'll text you and tell you when."

Tala started to sweat. "You know . . . um . . . I heard that the spring equinox was maybe a good time for cleansing energy."

Flo regarded her curiously. "It can be. I will do my calculations and let you know."

*

"Yuggh! What have you done to your hair?" Wolfie said.

Disturbed by the baffling pulses that had been pounding their stars all day, he and Zi'ib had expected Tala to come hurtling through the door spitting fury, and were shocked by the groomed apparition who sauntered in wearing a skirt and clutching bags of shopping. Tala glowered at him, but her expression, usually so sullen and intense, was strangely animated. "Missy's life stinks," she said, kneeling down to hug Elvis. "Did you find out anything useful about the Templars?"

"Not so far," Zi'ib said.

"We deleted a couple of messages from Wisdomseeker. Ridian's obviously mighty hacked off he's being ignored. Apart from that the whole day's been a complete write-off," Wolfie said, bitterly.

"No it hasn't." Tala allowed herself a little smile. "I've found some fragments of the Wisdom of the Wind."

"In some poncy hairdresser's?"

"No. A Chinese restaurant." And she poured out the story of Flo, and her grandfather's wisdom of wind and water, saving the revelations about the lo-pan, the magic square and the turtle till last.

"Flo says it means that the answers we seek are often staring us in the face but we don't recognize them. Like that line on Edgar's tomb about *de Monteneuf heirs inheriting a knightly calling*. It wasn't the secrets of the Knights Templar we had to find. It was Missy, heiress to the *knightly calling* of the de Monteneufs. Think of everything that family has done over the centuries. Their calling was obviously to help the bloodlines of the guardians."

Leaving the boys to digest what she had said, she ran to fetch the copy of the words on Sir Edgar's tomb.

"OK, Miss Know-all." Zi'ib grinned, pulling it out of her hands.

". . .de Monteneuf heirs inherit a knightly calling . . . a castle on Temple Stonham's sacred forest . . . here shall sweet wisdom's true adherents gather to begin their noble journey and follow the pilgrim pathways of the knights."

His face grew serious. "I thought this inscription was just a jumble of words to hide the coded clue to the whetstone. I never thought it contained other messages as well." He flipped open his laptop and searched for Temple Stonham. "The castle still belongs to the de Monteneufs. They hire it out for films and stuff." He looked up. "We've got to go there."

"How?"

"Simple. Missy's going to take us. We'll tell her it's for our research on the Knights Templar." He reached for Sarah's address book, took a deep breath, and left a message on Missy's mobile.

"I'm still petrified we'll overlook one tiny thing and mess up the whole search and then Mum will never—" Wolfie said.

"Listen," Tala said. "Flo says you find truth where different wisdoms meet. If something is really important, there are sure to be clues in more than one place pointing us to it."

Marcus Harrison was holding court in the back of the DT suite, attended by the ever-loyal Wayne. But even their most fawning lackeys were having trouble rejoicing in their good news.

"You jammy beggars," groaned Barry Cox.

"Yeah, how'd you swing that one?" said Gavin Wicks.

Marcus fanned himself with a pair of printed tickets and swung his feet on to the workbench. "That'd be telling. Course," he said with studied nonchalance, "it's just a friendly, but there'll be loads of England players there." Beneath his side-swept fringe, his eyes flicked across the room in search of Zi'ib, who was carefully applying a coat of varnish to a carved wooden box. Marcus gave Wayne a nudge which sent him swaggering over to Zi'ib's workbench.

"Oi, Charity Boy. Whatcha making? A *collection* box?"

He glanced round, to make sure his wit had been appreciated, and with a jerk of his fist knocked the box off the workbench into a pile of wood shavings. "Whoops."

Zi'ib bit his lip and bent to pick it up, just as Mr Sheriston, the DT teacher, came in.

"You should be more careful, Zi'ib," he tutted. "You've put a lot of work into that, now look at it. Get some thinners, wipe the lot off and start again."

Zi'ib retrieved the box and went in search of a rag, too

preoccupied to give vent to his anger. His dad had emailed that morning with news that the original trail of reports about his mother had led nowhere, but another tip-off was taking him back into southern Sudan. Zi'ib didn't know whether to be encouraged or dismayed.

*

To: esme@pastlife.com
From: ridianwinter@hotmail.com
Whichever child was weakening has stopped contacting Wisdomseeker. Investigate.

To: ridianwinter@hotmail.com
From: esme@pastlife.com
Don't worry. Forester says the children are very upset about Sarah. Her illness keeps them tied to the shop. I cannot see how they can be making any headway with cleansing the ley.

25

Lost and Found

Although it was a scramble for Wolfie, Tala and Zi'ib to get the papers sorted and delivered each morning and be ready to leave for school at eight-thirty when Sid arrived to open the shop, somehow they were managing it. Sid and Mr Forester divided the daytime shifts between them, leaving just an hour or so for the children to cover in the evening.

It was nearly closing time on Wednesday. Sid had taken Elvis and Monty for a run on the common, Wolfie was heating soup for Sarah, Tala was spell checking the article on the three-by-three magic square she had written for "Nikto Senki" to submit to the *EM* and Zi'ib was talking to Missy on the phone.

He put down the receiver. "Her dad says it's fine for us

to go to Temple Stonham, but she's got to contact the housekeeper to see about dates."

"Let's hope it's soon," Tala said.

"She says she's planned some big surprise for us. She wants to pick us up on Saturday afternoon."

"She's not taking *me* for a blimmin' haircut," Wolfie said.

The bell clanged and he hurried into the shop. The waiting customer was probably in his sixties, distinguished-looking with a head of wavy white hair and casual yet expensive clothes.

"Hello there," he said, casting Wolfie a quick warm smile. "I'm looking for Sarah Brown." He had a deep, mellifluous voice and was obviously excited about something.

"She's . . . upstairs. I can serve you," Wolfie said.

"Actually I've come about my dog. The police told me you'd found him."

Wolfie broke out in a cold sweat. The moment had come. The moment he had dreaded from the minute Elvis had strayed into the sweet shop and taken up residence. Although he had torn down all the "found" posters Sarah had put up in the streets, he hadn't been able to stop her informing the police. "Your . . . d-dog?" He wanted to shove this man out into the night and lock the door, but he'd only bump into Elvis on his way back with Sid.

"Elvis," insisted the man, his face crinkling with delight. "It was so kind of you to take him in." He pulled out his wallet. "There's a reward, of course. I can't tell you how much I've missed him. I've had him since he was a pup."

Wolfie stared at the man, trying to swim against a dreadful tide of inevitability. The irises of his eyes were unusual, a deep blue rimmed with black, and they shone with happiness. *The poor bloke. How terrible to raise a dog like Elvis and then lose him.*

From behind, he heard Tala say stubbornly, "We found him months ago," as if the passing weeks had erased the stranger's right to have his pet back. The man's gaze moved swiftly to her fierce face.

"I know. I'm so sorry. I was in the States visiting my daughter. I left him with my housekeeper. She was mortified when he ran off – put posters up, told the police . . . no luck." He held up a bundle of notes, counting them out with smooth deft movements of his thumb. "Here you go . . . fifty pounds."

Wolfie drew back as if the money were poisoned. The action touched off a thought in his misfiring brain. "Why didn't the police call us straight away?"

"I live in Surrey," the man said. Switching his gaze back to Wolfie, he laid the money on the counter. "Unfortunately the police don't put out nationwide alerts for missing dogs. I only started contacting other forces when I got back. Is he in the back? Can you call him? I'm in a bit of a hurry."

Zi'ib came through into the shop, lifting the counter

flap. It slammed down behind him, startling them all. "He's not here," he said. "We gave him away."

"Yes," said Tala, quickly. "This old couple took a real fancy to him so we said they could have him." She returned the man's penetrating gaze, certain he knew she was lying.

"Oh dear. Could you . . . give me their address?" the man said slowly. "I'll go round there right now."

Wolfie shrugged. "We don't know it . . . they were just passing." He glanced anxiously towards the common. He could have kicked himself. The man had seen him.

"You gave Elvis away? To strangers?"

"It was either that or the dogs' home," Tala said snippily.

"I've got to lock up now," Wolfie said, flipping the shop sign to closed.

"Look, I'll leave you my contact details and if you see this . . . couple again . . . perhaps you'd ask them to get in touch." Achingly slowly, the man patted his pockets for a business card.

Zi'ib thrust a pencil and a paper bag at him. The man seemed to have forgotten about being in a hurry and took an age to write out his details. At any moment the door would open and Elvis would come loping in, to be carried off by his rightful owner.

"I've given you my mobile number and the land line."

The man insisted on writing out his full address as Wolfie went round the shop pulling down the blinds.

They heard a scuffle outside. Tala wanted to scream. Sid

278

pushed open the door, the tinny bell sounding a death knell. Wolfie tried to speak. No words came out. Glancing up the road, Sid slipped two fingers in his mouth and whistled shrilly. He shook his head at Wolfie. "It's Mrs Baxter. She never bags up her rubbish properly, then she wonders why she's got every dog in the district sniffing round her bins. You wait, she'll be out in a minute moaning about the mess. Elvis! Stop that! Come here, now!" He slapped his leg.

The man rounded on Wolfie, hurt and indignant. "How could you look me in the eye and lie like that?"

"Who are you? What's going on?" demanded Sid.

"I've come for my dog, Elvis."

"Oh," Sid said, crestfallen.

There was a yelp from outside. Paws pattered on the step. A wet snout appeared around the door. The man rushed forward. "Elvis, Elvis, I don't believe it."

Neither did Wolfie, Tala, Zi'ib or Sid for that matter. The man was clipping a lead on to the collar of Sid's giant poodle Monty.

Sid flicked a glance at Wolfie, who raised his shoulders, too stunned to speak.

"You've got a bloody nerve," Sid said. "*Elvis* is down the road eating his way through the remains of Irene Baxter's Sunday roast. *This* dog is called Monty. And he's mine."

There was a dreamlike moment of unreality as the man let go of Monty and slipped silently into the street. As if trapped in aspic, no one moved. They just stood there stunned and immobile, only snapping back into control as his car screeched away.

"Bloody nerve," Sid said again. He whistled sharply. Elvis came bounding in, licking a shred of roast lamb from his whiskers.

"I don't get it," he said. "All that for a dog that's two parts wolfhound and ten parts Lord knows what. Don't get me wrong, he's a lovely animal, but not exactly prize stock. And if it's just some pet-napping scam you've only got to take one look at this place to see you wouldn't get much of a ransom."

All three children were too shocked to speak. The only things of value in the entire shop were three broken stars of Lupan gold. Was Ridian after those and Elvis too?

"I'm calling the police, we've got that bloke's address," Zi'ib said. He searched the counter and the floor for the paper bag. It had gone. "How did he do that?"

"I've heard about these types on telly," said Sid. "With a bit of sleight of hand here and a bit of suggestion there, they can con you out of anything. But don't you worry, from now on I'm not letting Elvis out of my sight."

The glass-panelled door of Frankie Fontaine's office offered a rippling view of a tall, lean figure pacing angrily.

"It's not good enough, Frankie. I need results."

The twinkle in Frankie Fontaine's dark blue eyes had morphed into a flinty gleam. "I'm sorry, Ridian. The bloke shouted Elvis's name. A great big dog came running in.

What were the odds of it being the wrong animal? Still, at least I got a chance to get the measure of those kids. They're going to need special handling when the time comes. It's the girl that's the tough one. But you just get them along to that SILK conference with the rest of them and I'll do what's needed."

Ridian nodded. He had requested SILK to add a talk on Spheres and interplanetary travel to the programme, certain it would guarantee the children's attendance. Once the minds of the Manus leaders had been downloaded into the bodies of those three brats none of them would ever need "handling" again.

"I'm terribly envious," admitted Mr Forester on Saturday when he heard Missy was coming round to discuss their trip to Temple Stonham. "Just think, the country seat of the de Monteneufs. It's a legendary point of power, you know, steeped in Templar mysteries. Don't worry, I'll look after Sarah while you're gone, but I shall expect a detailed report when you get back."

"Sure," said Tala. "Um . . . I noticed Nikto Senki emailed you an article on magic squares. Was it . . . any good?"

"It was excellent. In fact, I'm going to send him a complimentary ticket to the SILK conference. There will be a talk on Spheres and interplanetary ley travel that might interest him."

Tala's world tipped upside down and slowly righted. "Can we come?"

"Of course. I've been sent some invitations to the evening reception. You can come to that as well, if you like. It'll be a chance to meet some of the speakers personally."

"Who's giving this talk?" Wolfie said.

"Someone I've never heard of called Tristan Marchmont."

Wolfie's hands shook and a giddiness swept over him as he took a cup of coffee up to Sarah. The sight of her frail face lying on the pillow dashed away all thoughts of the Sphere. All that mattered was making her well.

Missy arrived with an armful of roses for Sarah. "OK," she said, reaching for a vase from the dresser. "This is the deal. We can stay at the house on the estate where Granny and Grandpa used to live. We hardly ever go there 'cos Dad didn't get on with them and I think the place makes him feel guilty, so it's mainly rented out. It's run by the housekeeper, Mrs Jessop. Dad calls her the dragon 'cos she's kind of scary. Anyway, she says it's free from this Friday for a week, then after that it's fully booked till June."

"Trouble is next weekend is Mum's birthday," frowned Wolfie. "She'll want us here for that."

"Why don't we take her with us?" Tala said, beyond caring if she sounded pushy. "A break from Thornham might do her good."

Missy squeezed her fists. "Wouldn't that be great? Hey, Mr Forester, why don't you come too?"

The old man flushed with pleasure. "Well, my dear, if you think this Mrs Jessop wouldn't mind, I would be delighted. I'll have a word with Sid and see if he'll look after the shop. He wants to put some of the produce from his allotment on sale so I'm sure we can work something out. And I'll give your schools a call and see if you can leave at lunchtime on Friday."

Missy's lips trembled into a smile as she texted a reply to Mrs Jessop.

"Come on, you guys," she said, pocketing the phone, "we'd better hurry or we'll be late for your surprise!"

26

A Ring of Power

Through the tinted windows of the Bentley, Tala watched streams of fans flocking towards a massive circular stadium of glass and steel. *Missy's big surprise is a football match. What a waste of time.* She focused her thoughts and hopes on the trip to Temple Stonham.

Missy took them up to a huge executive suite that opened on to a portioned-off section of the terraces. The stadium stretched below: a gleaming sweep of red and silver circling the bright green of the pitch. The air was electric with anticipation.

"Hi, Missy." A smartly dressed woman in her thirties came over clutching a large carrier bag. "It's a shame Mo's missing the fun."

"Meet Caitlin from INFASIC," beamed Missy. "Caitlin,

these are my friends Wolfie Brown, Tala Bean and Zi'ib Bakri."

"Zi'ib . . . Bakri? The boy from Sudan who got shot?" marvelled Caitlin, unable to believe that this tall, healthy boy was the dying child the charity had flown to England for treatment.

Zi'ib smiled, embarrassed. "If it wasn't for INFASIC – well . . . you know. So, thanks. I did write to the committee. . ."

"Seeing you like this is thanks enough," Caitlin said.

She handed them all red sweatshirts with I SUPPORT INFASIC printed across the front in rainbow lettering, to match the large INTERFAITH ACTION FOR SICK CHILDREN banner on the wall.

"I'll give out the rest," Missy offered, seizing the carrier bag.

"You angel," said Caitlin. "I need to find the photographer."

Wolfie, Tala and Zi'ib found seats at the back of the terrace while Missy handed sweatshirts to the other guests, who were mainly prosperous businessmen with glamorous wives. A few had children with them, decked out in brand-new red and white strip. Two older boys, one with dark greasy hair, the other fair, his head shaven at the sides, were hanging over the parapet gazing reverently at the pitch.

Catching a glimpse of their grinning profiles, Wolfie ducked for cover.

"Blimmin' heck, it's Marcus and Wayne."

"What are they doing here?" groaned Zi'ib.

Their frozen horror thawed a little when a mystified Marcus held up his INFASIC sweatshirt and bent forward to ask Missy what the logo meant. His lip curled and as soon as she moved away he and Wayne tossed their shirts aside and returned to their inspection of the pitch. In seconds Missy was back, picking up the shirts and standing over them while they put them on, which was not easy because they were a couple of sizes too small. Scowling, they pulled their scarves over the INFASIC logos.

"That's Marcus Harrison and Wayne Snaith," hissed Tala when Missy came tripping back.

"Yeah, I organized their tickets."

"Are you crazy? They hate charities."

"I know. You said. Oh, by the way, Flo texted me. She says the best time to do that Feng Shui thing at the apartment is March 20th round about five-thirty if you still want to come."

Tala felt the threads of Knowledge tighten and in honour of all the wisdoms of the world that understood the power of the equinox she raised her fists and let out a whooping, "Yes!"

A heavyset man in a fur-collared coat swept down the aisle and went round shaking everyone's hand.

"Who's that?" Tala asked.

"Bob Halligan, one of the directors of the club. He runs all their charity events."

The excitement of the sixty thousand spectators was beginning to build, sharpening their senses, uplifting them from everyday reality. Every eye was trained on the pitch as if drawn by an irresistible force, the tension reaching a crescendo as the referee blew his whistle. A collective shudder rippled the air and in an explosion of wild elation, the game kicked off. To the three bearers of the broken stars the electrifying power of so much mental focus directed on one small area of ground was almost frightening.

At half-time everyone was ushered to the bar area, where a bevy of waitresses plied them with food and drink. Bob Halligan, looking like an overripe tomato in his INFASIC sweatshirt, called for quiet.

"We've invited you here today to thank you for your generous contributions to the fundraising auction at tonight's charity ball. INFASIC do a fantastic job and those sick kids deserve all the help they can get. This year we've been overwhelmed by your generosity. A motorboat, two weeks in a luxury villa, and an appointment with one of Europe's top hair stylists are just some of the donations we've received. But the item that I shall be bidding for is the offer of time. Two young fans have offered to give up a whole weekend to do jobs for one lucky bidder – washing cars, gardening, cleaning windows, they're up for anything. So a very special round of applause for Marcus Harrison and Wayne Snaith!"

It was as if Marcus and Wayne had been dipped in stone. Only their eyes moved, widening in total disbelief.

"Come on, lads, don't be shy." Bob approached them, open-armed. "Where's that photographer? I want shots of these two on the website."

Marcus and Wayne walked slowly into Bob Halligan's embrace. "Here, move your scarves so we can see the INFASIC logos and step back so we get the poster in," he commanded.

Squirming with embarrassment, the two boys glowered at the circle of faces. Tala could not resist giving Marcus a little wave. His vengeful stare left her gasping.

"Hey, Bob, these guys are from Thornham, maybe we can get their picture in the *Thornham Gazette*," called Missy.

"Anything that drums up publicity for INFASIC," smiled Bob.

Wolfie was cringing, unable to believe what was happening. "They're going to kill us, they're going to kill us," he said through clenched teeth.

"Yeah, but it'll be worth it," snorted Zi'ib. Unable to hold in his laughter, he burst through the exit door and leaned against the wall, tears dripping down his face. Every time he wiped them away the thought of the look on Marcus's face set him off again. Contorted with giggles, Tala and Wolfie came running out to join him.

A blurred figure appeared down the corridor. Their laughter jammed in their throats.

It was the man who had tried to steal Elvis. His thick white hair gleamed as he opened the door of a suite up ahead. Voices gushed into the silence.

Hearts thundering, they crept forward. The glass walls along the corridor were etched with wide decorative panels, but by squinting through the gaps they could see some of what was happening inside. The suite was huge. On a plinth in the middle of the polished stone floor stood a three-times life-size statue of a footballer about to take a kick, hewn from white granite. It was just like the statue of the runner Zi'ib had seen at King Alfred's. Edging sideways, he caught the yellow slash of a Labs for Life banner hanging from the back wall.

He scanned the gathering, recognizing a number of teachers and coaches from the Labs for Life sports day. Mr Pinkney was there, and so was Hadley Hunter, talking to a pallid, balding man with glasses. It took Tala a few seconds to work out where she had seen his face.

"That guy," she whispered. "He's Stefan something or other, the weedy twin with the good-looking brother who was spouting about Battersea Power Station on that Zemogen press release."

Soft, insistent music vibrated the glass. Stefan seemed to be in charge of the event. With a proprietorial swagger, he mounted a dais and introduced the white-haired man to the crowd. A lean, dark-suited figure joined them. The turn of the third man's tanned, chiselled face twisted a blade in the children's hearts.

Ridian Winter.

The sight of him sent shards of anger, fear and revulsion exploding through their brains. Here was proof of Ridian's

289

connection with Labs for Life, proof he was behind the attempt to kidnap Elvis.

Stefan and Ridian stood to one side as the white-haired man began to address the crowd. He accompanied his words with curious gestures of his hands. Zi'ib tried the door. It was locked. They could not hear what the man was saying but, whatever it was, it held his audience mesmerized. The crowd grew dazed and motionless, their spellbound gaze never shifting from his face. It was as if he was controlling them with a slow-motion knob. Even Stefan stood frozen in time, his glass halfway to his lips. Ridian and the white-haired man began to walk among the static figures, poking and prodding them like stockmen inspecting a prize herd before slaughter. Ridian seemed pleased. At a word from him, the white-haired man returned to the dais and, with a few words and gestures, gradually reversed the slow-motion effect until the crowd were happily chatting and sipping drinks once more.

Wolfie, Tala and Zi'ib bolted back to the INFASIC suite, struggling to make sense of the eerie scene they had just witnessed. There seemed to be no point or logic to it at all. Yet the cry of their stars and every jangling nerve in their bodies was telling them that it involved the negative forces they had sworn to destroy. But the sighting of their old enemy in the flesh had whetted their weary spirits and brought a fresh and fiery edge to their resolve. It was up to them to ensure that whatever new evil Ridian was planning, it would all come crashing down when they conquered the darkness.

27

The Stone Princess

All the way to Yorkshire the children tried to suppress their feverish anticipation. But as Mr Forester turned off the motorway to follow the signs for Temple Stonham, anticipation changed abruptly to dread. They were risking Sarah's health on the gamble that this trip would save her. What if they had got it wrong? What if they were wasting these last precious days before the equinox, chasing some misguided notion that Missy de Monteneuf was the key to finding the spears? And even if she were, would they recognize them? Sarah, who had slept for most of the trip, woke up, as if their anxiety had pierced her dreams.

Mr Forester's van wheezed and groaned down twisting country lanes, and drew up in front of a pair of wrought-iron gates crowned with a riven eight-point star set above the motto "Trust in Truth". As the gates swung open, a glimmer of late sunlight caught the spikes along the top; they were pointed snakes' heads.

Passing down a long driveway cut deeply into banks of solid grey rock, they emerged into a wide, neatly turfed courtyard set around a fairy-tale ruin of a castle. With its six crumbling towers, it looked like a huge, half-eaten jelly on a big green plate. Beyond the castle, a sweep of ancient forest sloped towards the sky, broken here and there by outcrops of dark, glinting rock. From the middle of the courtyard rose a tall slab of grey, rough-hewn granite.

"Blimey," said Zi'ib. Sometimes he forgot how short a time he had lived in England and how many surprises this cold, mysterious country could still throw at him.

Mr Forester followed the track until they came to an imposing manor house of weathered stone, draped with creepers and topped by tall chimneys puffing smoke into the sky. He helped Sarah out of the van and for a moment everyone stood on the cobbles drinking in great heaves of cool sharp air. Elvis flung back his head and bounded off towards the forest. Wolfie tested the path. A crackle of crisp pure energy poured an etheric symphony of pulsings and soundings through his star. This was a route they must follow when they were alone.

They followed Missy through the porch into a wide hallway that smelt of beeswax and bracken and something old and warm like liquid, sun-drenched stone. Before them rose a staircase of age-blackened oak intricately carved with little birds and animals. Tala backed towards Zi'ib, not daring to open her mouth. Neither of them had ever been anywhere so old, so grand, so *English*. Only Mr Forester's grunts of delight and the scratchy patter of Elvis's claws on the flagstones broke the awed silence.

They entered a long oak-panelled room that looked out over a curtain of forest. A stout branch sputtered and hissed in a fireplace high enough and wide enough to stand in, sending curlicues of ash floating towards the darkly raftered ceiling. Green shaded lamps threw dim light across heavy oak furniture so sombre and aged it might never have been new.

"Who wants tea?" Missy asked, reaching for the silver tea things set out on the sideboard.

Balancing a shallow porcelain cup and saucer, Zi'ib bit into an airy morsel of cake and perched on the edge of a carved wooden chair, doubting if even a trip to Lupus could feel more alien than the stately time-worn world of Temple Stonham. Elvis stretched himself before the fire, as if utterly at home here. And it no longer seemed strange to the children that quite possibly, in another time, he had been.

"Welcome. I'm Diana Jessop."

Zi'ib jumped, nearly spilling his tea.

An elegant middle-aged woman, her thick fair hair pleated into a perfect chignon, was standing in the doorway, exuding an air of quiet control. She wore a tartan skirt, and a navy cashmere jumper with pearls at her neck. She nodded a greeting to Wolfie, Tala and Zi'ib, shook hands with Sarah and Mr Forester and took Missy by the shoulders, inspecting her as if she were a prize foal. "You must have been all of what, nine last time I saw you? Look at you now. You're a de Monteneuf through and through." Releasing Missy from her grasp, she made a sweeping movement with her hand.

"If you would all like to come with me I will show you your rooms." They filed meekly into the hall. "The drawing room and the dining room are both available for your use at all times. However, we have conservators working in the library and the smoking room so they are closed to visitors." She headed up the stairs.

Elvis bounded after her. Diana Jessop turned, raised one neatly arched eyebrow and he fled back down again. She strode along a long lamplit corridor, throwing open doors on to large wood-panelled chambers with four-poster beds hung with damask curtains and huge bathrooms with enormous winged baths, overhung with showers like great drooping sunflower heads. There were new smells up here – lavender, fresh linen and soap, the scents of wealth and luxury from another age.

"Dinner will be served at seven-thirty. Mr Forester, Missy said you'd like a tour of the castle. Would eleven o'clock tomorrow morning suit?"

Thanking her profusely, Mr Forester disappeared into his room. As soon as the clack of Mrs Jessop's heels had disappeared down the corridor, Sarah started to giggle. "It's like being in an Agatha Christie novel."

294

Missy's face fell. Sarah reached for her hand. "Which means it's the most wonderful place I've ever stayed in. And I'm going to enjoy every blissful minute of this weekend, starting with a soak in that wonderful old bathtub."

Ridian was worried. There was still no reply to Wisdomseeker's latest emails. Whichever kid had been succumbing seemed to have gone cold.

He opened a message from Esmé.

There will be nothing to report until Monday. They've all gone to Yorkshire with some rich kid called Missy de Monteneuf.

Ridian's eyes blazed hot and wild with fury.

De Monteneuf's kid? How had they met up with her? His people had told him that she'd been packed off to a boarding school in Wales. The last thing he wanted was those brats poking round Temple Stonham. The Manus Sacra should have torched the damn place centuries ago when they burned down Thornham Hall.

This called for radical action. The equinox was approaching. He fired off a new message to Nikto Senki.

At seven-thirty a booming gong summoned everyone to dinner. Heavy silver cutlery glinted in the light of the flickering candles and the children were glad that Sarah had made them put on clean jumpers and wash their faces. Mrs Jessop had made prune and cranberry compote for Mr Forester and roasted a huge rib of beef with Yorkshire pudding and piles of glistening vegetables for the others.

The food was so delicious that even Sarah managed a few mouthfuls.

"We really didn't expect to be looked after like this, Mrs Jessop," beamed Mr Forester.

"It's no trouble. I regularly cook for twenty or thirty. Mind you, I get caterers in for the film shoots so I can keep an eye on the crews. They've no respect for the house at all. Last time, I caught a sound man trying on a suit of armour."

Wolfie grinned, filled with admiration for anyone with the guts to dare such frivolity.

"When exactly was this house built?" enquired Mr Forester.

"Around 1600. Of course, the castle is much older; parts of it go back to the eleventh century."

"What about the house in Thornham?" asked Missy.

"Sir Guy built that around 1187 and the family divided their time between the two estates until Thornham Hall burned down in 1540."

"Such a tragedy," murmured Mr Forester.

"They say Sir Roger risked his life over and over again trying to save his possessions."

"Looks like our family's jinxed when it comes to fires,"

said Missy, ruefully. "Dad's still trying to sort out the mess at the New York gallery."

"Oh, I know," said Mrs Jessop. "The Rembrandt. Sir Simon will be heartbroken."

Mention of that image stirred thoughts in Zi'ib's brain, frail as wisps of smoke.

"So why didn't Sir Roger rebuild the Hall?" Missy asked, wishing the de Monteneufs still had a home in Thornham.

"He decided it was no longer safe for his family to stay so near to London." Encouraged by the wide-eyed attention of her audience, Mrs Jessop perched for a moment on the leather padded fender. "You see, the fire at Thornham Hall was no accident. Both wings of the house and all the outbuildings went up in flames at exactly the same time so there would be no chance of putting it out."

"Why would anyone *do* that?" cried Missy, incensed.

"Well, back then Templar families like the de Monteneufs were believed to have secrets, and secrets always attract enemies."

"What sort of secrets?"

Wolfie, Tala and Zi'ib were listening with such intensity their senses seemed to be tearing loose from their bodies.

"Mysteries handed down since the fall of the Templars in 1307. Officially they were protectors of the pilgrim paths across the Middle East—"

"Almost certainly a coded description of the ley paths between ancient points of power," cut in Mr Forester.

He wilted before Diana Jessop's glacial gaze. "So sorry. Do go on."

"There are countless legends associated with the Templars," she said crisply. "However, there was always a particular mystique surrounding the de Monteneufs because they were rumoured to have been singled out to perform a very special task."

"What task?" breathed Missy.

"To aid and protect the bloodlines of the wise, whose descendants would one day hold the fate of the world in their hands. And do you know, it was said that the reason they were endowed with their great wealth was to enable them to carry out this sacred duty."

"That is *so* not fair!" burst out Tala, starting to choke. "Why didn't the guys who had to save the world get the money?"

Mrs Jessop struck her sharply between the shoulder blades. "It's only a legend, dear, nothing to get het up about."

An inexorable vibration quivered through Wolfie's star, waking him from dreams of his father. The golden spikes shuddered against his chest, beating with a deep, mounting pulse that seemed to shake the very stone and mortar of the house. He padded to the window, pulled aside the heavy curtain and pressed his face to the glass. A silent call was sounding from the forest, mysterious and compelling as the howl of a wild wolf to its lost pack.

Pulling a jumper and boots over his pyjamas, he stole into the corridor. An eerie creak sounded in the darkness. He spun round. Tala was standing at her bedroom door. He turned the other way. Zi'ib was there, waiting at the top of the stairs, summoned by the primordial cry of Temple Stonham. They slipped out of the house into the strange limbo that falls between the coming of the day and the passing of the night. Elvis was waiting for them, fine drops of dew pearling his coat. They followed the path of energy flowing fresh and clear as a bubbling brook.

Skirting the tiny green shoots peeping through the dead leaves, they trod softly onwards, until they came to a wide lake wreathed in beckoning fingers of mist. They stood at its edge, sensing the path cutting straight across the dark waters to a little wooded island about ten metres out, wondering how they could cross. Elvis snuffled along the bank, ears twitching. After a moment he lifted his limbs like a thoroughbred horse, stepped on to the murky water and picked his way carefully to the island, where he sat down in the mud, looking very pleased with himself.

"Woah, weird," Zi'ib said.

Wolfie had broken off three long saplings, and tossing one to each of them, he set off across the lake, prodding the water for stepping stones as he went. Zi'ib and Tala pitched and wobbled behind, struggling to stay upright on the slimy pillars of granite hidden just beneath the surface. Relieved to reach the safety of the island, they swished their sticks, letting them twitch and bend to the eager pull of the energies.

Shafts of brightening daylight filtered through the trees, catching something pale among the leaves up ahead. Wolfie crept closer. It was a statue: a little white unicorn, rearing up on its hind legs, a long spirally twisted horn jutting from its forehead. The sculptor had breathed so much life into the stone that he wanted to touch it. The sudden memory of the unicorn in the tapestry in Missy's apartment stopped his hand. He swung round, seeking the dark outlines of a panther crouching in the foliage. All he saw was Elvis scrabbling happily in the undergrowth and Zi'ib and Tala pushing through the trees towards him.

Tala smoothed the flank of the little unicorn, tracing the tautly chiselled curves of bone and muscle, while Zi'ib stroked the finely wrought mane that streamed magnificently in the winds of the sculptor's imagination. Almost expecting a snort of moist breath to warm his fingers, Wolfie stretched out his hand and patted the delicate muzzle. At his touch the stone seemed to come alive, as if he had made the final link in a connection of mind, flesh and matter that had activated the whirring molecules in the carven rock. A shudder of vibration shook the statue, as if the very essence of the stone was changing. Like a mighty magnet it drew in a rush of energy from all around, whipping the surface of the lake into a thousand silver-topped wavelets as the energy funnelled up through the hollow core of the unicorn in a tightly spinning whirl that rocked the statue off its centre of gravity. The unicorn swayed, bucking violently beneath the children's grip until it crashed on its side. Horrified, they watched the beautiful horn roll into the mud, leaving behind a broken stump.

Stillness. Leaves stopped rustling. Birds stopped singing as the sucking wash of the energies retreated. Guilty tears welled in Tala's eyes. Why would the pure, positive forces of Temple Stonham lead them to something as beautiful as this little unicorn only to destroy it? Kneeling to inspect the damage, Wolfie peered inside the statue, surprised to see a thin shaft of light pricking through a tiny hole in each of its eyes. The plinth was circular, the lower part consisting of four tiered ridges that narrowed towards the bottom like an upside-down wedding cake. Zi'ib heaved it upright, trying to guide it back into the hole.

"Hang on!" Wolfie scooped the fallen soil from the tiered sides of the hole, patting them smooth. He sat back on his knees, puzzled. This stepped cavity was exactly the same shape as the well at Thornham.

"Mind out," Zi'ib said. He rocked the statue back into place and together they stamped the soil down with their boots.

Tala reached for the broken horn. It hissed and crackled, searing her palm. She snatched her hand away. The slender needle of stone was charged like a lightning rod, yet the rest of the fallen statue now felt cold and inert beneath her touch. Gingerly she lifted the broken end with a stick. It too was hollow. The inside was threaded, as was the stump on the unicorn's brow, so that once the horn was screwed on it would unscrew under the pressure of the forces spiralling up from within.

Tala let the horn drop back on to the soft leaves. Her hands were shaking. The boys turned to her, their stars singing at their throats.

"We've found the first spear," she breathed. "A spear of stone."

A flurry of nervous laughter gushed from her lips, like steam from a pressure valve. "But I can't even pick it up."

Behind them, forgotten, Elvis had been creeping towards the horn. He pounced, seized it in his mouth and ran to the lake, bounding across the stepping stones to the other side. By the time they had teetered unsteadily after him he had disappeared into the woods.

Through the trees, thin tendrils of smoke were already rising from the chimneys of the house. Zi'ib thought of the fire at Thornham Hall. Who else but the Manus Sacra would have wanted to destroy the de Monteneufs' secrets? He had a growing suspicion that Ridian Winter might have been responsible for the fire in the de Monteneufs' New York gallery. His thoughts returned to the Rembrandt. The original etching had been destroyed half a world away, but the newspapers had relayed the mysterious image of the alchemist's workshop straight into the sweet shop. Had the positive energies had a hand in that?

*

"Out! If I catch you upstairs again there'll be trouble."

Mrs Jessop was standing at the front door pointing into the yard. Elvis slunk past her with his tail between his legs and mooched off towards the stables.

Zi'ib ran across the cobbles. "Sorry, Mrs Jessop."

Although it was barely seven o'clock, the housekeeper was immaculately dressed and appeared to have been up for hours. She cast a cold eye over their muddy pyjamas. "You'll catch pneumonia. Go and have a hot shower and I'll bring you up some hot chocolate."

They raced up to Tala's room. There, gleaming white against the crimson counterpane, lay the unicorn's horn.

"Quick, we'll hide it in here." Tala emptied her rucksack on to the bed. Using felt pens and her copy of *My Travels in Atlantis*, they managed to nudge the spear of stone into the rucksack. She buckled it tight.

They were one step nearer to healing the ley. One step nearer to saving Sarah. But a single spear was not enough. With every nerve alive to the secrets of Temple Stonham, they ran downstairs to breakfast.

It was Ralph Jessop who met them outside the castle to give them the tour; a tall bluff Yorkshire man, he seemed amused to be telling Missy the history of her own family. "This was the old tourney court where the jousting took place," he said, panning a large blunt hand across the sweep of immaculate turf. "Imagine all the knights in their pomp and splendour, the excited crowds gathered to watch. And in those days the stakes were high – the knights were risking their lives as well as their honour on the tourney field. The locals used to call that stone over there the knight rider stone because the knights would ride in from all over England to gather in front of it before the tournaments and touch it for luck."

Another kinnection! A knight rider stone. Tala looked meaningfully at Wolfie. The lost standing stone she had sensed in Knightrider Street near St Paul's would probably have been used in exactly the same way. Obviously Ridian Winter was not the first to think of capitalizing on the power of sport to invigorate the ley grid.

Tight and trembly with hope, she took Sarah's arm as they followed Ralph towards the slab of grey rock, standing guard over the courtyard.

"What else can you tell us about this knight rider stone?" demanded Zi'ib.

"Not much," admitted Ralph. "Except it was here long before the castle and probably accounts for the name 'Stonham'."

"Thank goodness they didn't remove it to make more room for the jousting," Sarah was saying.

"The de Monteneufs would never have done that; real protectors of antiquity they were, even back then," said Ralph. "They weren't mean with their money either and heaven knows they had enough of it, but they never threw anything away." He wagged a playful finger at Missy. "So don't you go having a clear-out when all this is yours."

Something leaden pressed Missy's heart. Maybe it was more than guilt that kept her dad away from Temple Stonham. Maybe he shunned the burden of this ancient castle with all its traditions and troublesome secrets that she, one day, was destined to inherit.

"See these markings here?" went on Ralph. "The de Monteneuf knights used to score these vertical lines with their swords before they went off to the crusades and slash them with these horizontals when they came back, to complete a sign of the cross."

They ran their hands across the cool stone, saddened by the single slashes made by nameless swordsmen who had fallen in distant lands. Ralph led them on through a pair of enormous iron-studded oak doors into the great hall of the castle.

It was an immense space, with a long low hearth and a roof of curving timbers supported by slender-shafted columns. What made it extraordinary were the carvings encrusting every inch of stonework: a snarling bestiary leaping from legend and nightmare to roam a petrified forest of pillars. Gasping and pointing, everyone gazed around in wonder.

"The de Monteneufs brought masons from all over Europe to do these carvings and they rivalled the decoration of some of the great cathedrals," explained Ralph proudly.

"Indeed," murmured Mr Forester.

Wolfie wandered over to an archway, drawn by its

tracery of flowers and serpents, delicate as spun sugar. He touched the smooth under-curve of a leaf, amazed to see the darkened shape of his finger showing through the parchment-thin stone.

"Hey, Mum, look at this," he called.

"There's a tale about that archway," said Ralph. "It's said that the master mason who oversaw the building of this hall was a cruel, exacting man who took an ungodly pride in his own skill. One day a young French mason arrived asking for work. He was sickly and thin and the master only took him on because one of his apprentices had fallen ill. The other masons shunned him, calling him a gypsy, and when this lad said he was called Armel, they mocked him because that name was from the old *Arth-mael*, meaning 'stone prince'. Well, soon after that the master went off to the quarries to pick out some new stone, leaving detailed instructions as to the work each of his men should do in his absence. He assigned that arch to Armel, ordering him to carve it with a simple pattern of chevrons.

"But Armel took it on himself to carve the decoration you see now, and when the master came back and saw it he was incensed with jealousy and he seized a thick staff, dragged Armel into the courtyard and beat him till he nearly died. Sir Piers and Lady Anne came rushing out and found Armel collapsed on the ground and the master mason raining blows on the lad's poor broken limbs. And Sir Piers, he snatched the staff and struck the master down in front of everyone and dismissed him from his service.

Then Lady Anne had Armel brought into the castle so she could dress his wounds and when she peeled off his bloody clothes, lo and behold, she found *he* were a girl. Well, that caused a right ruckus because in those days there were strict rules about who could become a mason and women certainly weren't allowed.

"This poor lass, whose real name was Armelle, took months to recover. And while she was convalescing in the castle she fell in love with Sir Piers's son Henry and he with her. Despite their difference in station, Sir Piers gave the pair his blessing, saying Armelle was truly a stone princess whose artistic skill was worth far more to the house of de Monteneuf than any lands or titles. They were married in the church at Thornham and for a wedding present Armelle gave Henry a unicorn carved from a piece of stone as white as linen, which she got shipped over from her home in Brittany. And he set it up where all the villagers might see it."

"Of course the white unicorn is a perennial symbol of pure positive energy," murmured Mr Forester, making a note.

"I wouldn't know about that," said Ralph. "Armelle told the villagers that if ever there was a threat to the de Monteneuf lands the unicorn would weep tears of blood and shed its horn. And when the danger had passed its tears would dry up and its horn would grow back."

"What happened to the statue?" asked Wolfie, his head spinning.

"It stayed in Thornham until the fire. And then Sir Henry's son Roger brought it up here and erected it on the island in the lake. And I'll tell you something strange, there are stories that sometimes, when there's thunder in the air, the statue gets magnetized and attracts anything metal."

As Ralph turned to answer Missy's excited questions about Armelle, Wolfie pulled Tala and Zi'ib behind a pillar. "I bet a black ley counted as a threat to the de Monteneuf lands," he whispered. "And I bet you anything Armelle designed that unicorn statue to go over the well at number forty-five."

"The sides of the well *are* the right shape for the base," Tala said.

"It's not just that. The water in the well is all red, full of iron."

"So?"

"You heard what Ralph said. Sometimes the stone gets magnetized. That would happen if the energies round it got infected and their vibrations changed. Once the statue was magnetized the iron-rich water would be drawn up through its insides and come out through the holes in its eyes like tears of blood.

"What's the point of that?" said Tala.

"It was an early warning system telling the villagers there were bad energies around that needed to be cleansed. And the heightened forces spiralling up through the horn would unscrew it so it could be used to spear the ley."

"Cool," said Zi'ib.

Tala ran over to Ralph. "Did Armelle carve anything else?"

"The beating left her too weak for stone masonry. But after the birth of her first son she began a series of three tapestries telling the story of a hunt. She worked on them right into her old age and the story goes that the day she finished the last one was the day she died."

Wolfie came rushing over. "Where are these tapestries?"

"Sir Simon's got the one showing the prey down in London. The one depicting the chase is here being restored. Unfortunately the one showing the kill didn't survive the fire."

Wolfie watched his mother, tired out already, slumped on a stone ledge by the hearth. The stakes were high. If he missed the slightest clue, he would spend the rest of his life reliving and regretting his mistakes.

Biting back his frustration that the third tapestry was missing, he asked Ralph if they could see the one of the chase.

"It's being cleaned and repaired in the smoking room," Ralph said. "You'll have to ask Diana."

Wolfie rattled the door to the smoking room on the way in to lunch. It was locked. Quietly desperate, he hardly touched the soup and home-made bread laid out in the dining room.

"Mrs Jessop, please can we have a look at the tapestry

that's being restored?" he asked as soon as the housekeeper came in to clear away. If she said no, he'd already decided to break into the smoking room that night and take the consequences.

"We'll be really careful," pleaded Missy, anxious to please her friends.

"Well, since it's you, I suppose it will be all right." She handed her a bunch of labelled keys. "Leave the room exactly as you found it and do not touch the tapestry or *any* of the conservator's equipment."

Missy pulled a face behind the housekeeper's back. Leaving Sarah and Mr Forester snoozing by the fire, she led the way to the smoking room.

Although the furniture was spotless and arranged with military precision, the room had a homely, lived-in feel that even Diana Jessop had failed to expunge. Pipe racks and photographs cluttered the desk and the cushioned sofas were invitingly saggy. Wolfie marched straight over to the large trestle table set up at the far end and switched on the angled magnifying lamp clamped above it. A soft light spread across the tapestry hunting scene pinned flat to a padded frame. Windswept clouds, spangled as if by distant stars, melted into a vista of mountains and rivers, and in the foreground, bands of mounted nobles in furred robes burst through turbulent waves of forest foliage, worked in threads of green, brown, yellow and gold. With their dogs at full bound and their banners, bearing the crest of the riven star, kicking in the wind, they galloped through a mystical forest towards a unicorn caught in a thorn thicket.

Three quarters of the tapestry had been repaired with exquisitely tiny stitches. But in the shadowy undergrowth beside the unicorn gaped a patch the size of Zi'ib's palm, where the dark wool had worn away, exposing ravaged cotton warp threads, thin and pale as broken harp strings. On a little table to one side lay the conservator's tools: narrow hooks and scissors, needles of all sizes and myriad spools of coloured wool and silk.

Missy looked on, bemused to see how excited the others were about this faded relic. "Hey, look," she said. "The dog by the little drummer boy looks just like Elvis."

They hardly seemed to hear her.

Entranced by the intricate beauty of Armelle's threadwork, Tala and Zi'ib were focusing on the unicorn, willing it to tell them exactly what to do with the horn of its stone counterpart. Wolfie took a mental step back, viewing the tableau as if it were a comic strip, letting the story that Armelle had set out to tell unfold in sequence.

If Mr Forester was right, and the unicorn in these tapestries represented pure positive energy, it was easy to see that in the panel in Missy's apartment pure energy was being preyed on by dark forces manifested in the shape of the panther. And in this panel, the mounted nobles, converging from all sides of the forest, were hunting those dark energies down.

"Can we, er . . . borrow your camera?" Wolfie asked

Missy. "I'd like some shots of this . . . so I can do a drawing of it when I get back."

"I think I left it up at the castle." She saw the insistence in his eyes. "No worries, I'll go get it."

"Quick, look for hunters with spears," he urged as the door closed behind her. He swung the magnifying lamp across the tapestry. Letting out a whoop of triumph, he found a jaunty figure in a red cape holding a white spear with a twisted shaft. "We were right. This is a spear of stone!"

Tala peered into the magnifying glass, breathing in shallow gasps. Another rider, cloaked in green, wielded a gilded spike. The haft was shaped like the head of a red-eyed serpent.

"A spear of gold . . . with a snake's head handle." She looked up in wonder. "The pin that injured Elvis. It was a snake with ruby red eyes. With all the upset about the burglary we hardly looked at it." She pursed her mouth. "It was right under our noses all the time. Just like Flo said."

As if shaping wisps of recollection, Zi'ib was murmuring, "Stone, gold. . ."

Wolfie turned his attention to a noblewoman in a heart-shaped headdress, who had dismounted and was extracting what looked like a brown, handleless dagger from the ground. "A spear of wood, maybe?"

Tala frowned. "Not sure."

A second noblewoman wearing a flowing robe of azure

blue appeared to be unarmed. She rode with one hand held high, as if rallying her maidens to the chase, but her fingers were curved. Through the magnifying glass, Tala traced a line of pale thread, outlining the shape of a tapering javelin grasped in her hand. "A spear of air . . . no, glass," she suggested. "Did they have glass back then?"

From a haze of memory Zi'ib was plucking vivid glimpses of words spelled out in ancient scripts. He burst out. "Not glass, *water*! It's stone, gold, *earth*, *water*. . ."

"How come?" demanded Wolfie.

"That Rembrandt etching that got destroyed in the fire at Missy's dad's gallery. Those were the words in the books scattered round the old alchemist's feet."

Wolfie turned the magnifying glass to full power. Beneath the lens he saw tiny drops of liquid streaming from the shaft. "You're right. But you can't do much damage with a spear of earth or water."

"You can if you fire the earth and freeze the water," Zi'ib said.

"It can't be any old water and earth."

"By your wisdom you will know them."

"What?"

"That's what Dad told us."

The secrets of the ancient energy healers had survived piecemeal and fragmented, handed down through the centuries in rhymes, inscriptions and paintings. And now, all the strands of that ancient lore that had brought the children to Temple Stonham were shooting back and forth through their heads, swifter than the shuttle on Armelle's loom as they tried to weave a taut, clear pattern from the ravelled threads.

"Water. The healing well at number forty-five," said Tala. "That's where we've got to take the water from. Remember the rhyme on the arch: *Take a needle from these waters to relieve the world of strife.*"

"What about the spear of earth?" Wolfie said. "I s'pose we could get some earth and fire it ourselves."

"Fired earth." Zi'ib rolled the words across his tongue, prodding it for meaning. "Fired earth, that's terracotta. It's what pots are made of."

Wolfie ran with the idea. "The broken bits of Mum's planter." There would be justice in that, he thought, if unwittingly the panther had created one of the weapons of its own destruction.

There had been five words in the books in the Rembrandt etching. Zi'ib snapped his fingers, trying to picture the fifth. "*Sound.*" Weird, that couldn't be right. They searched the band of riders for guidance and saw the great hound running beside the drummer boy with his little black drum and recalled the boom of the metal pan in the outhouse that had shaped the sugar on the hotplate into a spear of sound.

"Spears of stone, gold, earth, water, sound. We've got all five," Zi'ib cried, jubilant.

"We're nearly there," murmured Wolfie, determination throbbing in his blood.

"*Seize the hour to smite the dark, And Michael's spears shall find their mark*. We know *when* to smite the dark – the moment of the equinox – and we've got the five spears to do the smiting *with*. All we need to work out now is exactly *where* to do the smiting so they find their mark."

"Five spears, so five places along the path of the contaminated ley," said Zi'ib.

Wolfie's soaring spirits crashed. "That's what Armelle would have woven into the third tapestry that got destroyed in the fire."

"Just remember what Flo said about finding important stuff where different wisdoms meet. That information's got to be somewhere else."

"OK, so where else have we heard about smiting?"

Tala gave a little yelp and flapped her hands at Zi'ib, trying to draw out the words. "Come on, what was that line in Esmé's book – you know, the far memory of King Sargon when his kingdom was threatened by a fiend?"

"Um, something about sickness, mayhem and angry youths."

"That's what the dark energy *caused*. What did Sargon say to the warriors he sent to destroy it? 'I, Sargon, command you to silence the roar of the dread fiend' . . . then what? Hang on, I'll fetch the book."

"No!" said Wolfie. He had screwed up his eyes, and painful as it was, he was forcing himself back to that awful moment burned on his memory when he had stood alone in the yard in thrall to the dark energies and watched Tala

315

and Zi'ib reading Esmé's book through the kitchen window. In a cracked voice he cried out, "'Smite its tail and cankered heart! Pierce the hump of its writhing back and wound its head and throat that I might have peace in my kingdom'—"

"Are you OK?" Missy was watching him from the door.

"Oh yeah, I'm just . . . practising for our school play,"

"Great, get tickets for me and Dad. He loves Shakespeare."

She handed Wolfie the camera.

"What? Oh, thanks." As he fired off shots of the hunters entering the contaminated forest, the thought of Sarah returning to the polluted sweet shop suddenly filled him with dread.

He blurted out, "It's done Mum so much good being here. I wish she could stay on for a couple of days."

Missy smiled. "Why not, I'll talk to Dad. Come on. Let's take Elvis out."

"I'd be grateful if you would lick the cobbles clean after you've walked on them," said Wolfie in a pitch-perfect imitation of Diana Jessop as they crossed the yard. He swung round and saw her watching them from the kitchen window. Exploding into nervous giggles, they charged up the hill.

"Happy birthday!"

Everyone burst into Sarah's bedroom and laid her presents on the bed. There was a hand-painted sign advertising Brown's Traditional Fudge from Wolfie, the willow-patterned plate Tala had bought in Strowger's, a pair of silver earrings from Mr Forester and a bottle of hand-pressed bath oil from Missy. Zi'ib stood twisting his hands together as she unwrapped the carved wooden box he had made in DT and when it came to his turn to be thanked and hugged he felt a little piece of ice melt inside him.

Sarah unstoppered the bath oil. "Mm, gorgeous smell. What is it?"

"White sage," said Missy. "One of Mom's favourites."

"Or to give it its proper name, *Artemisia ludoviciana*," smiled Mr Forester. "An aromancer told me that sage is the fragrant herb that helps fight bad energies. Perhaps having you around will help me find a solution to our problem ley at Thornham!"

Missy grimaced. "That energy stuff creeps me out. Hey, Sarah, I talked to Dad last night and he agrees with us that you should stay on here for a couple of days."

"I couldn't."

"It's already been arranged," said Mr Forester. "I'm staying at the shop till Friday. Ralph will drive you to York station and I'll pick you up from King's Cross."

"Don't worry, you'll be back in time for Jenna Falkirk's opening," said Missy.

Sarah sank into the pillows. "Then . . . thank you. I wish I could think of a way to thank Mo."

"There is one thing he'd really like," Missy said.

"What's that?"

"A pot of Saravita."

And Missy told Sarah all about Agnes's painting of her baby son sitting in front of the outhouse among the purple Saravita, and Mo's failed attempts to get hold of the mysterious star-flowered herb.

Once home, Mr Forester went straight to sleep in Sarah's room, tired out by the long drive. Tala rushed to retrieve the snake hatpin from the larder door, wondering what tortuous path of kinnections had brought it to Thornham. Wolfie unfurled their map of Thornham with the thick black line of the contaminated ley inked from Thornham right up to the banks of the Thames. King Sargon had spoken of five points where the "dread fiend" must be speared and after a bit of wrangling they agreed that the *tail* had to be the shop, its *cankered heart* the old foundations where the contamination had begun, the *hump of its writhing back* the crest of Dodd's Hill, its *head* Missy's apartment and its *throat* the basement of the de Monteneuf Tower. The equinox fell on the following Tuesday. The precise instant, according to the internet, was 5.32 p.m. To be certain of getting to Missy's in time after school, they decided to spear the three points at Thornham early in the morning before their paper round.

They were exhausted now, wound up with anticipation. Just before bed, Zi'ib made a hurried check of their emails. A message flashed on to the screen. A spasm of horror sent

318

him stumbling back from the laptop. He called out to the others.

The message was from Ridian Winter.

Wolfie, Tala, Zi'ib,

I have faced the truth. If the Manus Sacra had been destined to rule the inhabited worlds the leys would never have allowed them to be annihilated. Their destruction has rendered my life on this alien and backward world meaningless. I have no choice but to return to Lupus a broken man and face whatever punishment awaits me. I have travelled deep into the hidden realms of wisdom and discovered how to open cosmic gateways even without the Sphere. It can be done using dark energy. So let us strike a bargain. Delay your attempt to cleanse the black ley for two weeks and in exchange, when I open the gateway to return to Lupus, I will allow Arion and Kara to return to earth. Agree to my request and when those two weeks are up, I will tell you where to find Zi'ib's mother. I will also instruct you in a method of taming black streams perfected by the great sage Nessus himself, so that you can lift the contamination from Sarah Brown.

You have no guarantees and no reason to trust me, but I am your only hope of achieving your hearts' desires.

Ridian Winter

Wolfie felt a pain growing inside his chest and spreading through his limbs. Everything around him was shrouded in a red fog of anger. Anger at Winter for using their parents as bait to tempt them, anger at himself for feeling tempted.

Tala was gazing at the screen, her face sullen and expressionless, yet her star throbbed with longing to believe this man who was offering to bring her mother home. And Zi'ib, icy, feverish, clammy, his whole body shaking, was staring and staring at this promise to tell him where his mother could be found.

Wolfie had weakened once and now it was his turn to be strong. He leaned towards them and shouted so loudly it hurt his throat, "He's lying!"

"W . . . we can't be certain," stammered Zi'ib.

"Yes we can. We know he's Wisdomseeker. Just to prove it, check his IP address."

Zi'ib moved to the computer as if dragging a heavy weight. His fingers pecked the keys. "Yeah. It's the same as Wisdomseeker's."

"So think about it logically. We know Ridian is Wisdomseeker. So we know he's been trying to stop us healing the dark energies for weeks."

"Yeah, but that could be so he can get back to Lup—"

"Shut up! If he was telling the truth about wanting to go back to Lupus he'd have made us this offer ages ago. We saw him at the football match. He wasn't a broken man. His life here isn't meaningless. He was testing out that mass hypnosis stuff for a reason. He's got a crystal dome at the Zemogen HQ all ready to house the Sphere. He's stolen two of the Stones of Knowledge and he tried to clone *and* steal the Saravita. He tried to kidnap Elvis; he got Esmé to pretend Kandass was sending us messages. Why do any of that if he's planning on going back to Lupus? He knows he'd face instant imprisonment. He wants that dark energy for some creepy scheme that has to involve resurrecting the power of the Manus Sacra and taking over the ley grid. He's a scholar; he wants the two-week delay because he knows the equinox is the time to decontaminate the ley. This message is his last-ditch attempt to stop us."

Tala took a deep breath. "You're right," she said miserably.

Zi'ib's face furrowed with fury. "So we email him back and tell him we know he's a lying, two faced—"

"Wrong," cut in Wolfie. "He's desperate to protect those negative energies. Who knows what he'll do to stop us decontaminating the ley? We'll email him back and tell him we agree to his deal and we'll meet him in two weeks' time. That way we keep him off our backs till Tuesday and that's all that matters."

They knew they had one chance to change the vibrations of the corrupted ley from negative to positive. They were sure they had done everything that their combined Wisdom of the Forests, Mountains and Rivers and the forces of the positive leys had guided them to do. They had gathered spears of different primal matter from all across the world and arranged for Flo to bring her Wisdom of the Winds. They had located the five points along the length of the ley where they must plunge those spears into the earth. They had found the whetstone that would set the matter in those spears resonating at the precise frequency to effect the transformation. And they had found the exact moment when the rotation of the earth would magnify that effect to the necessary power. But was it enough to transform the great sweep of malicious energy scarring the landscape into a current of bright positive force? Was it enough to wreck Ridian's plans? Was it enough to save Sarah?

As Ridian Winter and the three bearers of a broken star made ready for the critical moment of the equinox, the fires within the Sphere of Lupus burned bright, weaving together strands of their opposing endeavour, twisting wisdom, ignorance, strength, weakness, hope and purpose ever tighter around the warp thread of dark energy. Slowly a pattern of the Sphere's own cosmic making was emerging.

28

Equinox

It was three-thirty on Tuesday morning when they entered the outhouse to lay their strange armoury out on the workbench: the blue whetstone they had found hidden beneath the brass of Sir Edgar de Monteneuf in St Michael's Church; the horn of a medieval unicorn carved by Armelle from stone quarried in Brittany; a golden hatpin with a snake's head hasp, fashioned by a Mogul goldsmith and stolen by Esmé many years before from the Maharani of Jaipur; a small black pan that shaped a spear of sound when struck, forged by an ancient blacksmith of southern England; and a shard of terracotta from Sarah's broken planter, crafted by a Navajo potter. Zi'ib added his torch, a metal ladle and a trowel to the pile.

Tala came in carrying an old Thermos flask. Inside was a spear of ice, made from water from the healing well frozen in a mould cut from an old Frescos bag and sealed together with a damp cloth and the tip of the iron, the way she sealed the bags of Fidgits.

"Ready?" asked Wolfie.

Elvis stood beside him, strong in spirit, as Wolfie raised the whetstone. One by one they ran the spears across its rough blue shaft, rousing the infinitesimal particles within each one to a keen, vibrating, battle-ready fury. The rasp of the whetstone across the black pan scraped away the tarnish of years to reveal a shimmer of bright metal engraved with a little golden serpent, coiled in a figure of eight, swallowing its tail.

"I'm not taking any chances," Tala said firmly. "To prove that none of our wills are weakening, we're each going to wield one of the spears completely on our own."

"I'll go first," Wolfie said.

He chose the golden hatpin and grasped it tightly, his fingers thrumming to the resonance pulsing through the metal. He took a deep breath and walked out into the yard, glad of the light spilling from the outhouse. A pair of crows fidgeted on the telephone wire, semi-realized manifestations of dark energy, predatory, single-minded, determined to survive. A foul, sickly stench filled his nostrils. He felt the blazing weight of the panther's gaze. Filled with dread, he looked up. The creature was larger, stronger than before, crouching black and beautiful by the wall, twitching its tail. It exuded a deep, chilling melancholy that filled him with longing for his father. And he saw a vision of Ridian summoning the dark energies to open the cosmic gateway and Arion stepping through it holding out his arms to his son.

Lies! Lies! Wolfie dashed the image away. In a sweep of anger the crows flew at him: one steel pick of a beak stabbing into his fingers, ripping flesh from his knuckles; another snatching at the glittering spike. Blood spurted from his hand and in a frenzy of pain he ducked his head, batting the birds away and stamping the pin down, down into the earth with his trainer. With a dreadful snarling hiss the panther sprang over the wall and the birds backed off, but slowly.

The battle had begun.

"Come on." Tala grabbed her bike. Dizzy with pain, Wolfie wobbled after her, barely able to grip his handlebars. As they approached the old foundations the dark ley was waiting, its palpitating discord bombarding them with arrows of confusion and despair.

Tala knelt by the foundation stone, jabbing the ground with the trowel until she had loosened the soil. Fear dripped down her spine. She twisted round. The menacing creature hovering over her was her own shadow shaped by the flicker of Zi'ib's torch. As she shook the dripping ice spear from the Thermos a weight of darkness came crashing down on her resolve, churning up her yearning and grief. Ridian's insidious bargain was shaping her doubts into an image of him flinging open a cosmic gateway to let her mother through. Blinded by tears, she raised the icicle with both hands and threw back her head. The dark unknown lashed out, smashing her skull against the foundation stone. Blood trickled down her neck. Fighting the pain, she gripped the cold slippery spear and plunged it into the crumbled earth.

She and Wolfie struggled up Dodds Hill after Zi'ib. A morbid stench permeated the air around the smashed telegraph pole. Bracing himself for the appearance of the panther, Zi'ib ran the torch over the street, searching for the faintest crack in the paving that would allow him to sink the spear of earth into the underbelly of the hill.

His was the darkest battle. All it needed for Ridian to give him his heart's desire was a map location telling him where the Manus Sacra had dumped his mother. He glanced angrily at the others waiting by their bikes. It was all right for them. Arion and Kara might be trapped on Lupus, but at least they were safe. His mum was in danger. She *needed* him to make a deal with Ridian. Sarah would be all right. . . In two weeks' time Ridian would show them a way of cleansing energies that didn't depend on the equinox . . . it would be fine . . . he had to give it a try . . . he had to—

A car door slammed, snapping the spell of the dark energies.

"It's four-thirty in the morning. Would you mind telling me exactly what you are doing?"

He spun round. PC Mott was striding towards him.

"I, er . . . dropped my keys last night and we came back

to find them," Zi'ib said quickly. Crouching down he shone his torch along the kerb, sickened by the vile rotten-egg stink drifting up from the gutter.

"I've had it with you three," barked Mott. "If I find out there's been so much as a broken window round here you're going to be for it. You've got five minutes to find your keys and get out of here."

Zi'ib's eyes darted in panic, desperate for any kind of opening in the ground. Through a pulpy mess of leaves his torch beam caught the edge of a drain cover. He kicked it clean. The light shone through the metal slats on to a circle of oily water rippling to the insistent rhythms of the black energies. In a flash he dropped the spear of earth into the dank waters.

"I saw that, you little beggar," cried Mott, pulling Zi'ib away. "What did you just throw down there?"

"A . . . a bit of chewing gum."

"Get out of here!"

They had successfully driven three spears into the tail, heart and back of the "dread fiend". And after school at the de Monteneuf Tower they would plunge two more into its head and throat.

Dirty and dishevelled, they cycled home, Elvis still limping slightly, loping by their side. The vibrations from the dark ley had changed to a deeper pitch of discord that resounded in their heads like the bellowing cry of a wounded beast. And all through that day, as they prepared themselves for the final onslaught at Missy's apartment, their blood twitched and trembled to that dark angry groan.

To avoid the skips and scaffolding blocking the entrance to the de Monteneuf Tower, Johnny dropped Elvis and the children in Lambspring Passage and took the Bentley round the back way to the car park.

Sarah had asked them to take along a pot of Saravita as a thank-you present for Mo and all the way up in the lift Tala hugged it to her chest, as if it would protect her from the sickly, suffocating vibrations shaking the building. She and Zi'ib gazed in awe at the luxury of Missy's home, stopping only briefly to look at the tapestry before running out on to the terrace. Across the river, directly ahead, the chimney of the Tate Modern brushed the sky.

"Tala! I am so glad you have come."

Flo was calling from the terrace, where she had set out her lo-pan, a bundle of copper spikes and three great concave mirrors, large as shields, in octagonal wooden frames, which she was covering with red silk cloths embroidered with golden serpents. Tala introduced Flo to the boys and set the Saravita down beside Bonbon's lawn. Ignoring the activity around him, the little tortoise went on chewing a lettuce leaf.

Flo explained that she was going to attempt to reharmonize the disturbed energies currently in the building and create a powerful barrier against any infected forces that encroached on it in the future. Wolfie, Tala and

Zi'ib listened carefully, willing this wisdom of the wind to aid their own assault on the dark ley.

Zi'ib unpacked a bundle of dried sage, and with Flo's permission pushed it into one of the planters and set fire to it. She turned to inhale the pungent smoke, nodding and smiling her approval.

They had decided to create the spear of sound up here in Missy's apartment, and save the spear of stone for the basement of the building.

"Er, Missy, any chance of a cup of tea?" said Wolfie. "I'm feeling a bit queasy again."

"Sure," she said, making for the kitchen. "I've ordered in cakes and sandwiches, too; I'll go unpack them."

"Quick, round the other side," Wolfie whispered, heading down the terrace. Zi'ib's rucksack bounced on his back and Tala ran with the little iron pan humming in her hand. They gaped at the view of the city, sensing the line of the Thornham ley passing through the base of the de Monteneuf Tower across spires, towers and offices towards St Paul's Cathedral and Paternoster Square.

"Hurry," Zi'ib said, handing Tala the ladle.

A fire alarm erupted, blasting the air with rolling shrieks of sound. A stream of workers gushed through the doors of a neighbouring office block.

Time was running out. Tala reached over the glass parapet, dangling the pan, and struck it again and again with the ladle. The wail of oncoming fire engines swelled the cacophony below, swallowing the sound. She leant out further and beat harder. She felt something give. The glass panel shifted beneath her weight, toppling her sideways. As she reached to steady herself, the pan dropped from her hand and crashed into the empty skip fifteen storeys below. The slam of metal on metal rang out through Lambspring Passage like a cannon boom. Missy came running to see what was happening.

Together they leaned down to watch the spectacle below. One by one the sirens fell silent but, like oil separating from water, the boom of the little pan hovered in the air, billowing out as rich and sombre as the after-chime of a great church bell.

"What's that weird noise?" Missy said, jamming her fingers in her ears. "It's making me feel funny."

Downriver, Ridian Winter entered the empty conference hall of Zemogen's Battersea HQ. The architects had transformed the shell of the central boiler house of the old power station into a cathedral-like space of pale stone and steel and in accordance with his instructions designed the immense crystex roof dome so that the refracted light beams passing through its facets converged on a black and white compass star set into the centre of the marble floor. To the directors of Zemogen the star was an attractive decorative feature. To Ridian it was a powerful ancient glyph that contained at the heart of its geometry the infinite, barely penetrated mysteries of the three-by-three magic square.

Ridian had encouraged the chairman of Zemogen to purchase the derelict power station because it stood on a crucial exchange point in the earth's nervous system. Yet even he did not comprehend the significance of the primordial tricorn of power lines winding between this riverside site, the de Monteneuf Tower and the Tate Modern Art Gallery, like the wires of a vast electrical transformer. This circuit had waited for millennia for an exceptional combination of time, matter and consciousness to activate its power.

Ridian punched a code into the keypad of the conference hall. With a satisfying clunk the doors locked shut around him. He flicked a switch. Instantly the smart glass interior windows turned opaque. He typed in a second code and heard the grind of rollers as the dome above the power station slid open to the sky. He laid his Lupan star in the centre of the black and white compass star on the floor and from a metal case removed two Stones of Knowledge: the granite obelisk he had stolen from the Browns' outhouse and the stone support he had taken from the old bench on Thornham Common. He unstoppered a phial of desiccated Saravita and sprinkled it into a glass tank crawling with black ants. He had failed in his bids to obtain a fresh Saravita seed or larger, fully realized elementals and could only pray that the combined power of this pure primal matter would be enough. On each of the eight arms of the star he placed a piece of white crystal mined from the wastes of Alaska. He checked his watch.

5.05 p.m. He had exactly twenty-seven minutes until the magical moment of the equinox when the tilt of the planet would reach the critical balance point that would activate the magnetic forces he needed. He closed his eyes, steadied his thoughts and entered into the place in his mind that his ancestors had named the Hidden Realms of Wisdom. And there he waited, with the full weight of his mighty will directed towards the lost Sphere of Lupus.

As soon as Missy had dashed back to the kitchen, Wolfie, Tala and Zi'ib slipped down the hallway and took the lift to the sub-basement. The tiled walls shivered to the beat of the air conditioning units keeping the upper building at a perfect temperature. Down here the air was sickly and intense, smothering their skin like damp rags, pressing on their minds, sapping their spirits. They forced themselves through a maze of corridors, following the pull of the dark energies. Ahead stood a battered metal door painted the colour of dried blood. For a second they hesitated. Tala shouldered it open. A blast of foul air spat through the gap. She shrank back. Screwing up their courage, Zi'ib and Wolfie pushed past her, down slippery steps into the groaning guts of the building. Strands of dirty light threw misshapen shadows on to clumps of pipework, pulsing to the oily drip of water. Wolfie gripped the unicorn horn in his sweaty hand and pushed on between hissing spectres of steam. A hairline crack zigzagged beneath his feet, opening into a raw-edged fissure that ran the length of the room.

"Here," he gasped.

They knelt at the edge of the narrow crevasse, using the combined focus of their minds to seek out its weakest point. Desperately trying to hold the point in his sights, Wolfie raised the spear of stone. Blood blossomed from his bandaged wound as he plunged the twisted horn deep into the gap. The tip smashed into concrete. A blast of malice struck back, jarring his bones, ripping pain through his arms, weakening his muscles to quivery pulp. Even with two hands he barely found the strength to raise the horn once more. His eyes scoured the dark slash for the strike point. Wounded and angry, the dark energies were attacking his senses, shattering his will. Tala and Zi'ib threw their hands around the twisted shaft. Choking and gasping, the three of them brought the spear down into the fissure and felt it slide deep into moist soil, like a skewer through rotten flesh. Pain split their heads. They staggered back as a gust of foulness screamed up from below, rolling over them in a fetid wave of fury.

5.27. The moment of the equinox was approaching.

"L-let's g-get out of here," Wolfie stammered. Choking and gagging, they left the horn in the crack and hurtled back through the boiler room, pounding down dark corridors spiked with sudden jags of white that popped and crackled from the fizzing strip lights.

Flo had embedded her copper spikes, like strange metallic saplings in a row of planters, and positioned her mirrors so they faced directly on to the river. On the decking between the Saravita and Bonbon's tray of grass lay her lo-pan, its compass needle spinning crazily. She said excitedly, "I felt a shift just now, a subtle change in the vibrations. It's nearly time."

Tense seconds of agony and expectation ticked by. Elvis whimpered softly. Only Bonbon seemed untouched by the moment. Tala watched him paddle across his little lawn on slow, determined feet, snap up a curl of lettuce and pause to cast a curious eye over the untried territory of the lo-pan.

Along the stream of negative energy running from Thornham to Lambspring Passage, the sonic vibrations from the five spears were resonating through the earth, amplifying in sympathy as the waves of positive vibration rolled on from one spear to the next, swelling towards the mouth of the black ley. And there, on Missy's terrace, as the world tilted inexorably towards the equinoctal point, a reciprocal harmony was building. The tiny, dynamic, ever-dancing particles of matter within three broken stars of Lupan gold; an ancient elemental beast, strong and pure in power; a Saravita plant, native of another world; a lo-pan with a base of crystal mined from the wastes of Alaska; and the concentrated minds of three children of mingled blood, all drenched in the heavy vapour of burning sage, were responding to the song of the spears. This convergence of pure matter was creating a strange and potent alchemy that rivalled the power point that Ridian Winter had created downriver at Battersea.

In the shuddering melancholy of the waves of negative energy the sonorous positive undernote was rousing every fibre of the children's being. They marvelled, almost afraid, as their inner "sixth sense" responded to the play of the changing vibrations, creating patterns and connections in their heads far stronger than any they had ever experienced, even when dowsing. Suddenly they knew something was wrong. One small vital element in the building harmony was missing.

5.31. One minute to go.

Ridian turned his eyes to the sky, focusing his will. At the moment of the equinox, the crystal barrier that he had built in the basement of the de Monteneuf Tower would divert the flow of negative forces and send them cascading towards the Zemogen HQ. This flood of power would activate the molecules in the circle of pure matter he had built on the compass star, creating a pull of negative energy strong enough to draw the Sphere down through the open dome. He rose and, as he reached out his hand, ready to close the dome over that longed-for orb, he smiled to himself, imagining what the feeble-minded inhabitants of this world would make of something as perfect and powerful as the Sphere of Lupus.

Tortured by the prospect of failure, Wolfie rummaged frantically in the rucksack for the whetstone. He was ready to strike it against anything and everything in sight in a last desperate hope of hitting the right vibrant note to complete the transformative harmony. Tala saw Bonbon scrabbling towards the lo-pan with its inner ring of numbers arranged around a space where the five would be. She thought of the turtle who had risen from the river with the magic square mapped on its shell. With a shriek she scooped up the little tortoise and lowered him towards the centre of the lo-pan. At that moment Flo snatched the cloth from the mirror, its polished surface blazing like a disc of fire as the five dark dots on Bonbon's under-shell met the inner circle of the lo-pan, completing the powerful pattern of the three-by-three magic square.

The wheel of the year tipped over into light, raising the pitch of vibration sweeping through the speared ley towards breaking point. With a violent shudder, the raging waves of transforming energy slammed into the protective wall that Flo had built with her mirrors and Ridian had unwittingly reinforced with his row of crystals. So strong was the barrier now that instead of veering off towards Battersea, the energy ricocheted back across the Thames to Tate Modern, activating the primal triangle of power connecting the Tate, the de Monteneuf Tower and Battersea Power Station. The three ancient sites came alive as if fired by a giant switch. The circle of matter created by Ridian erupted, sending its own barrage of charged particles whizzing straight towards Tate Modern. The two torrents of force crashed together, creating for one blinding moment a jagged finger of fire that reached into the sky and ripped down through the roof of the gallery.

Wolfie, Tala and Zi'ib felt a great sigh shudder through the de Monteneuf Tower. They ran to the edge of the terrace, their muscles light and easy, the crackle of crisp clear energy filling them with wild joy.

"Blimey, we did it," gasped Zi'ib.

29

Baffled Boffins

Lightning strikes Tate Modern. The Times was running a front page photo of the interior of the Turbine Hall. Beneath a hasty patchwork of wrinkled tarpaulins, a glowing, globe-like object appeared to be hovering in mid-air. The strapline read: *Guerrilla artist – genius or vandal?*

Every paper had a story about a mystery artist who had somehow managed to sneak in through the damaged roof of the Tate and install an extraordinary floating artwork in the Turbine Hall. The *Sun*'s headline was *Ball of Fire Baffles Boffins*. Zi'ib switched on the breakfast news and caught a glimpse of a shimmering globe of light before the shot cut to a discussion in the studio.

". . .it's an extraordinarily enigmatic piece," a man with a plummy nasal voice was insisting. "It seems to inhabit both physical and psychological space, offering each viewer a dazzling and very intimate encounter with light and form. There are even reports of it giving off a curious music, but I have to say I didn't experience that myself."

"So you'd call the artist a genius rather than a vandal?" asked the interviewer.

"Absolutely. And the very act of installing it on the eve of Jenna Falkirk's opening subverts all the hype that surrounds the pieces usually exhibited in this space." He glanced nervously at the attractive red-haired woman on his left, as if she might take offence. "The anonymity of the artist makes a mockery of the cult of celebrity dominating today's art world."

"Jenna Falkirk, as a 'much hyped' celebrity artist, how would you respond to that?" demanded the interviewer.

"I quite agree with everything Ben has said," Jenna replied with quiet dignity. "This strange sculptural form is the perfect foil to my own work in so many ways. I have called my installation Earthbound because it uses solid blocks of clay from all over the world, firmly anchored by gravity, whereas this piece is ethereal, translucent and appears to obey no rules of physics at all."

"So do you think it was deliberately put there to counter Jenna's work or was it just an opportunistic act?" the interviewer demanded of a spokeswoman for the Tate.

"Who can say?" she replied. "But if it hadn't been for the freak lightning splitting a hole in the roof, I don't see how the artist could have got the piece into the gallery. To be honest, what intrigues me is not *why* the artist put it there but *how* he or she is getting it to float in mid-air. If it's all done with magnets, where are they?"

"Are you going to have it removed?"

"Not immediately. It is an exquisite piece that has earned the right to be exhibited in a major gallery, and since Jenna has no objection to it remaining there, neither do we."

"And finally, any ideas who the artist might be?"

"None whatsoever. But given the difficulty an outsider would have in breaching the gallery's security, it may be someone who works for us."

The shot cut back to the Turbine Hall, where a cluster of bemused curators, workmen and guards were gathered beneath the glowing orb. The cameras panned across their upturned faces.

"Is this the face of genius?" asked the presenter. "Or this? Or this? If you have any clues as to the identity of the mystery artist, please call, email or text us."

Tala threw herself across the sofa, a deep sob rising from her throat. Months before, when the children had discovered the first Stone of Knowledge, they had seen a vision of the Sphere. In a state of heightened awareness they had glimpsed its power as well as its beauty, something which the television screen could never convey. But there was no doubt in her heart that the mystery orb in the Tate was the Sphere of Lupus. This was the longed-for scrap of primal matter that held the keys to the cosmic gateways that could bring her mother home.

All through the night, Ridian Winter waited beneath the open dome, refusing to move, refusing to countenance failure. He knew his plan had failed. He also realized that something very disturbing had happened to the forces converging on the Zemogen HQ. As the stars faded, giving way to pale morning mist, he rose on heavy limbs and closed the dome.

"News is coming in that art collectors from all over the world have begun a bidding war for the orb in the Tate," announced the breakfast-show host.

"No!" cried Tala. "What if someone locks it away where we can't get to it?"

Wolfie's spirits plummeted as an even worse thought occurred to him. "What if Ridian buys it?"

"The Tate can't sell it to anyone, it's not theirs," said Zi'ib.

"They might lend it out in exchange for some massive donation."

Tala jumped up, her eyes wild. "We've got to say it's ours."

"Like anyone's going to believe that!" said Zi'ib.

"Yeah," scoffed Wolfie. "Since when have *we* been guerrilla artists?"

She looked at him steadily. "*We're* not, but Nikto Senki is."

He scanned her face, weighing the idea. "Nah, we'd never get away with it."

"We might if we got Mr Forester involved," she said thoughtfully.

"We can't tell him it's a celestial Sphere – we're s'posed to be normal kids, remember? How would we know something like that?"

"*We* don't tell him it's a Sphere. Nikto Senki does; he's the expert."

"OK, then what?"

"Senki says he's so worried the Sphere might fall into the wrong hands, he's willing to pretend he's the artist who made it as long as he doesn't have to meet anyone face to face."

Zi'ib opened his laptop, half grinning, half grimacing. "This is crazy! But what have we got to lose?" Hurriedly they composed and sent the message.

Tala ran upstairs, shouting to Mr Forester to come down to see the news and take a look at an email from Nikto Senki that had just arrived in the *EM* inbox.

They delivered the papers that morning in double-quick time, mostly to the wrong addresses.

"I'm so glad you're back," said Mr Forester, looking furtively up and down the yard before closing the back door. "You were quite right to alert me to Senki's message." Pointing a trembling finger at the television he said, "The minute I saw it I thought great heavens . . . that orb has all the attributes of a cosmic Sphere. I told myself it was madness to even imagine it could be such a thing until I saw the message from Senki. He is absolutely convinced it is a Sphere and he's quite an expert, you know. It's absolutely extraordinary." He collapsed into a chair. "What a wonderful thing the cosmos is, striving always for harmony despite the destruction caused by man. This Sphere is exactly what the world needs to earth the current of the revived energies and steady them until the world has relearned the ability to live in harmony with the forces of the cosmos."

"That's great, Mr Forester," said Tala.

"Senki is right, however. We have to protect the Sphere and we have to keep its true identity a secret. The plan he has come up with is ingenious. Although it involves a rather complex deception, for the greater good I have decided to comply." He gazed up at them, his thick white eyebrows furrowed into a deep frown. "I know it's a lot to ask, but will you help us? Will the three of you join me and Nikto Senki to become the secret guardians of the celestial Sphere?"

"Er . . . sure . . . why not?" gulped Zi'ib.

"Oh thank you, I'm so relieved. And I'll tell you something else that's very strange. I had a message from SILK. A number of dowsers are saying that the dark ley has suddenly been decontaminated. It defies all logic, but the two events may well be *kinnected*."

Red-eyed and weary, Ridian dragged the metal suitcase full of matter through reception. With a nod at the security guard, he picked up a newspaper from the front desk. A cry of rage rang through the deserted corridors of Zemogen International. He ran to his car and tore across London, screeching towards the South Bank. As he neared Tate Modern, he hit a fresh running stream of bright energy. Anger and disbelief gave way to terrifying loneliness. Not only had the Sphere slipped from his grasp, all the pent-up power of the dark forces that could have released the minds of the Manus Sacra from the nether void had been sluiced clean.

"So what do we do now?" panted Wolfie when Mr Forester had gone to get dressed.

Tala said, "Senki contacts the Tate and tells them he made the Sphere – we'll give it some poncy name like Jenna Falkirk's Earthbound thing – and that Mr Forester is his front man, agent – I dunno, whatever it is artists have."

"OK, if it's the opposite in every way to Jenna's lumps of clay, let's call it . . . Skyborne," suggested Zi'ib. His fingers sped across the laptop.

My name is Nikto Senki. I created the orb. I call it Skyborn. It is not for sale. Please refer all enquires about my work to Mr Remus Forester, editor of the Earth Mysterian *magazine.*

"Duh! Skyborne's got an e at the end," Tala said, leaning over to correct his spelling.

Zi'ib caught her hand. "Leave it. Skyborn's good. It's kind of like the Lupan bit of us."

*

That evening Mr Forester invited Missy round for supper to welcome Sarah home. Sarah walked into the kitchen still frail, but with a steady step and brightness in her eyes.

"I've only been gone a few days," she laughed, taken aback by the children's emotional greeting.

"I've brought Agnes's painting to show you," Missy said, dancing from one foot to the other. "You said how much you wanted to see it."

Sarah lifted back the tissue. Her face lit up with astonishment at the skill of her humble ancestor. She studied the figure of the little boy with the purple flowers clasped in his fat fist for a long time, before taking the portrait to her easel and holding it up beside her painting of Missy. Suddenly the old familiar Sarah was there in her smile. "That's what it needs! Some stems of purple Saravita falling from Missy's hand. Agnes, you're a genius! This painting must be worth a fortune," she said, folding it back into the tissue paper. "I'm amazed Mo let you take it out of the house."

Missy reddened. "He doesn't know. He and Mom are still away. "

"They've been gone for ages."

"It's all the problems caused by the fire in the gallery. They'll be back tomorrow for Jenna's opening and I've been spending so much time with you guys I've hardly missed them."

Ridian had been fighting too hard and for too long to give up now. With the dogged fervour of the fanatic, he convinced himself that these setbacks were merely trials to test the worthiness of the Chosen. He had informed Esmé and Stefan of a minor setback to his plans and then he swore to the spirits of his masters that somehow he would unleash the powers of dark energy and release them from the nether void. But first he must neutralize the power of those misbegotten brats. Either he must have their stars or they must die.

30

Pilgrim Paths

The vast and crowded Turbine Hall at Tate Modern was as hushed as a landscape smothered in snow. Every face was gazing up at an object of such exquisite beauty it stilled all conversation to whispers. Twisting almost imperceptibly within a play of glistening light fibres, the Sphere burned with an opaline fire, giving off a sweet, soft sound, sonorous as a fingertip on glass.

Wonderstruck, Mr Forester moved towards it, but it was almost too painful for Wolfie and Tala to look at, so filled were they with longing and hope. Sarah was dragged away to join a group of contemporaries from art school. As if in a dream, the children slipped through the crowd to where a journalist was interviewing Jenna Falkirk. They stood, blinking at the Sphere, listening to her voice.

"I used clay for my installation because clay is the earth

that nourishes us, the stuff of life, the raw material for pots — which were some of the earliest artefacts to be decorated and the first medium used for writing, which is why the Arabs called it the Clay of Wisdom."

The crowd swept them on towards a series of enormous terracotta blocks ranging in colour from creamy white to reddish black, piled one above the other in a seemingly random arrangement, to create a grid of towers and passageways large enough to walk through. They filed through the narrow gaps like pilgrims treading an ancient maze. As they walked, they became aware of a pattern that was not random at all, but sang to their stars of shape and number. Four blocks in the first tower, nine in the second, then two. They turned into the next row: seven blocks, then five, then three. They turned again: eight, then one, then six. The blocks in each row, whether horizontal, vertical or diagonal, all added up to fifteen.

Earthbound was a huge three-dimensional three-by-three magic square. And its power was palpable.

Three pairs of green eyes flecked with gold stared at Jenna, sensing the hum of the *kinnections* that had enlisted her as an unwitting foot soldier in their battle against the dark.

Mr Forester pulled them aside and whispered, "The proportions of the magic square inherent in this artwork must have helped to draw the Sphere into the Turbine Hall. It's safe enough now, but how are we going to protect it once it leaves the Tate?"

Missy, who was standing lonely and fidgety at her father's side, spotted them and came running over.

"Amazing, isn't it? Dad's going crazy trying to track down the artist. He wants to buy the orb for his new gallery."

A little after six a.m. Sarah's astonished shout of "Quick, look at this!" brought Wolfie, Tala and Zi'ib thundering downstairs.

"What's up?" panted Wolfie.

"That artist who made the orb. He writes for *The Earth Mysterian*."

Beneath *The Times*'s headline *My name is Nikto Senki* was a huge blow-up of the "self-portrait" Wolfie had drawn.

"It says they got his picture from the *EM* website."

The children cycled crazily round to number forty-five. Mr Forester was standing on the front steps in his best suit, posing for a photographer. He looked totally unfazed when a TV news van swung into the drive.

"We're never going to pull this off," said Zi'ib, flattening himself against the hedge.

"We will if we keep our nerve," Tala said.

An eager young woman leapt from the news van.

"Remus Forester?" she cried, thrusting a microphone in his face.

"Yes, my dear."

"How long has Nikto Senki been writing for your magazine?"

"Not long."

"He posted messages on your discussion board about celestial Spheres. Is there any possibility. . .?"

"His posts on the website are all part of the performance element of his installation at the Tate. Even this interview you are doing with me is in some way an extension of his art."

"He's good," grinned Zi'ib.

"Yeah, but what's *Senki* going to do when the Tate tell him to come and take his orb away?" demanded Wolfie.

Tala tossed her hair. "He's going to put it on permanent exhibition at the de Monteneuf gallery in Thornham."

"Oh yeah, and how is he going to get it there?"

"The Book of Light said the Lupans transported it in a basket, so we'll catch it in a net and bung it in a removal van."

Ridian switched off the television. The use of the fictitious Senki to get possession of the Sphere was a masterstroke. He must strike back and destroy the children's power once and for all. The SILK conference at the Zemogen HQ would provide the perfect opportunity. The kids were sure to turn up, desperate to hear the talk on interplanetary travel. If they had not ruined his plans, the Sphere would be floating safely in the Zemogen conference hall, firing his Link of Light to the minds of his Manus Sacra masters. By now they would have told him how to release them from the nether void and he would be preparing for the first batch of human units to attend his exclusive evening reception. Once there, Frankie Fontaine would have had no trouble at all in hypnotizing those wretches into perfect compliance while Ridian downloaded the minds of the Manus Sacra into their worthless bodies. As it was, Fontaine's skills would be put to a slightly different use. As soon as those brats had been dealt with, the Chosen *would* prevail.

Tala raced into the kitchen and snatched up the ringing phone.

"Tala? Tala, is that you?" It was the voice of Dr Walker. "Are you ready for some fanatastic news? Your dad's woken from his coma. He can't speak yet, although he's trying. And with the amazing new drug therapies we'll be using to help him recover, I can give you my word he's going to be fine."

A breathless croak slipped from Tala's lips.

"I have to go back to him now. I'll keep you updated, but I don't think it will be long before you can take him home."

Tala turned to the others, working her mouth before the words would come. "It's Dad. He's woken up."

Tala looked at Wolfie and felt her heart rip in half. She was ecstatic about her dad and at the same time distraught that soon she would be going home and they still had not discovered how to unlock the gateways.

"Don't worry," he said. "Just keep your fingers crossed

that this Tristam Marchmont bloke comes up with the answer at the SILK conference."

"I know, but what do we do if Ridian Winter sees us?"

"He can't touch us if we stay with the crowd," Wolfie said with a show of bravado he did not feel.

31

A Battle of Wills

Delegates of every age, gender and nationality were picking their way through the rows of chairs in the Zemogen conference hall, waving their programmes at acquaintances or helping themselves to coffee from the refreshment stands. Every glimpse of a tall, dark-haired man sent the children's pulses into overdrive.

An enormous screen at the back of the platform displayed ever-changing images of ancient power points. Beneath the great glittering curve of the dome ran a layer of internal windows, giving on to technical suites that controlled the visual effects and sound for the presentations. Mr Forester clutched his notes nervously. "My goodness, there must be over a thousand people here."

"You'll be brilliant," Tala said, squeezing his arm.

A single black ostrich feather headed through the crowd, moving towards them with the determined menace of a shark fin slicing the waves.

"Remus!" It was Dame Esmé, draped in purple silk, her neck hung with strings of polished jet, wearing a pillbox hat of puce taffeta topped off with a nodding feather. "I've reserved places for us right at the front."

The children had no choice but to follow her down the aisle.

Mr Forester was the second speaker of the morning. Quickly overcoming his nervousness, he talked animatedly about the need for the world's museums to re-identify the ancient artefacts in their collections. "We don't have to reinvent the wheel to create tools to husband, tame and harness the enhanced energy flows our planet is now experiencing. All we have to do is remove the term 'ritual object' from our lexicon and subject any museum pieces labelled as such to rigorous scientific investigation."

While the audience applauded, a message flashed up on to the screen.

"Oh look," Dame Esmé said, leaning across to the children. "The talk on cosmic gateways has been cancelled. Of course, you do realize that Tristam Marchmont doesn't exist. Ridian Winter had that talk put on the programme just to make sure you would attend."

Tala went rigid, too proud to let Esmé see her cry. Inside, humiliation, self-pity and disappointment engulfed her and she gave herself up to the wretchedness crashing from Wolfie's star.

"Come with me," said Esmé. "Ridian Winter wishes to talk to you privately."

If he wants to talk to us, he'll have to do it where there are other people around," said Zi'ib.

"I'm not sure you are in a position to dictate terms," Esmé said, nodding at the screen, where an advertisement for Vasco Pharmaceuticals was now playing on a loop.

"*A Zemogen company, pushing the boundaries of science to bring you hope and health*," purred the voiceover while the screen showed an emaciated figure lying on a hospital bed connected to a mass of tubes and drips.

Tala gasped. "It's Dad."

"You wouldn't want Zemogen to stop funding his treatment at this critical stage of his recovery, now would you?" Esmé gestured towards the aisle. "After you."

The detail of every sound, smell and sight seemed to magnify as the children followed her strutting little body up in the lift to the technical floor. She swept them through a set of swing doors into the sound suite. Curious to hear what Ridian had to say to them, she slipped through a side door into a darkened recording booth divided from the sound suite by an interior window. Peering through a small gap in the curtains, she flicked the switch marked intercom.

Wolfie, Tala and Zi'ib entered a huge, dimly lit room with a sound-mixing desk at one end and a sunken, leather-lined seating area at the other. Three dark-suited men stood by the wall staring straight ahead, their hands clasped demurely in front like hard-faced choirboys. In the middle stood three metal chairs arranged in a tight semicircle. Ridian turned from the floor-length tinted windows, where he had been staring down at the auditorium, and came towards them. The silence of his footfall on the thick carpet and the stuffiness of the room combined to deaden the children's senses and add to the dreamlike feeling of unreality.

With a sour smile Ridian motioned towards his henchmen and said in an obscure dialect of Swahili, "Curiosity is just about the only vice these men do not possess; however, I prefer to keep our conversation as private as possible. Congratulations are in order. It was quite a feat to cleanse that dark ley *and* capture the Sphere. But what good is it to you if you don't know how to use it?"

"Dad will show us how to open the gateways," said Zi'ib.

Ridian gave a scornful laugh. "He's just a jobbing explorer who can't even restore your Link of Light. It takes the skill of a great scholar to unlock cosmic gateways. So you see, without my knowledge, the Sphere is worthless to you. Unfortunately, without access to the Sphere my knowledge is worthless to me. But I assure you I will get hold of it eventually, so why don't we come to an arrangement now?"

"We'll never do a deal with you, Ridian. Not now, not ever!" cried Tala. "So you might as well give up and let us out of here."

"You may go as soon as I have your stars."

Their hands moved instinctively to their throats.

"Your meddling ends now. Surrender your stars willingly or I will be forced to remove them from your lifeless bodies."

The children turned to run. With swift menace the thugs blocked their way.

"Give me your stars!"

Something inside Wolfie, not bravery or recklessness but an overwhelming sense of right and wrong, spat a "No!" from his mouth.

"So be it." Ridian snapped his fingers. In a heartbeat the waiting thugs grabbed the children from behind and rammed them into the metal chairs, strapping their legs and torsos to the seats with plastic zip restraints that bit into their flesh and crushed their ribs.

Ridian dismissed the men. Horrified, the children watched them leave. He must be planning something worse than torture by his goons. Ridian pressed a remote control. A side door slid open. Frankie Fontaine came out, moving towards the children as smoothly as sump oil oozing from a cracked pan. They tried to look away, but couldn't drag their focus from his pink expressive mouth or stop the gentle croon of his honeyed voice from winding clammy fingers round their minds.

Esmé crumpled against the glass of the darkened recording booth as if watching a spectre rise from the grave. Her world was unravelling. This was her once beloved Frankie, grown old. And the voice that had whispered to her of love was now working its greedy hypnotic spell over the children of mingled blood.

And suddenly Wolfie, Tala and Zi'ib were so, so tired they just wanted to sleep. The voice drifting through their fuddled thoughts was so calm, so appealing, and if they just listened it was going to be all right. Why shouldn't they surrender their stars to someone who really understood their power? If they just lifted those broken scraps of metal from their throats and dropped them into Ridian's outstretched palms, they could go back to being kids again, free of the terrible crushing burden of their stars. They knew they should tear their eyes from those insistently moving lips, yet their muscles were in thrall to the mesmeric power of the voice that was slowly, slowly dragging their wills into a soothing sea of temptation. Already mourning their loss, their heads sank forward. Ridian wanted their stars and he must have them. With a sob of misery, Tala unhooked the thin silver chain around her neck, the boys fumbled with the grubby knots of string around theirs and, as if in a dream, they lowered their stars towards Ridian's waiting hands.

But the broken stars were not theirs alone to surrender. Each golden fragment, forged in the fires of understanding, was half of a whole whose indivisible essence was nested and entangled in the matching halves

358

hanging at the throats of their Lupan parents. Activated by the children's ebbing resistance, a frail filament of their Link of Light strove to reconnect. Along the river at the Tate Modern, the Sphere spun faster, flushing with pearly tints of milk and fire as three energy threads shot from the spikes of the children's stars, fanning out across earthly sea and cosmic wasteland to the halves still worn by Zane, Kara and Arion. And over the taut spans flowed strength, warm and sustaining, and the children could feel the pull of a connection unseverable by time or place, reaching into their hearts. And suddenly there were not three minds battling the insidious powers of Frankie Fontaine but six, and the children's exhausted spirits were raised up by the determined wills of Arion, Kara and Zane.

With an anguished cry they snatched back their stars. Ridian leaned into their faces.

"You leave me no choice."

"We'd rather die than give you our stars!" yelled Tala.

"How admirably noble. How infinitely stupid," snarled Ridian as he left the room.

"You're quite something," Frankie said admiringly as the door clicked shut. "Wills of iron. But I'm afraid for my next trick, it doesn't matter what your minds are doing. All I have to do is get your bodies to obey."

Tala squirmed in her seat, rocking backwards and forwards. "Keep moving," she shouted to the others, "don't look at him."

Wolfie and Zi'ib drummed their feet and shouted, putting Frankie in mind of oversized toddlers throwing tantrums in their high chairs. He started to laugh: a deep, soulless, chilling laugh.

Esmé watched, sickened by the realization that she had mourned her life away for a monster. Even her heartache had been a meaningless mockery.

Snap! Frankie's fingers clicked. The children grew still, frozen by the power of his hypnotic skill. He jabbed the remote. The floor-length window overlooking the conference hall slid open. Voices drifted up from below on a gust of cool air. Tala tried to scream but her body was no longer hers to control. Frankie slit the plastic restraints with a penknife.

"OK. I'm going to start counting. When I get to five, you are going to stand up. When I get to ten, you are going to start walking towards that window, slowly and steadily, so I've got enough time to get downstairs. And you're going to keep on walking until you hear me say one hundred." He added almost wistfully, "Though you won't be around to check that I actually get that far." With an arid smile he began counting down to the moment when the children would begin their walk to certain death.

"One . . . two . . . three . . . four . . . five. . ."

Deep in hypnotic trance, Wolfie, Tala and Zi'ib stood up,

their bodies mere puppets unable to do anything but obey Frankie's command.

Gripped by hatred for the man who had spurned her love, Esmé hurtled out of the recording booth. Frankie tilted back in surprise.

"Muriel?"

"Stop this now, Frankie."

"What's it to you?"

"You owe me, Frankie, and I . . . I know these kids. Give me the remote."

"I owe you nothing, Muriel. I never asked you for a bean. You were so desperate to keep me you just kept on giving." He chuckled. "It wasn't as if men were queuing up for your affections."

Tears pricked her eyes. "I loved you, Frankie."

"Then you were a fool."

She ran at him, lunging for the remote.

"Six, seven," cried Frankie.

They struggled, whirling round and round, locked in a clumsy caricature of their first fateful dance.

"Eight. . ."

The flat of Esmé's hand smashed against Frankie's teeth, ramming the words back down his throat. He slammed her violently against the desk, dropped the remote and pounded it beneath his heel. "There you are, Muriel, all yours." With remarkable agility for a man of his age, he made for the door, crying, "Nine. . ."

Esmé was on her knees, scrabbling for the broken pieces of the remote.

"Don't do it, Frankie; prove you're not a monster," she begged.

"Ten," said Frankie. And he was gone.

Like driverless cars slipping slowly and inexorably downhill, Wolfie, Tala and Zi'ib began to walk towards the open window, their eyes fixed on empty air.

"Stop!" commanded Esmé. She gripped Wolfie and Tala by the arm and dug her heels into the ground, crying out to Zi'ib to turn around.

Zi'ib plodded on. Fired by a robotic strength, the other two dragged Esmé onwards across the carpet.

"Turn around! All of you!" she cried. "Help me! Somebody help me!"

The children didn't waver in their course. Esmé let go and made a vain attempt to close the window. Stumbling in her high heels, she wrenched at the mixing desk, trying to drag it over to block the gaping space. The desk was bolted to the floor. Kicking off her shoes, she darted in front of the shambling children, frantically snapping her fingers, crying out their names. They plodded on like clockwork toys, swaying to an unstoppable rhythm.

"Stop! Turn back!"

Esmé flung out her arms to block their path. Onwards they came and backwards she went, step by step, until the cold steel of the window frame brushed her fingertips and the cool air of the auditorium blew against her neck.

"Oh, please, please stop!" cried Esmé. "The world needs you; the leys need you. You can't die at the hands of a cheap trickster. That's all this is, just a trick."

Just a trick. Frankie had said keep walking till he said one hundred.

Yes, yes, of course that was it. "One hundred," Esmé shrieked. "One hundred!"

But Frankie had primed the children to respond only to *his* voice reaching the count of one hundred. They were almost upon her. Her mouth was dry. She teetered on the edge of the window, biting her tongue to make the saliva flow. Summoning every ounce of her acting skill, she snatched a deep breath and threw back her head. Her stockinged feet slid beneath her, her toes groped vainly for purchase on the smooth carpet and she tipped backwards into the conference hall, a tumble of purple dropping down and down, the feather on her hat twisting in her wake like a storm-tossed bird as she cried out in the rich mellifluous voice of Frankie Fontaine, "One hundred!"

The children halted, blinking down at the auditorium.

A straggle of delegates were returning from lunch. Some watched in horrified silence; others screamed as Esmé's plummeting body hit the back of a row of chairs and slumped on to the marble floor. The fragile bonds of her life were loosening fast but she was smiling, filled with the deepest happiness she had ever known. In the only selfless act of her life, she had helped the children of mingled blood, just as Kandass had once helped the green-eyed wanderers to hide the Stones of Knowledge. Collapsed across the inlaid compass star, she gazed up at the overarching beauty of the dome, glimmering with all the colours of sun and moon, and in its fiery facets she saw the seamless threads of destiny connecting the power of the leys to the bloodlines of the guardians and all the myriad filaments reaching out to the righteous helpers born to aid their task.

The children had recovered quickly enough to get to the lifts before the security guards came charging upstairs, and now they were pushing through the circle of shocked onlookers to kneel at Esmé's side. Tala took her hand.

"We owe you our lives," she whispered. "How can we ever thank you?"

Esmé smiled as she gazed into their stricken faces. "You are my reward," she rasped. "Don't you see? It was *me*, me all along. I was the one the positive energies sent to save you. My life did have meaning. I was born to help *you*."

"Then stay, and go on helping us," pleaded Zi'ib.

The fine membrane between life and death shimmered before her and Esmé approached it feeling happier and nobler than she had ever imagined possible. She smiled and with her last rattling breath whispered, "I will be with you in spirit."

From a window high on the opposite side of the conference hall, Ridian had watched the scene unfold. Now Tala felt the laser-hatred of his gaze. She looked up. For one unfathomable moment two sets of green eyes flecked with gold locked across the vast space before he stepped back into darkness. Numb and dizzy, Tala moved aside to let the ambulance men through, aware, amidst the shouting and chaos, of the pulses of her mother, Arion and Zane still spreading through her, warm and enveloping as if the battle to save the star from Ridian's clutches had plugged that strange otherworldly device back into an electric current.

She turned, searching the hall, and saw Wolfie drop on to a chair holding his head, and Zi'ib press his hand hard against his throat. It was suddenly too much. In the whirling turmoil of their own distress one of their parent's stars was suddenly caught up in a drama of its own, beating wildly, pounding them with anger, anticipation, horror and hope.

They sat up late that night with Sarah and Mr Forester talking softly about Esmé, wishing they could share the tale of her heroism and the trauma of their own brush with death. But of course they could not, and neither could they still the violent emotions growing ever stronger in their stars. Yet they knew, even before the shrill of the phone pierced the quiet and Zi'ib gasped into the mouthpiece that the turmoil came from Zane.

He had found Zi'ib's mother.

The exquisite shock of joy left Zi'ib gaping and stuttering, barely able to breathe as iron bands of misery sprang open, loosening his chest for the first time since she had been abducted by the Manus Sacra.

Zane had discovered Shadia lying weak and fevered in a deserted village where her captors had abandoned her. He was flying her to hospital in Khartoum that night and wanted Zi'ib to fly out the next day.

Zi'ib leaned against the wall, his ecstatic relief touched by shades of disbelief, sadness at time with his mother irrevocably lost and the knowledge that he was leaving Thornham.

Tala and Wolfie's happiness for him was matched only by their anguish at watching their dream of bringing Kara and Arion back from Lupus fade away. They had the Sphere and the Sphere held the key to the gateways, but even by pooling their wisdom, that key might take a lifetime to find. The power of the leys that had brought them together was now pulling them apart like a careless child ripping petals from a flower, and soon Tala too would be going home to her father.

Epilogue

Wolfie stepped out on to the metal walkway circling the dome of the newly renovated corset factory. Before him, almost within touching distance, the Sphere turned serenely on a pivot of air, protected by a floor of toughened glass from the noisy preview party taking place below. In a moment he would go down to hear Mo introduce Sarah as the de Monteneuf gallery's first artist-in-residence and he would stamp and cheer when she unveiled her portrait of Missy. But for a few minutes longer he wanted to stay up here and watch the curved symmetry of the Sphere glistening like a bubble afloat on liquid eternity, listen to the sweet strange swell of its mysteries and think about his father. He could bear it because the great, grizzled warmth of Elvis's head was pressed against his hip.

For many weeks after Tala and Zi'ib had left, he had felt like an empty husk of a person, able to talk and breathe and function while inside there was nothing. He had railed at the unfairness of life, hated himself for feeling so envious of Zi'ib and sworn at the locked gateways for keeping his father on Lupus. Gradually, however, the anger had burned itself into faintly glowing embers. He was not alone. Sarah had bought him a laptop and he and Zi'ib emailed every day, Zi'ib telling him about life in Khartoum, his dad's new job at the university and his mum's steady recovery from her ordeal. Tala emailed when she could and sent him sharp funny letters that made him ache to see her fierce, brave face. And he updated them both about life in Thornham now that Sid was running the shop and Sarah was painting full time in her studio in the de Monteneuf gallery. But it was the ties that bind through darkness unto death that had stopped him from falling apart, filling his star with the constant buzz and beat of Zi'ib and Tala, Kara and Zane, and strengthening day by day the deep, instinctive bond with his father Arion.

Footsteps sounded behind him. It was Mr Forester.

"The ways of the leys are manifold and subtle, Wolfie. I know now that they brought me to Thornham so that you and I would become protectors of this precious Sphere until this world is ready to embrace true wisdom. It is a heavy burden that we carry, but one we are honoured to bear."

The boy, the dog and the old man stood for a moment longer gazing at the glistening orb, their heads filled with fathomless thoughts without images, and then the old man placed a hand on Wolfie's shoulder and guided him gently towards the stairway. "You know, I always thought that the leys brought you and Zi'ib and Tala together for a purpose. And, although I never managed to work out what that purpose might be, it's quite possible that one day the leys might do it again."

APPENDIX 1

ref. p.31

Extracts from THE BOOK OF LIGHT

In the dark days before the secrets of the living worlds were known, there dwelled at the foot of the Centaur a warrior race who sought dominion over all other races. They commanded their scholar slaves to collect all the Knowledge of the earth and the seas and the skies. But the wise slaves feared the evil purpose of the warriors and secretly planned their escape. The bravest among them was Seth, the son of Akmon, who was but a boy. In the dead of night he stole the great treasure of the warriors, placed it in a basket and led the slaves into the starless Wilderness, homeless fugitives in search of refuge.

Many died on that journey and only a small band of the strong in spirit came safely to a treeless world buried beneath the ashes of a great volcano. By the light of the twin moons Dido and Elissa, they journeyed to a ridge of white mountains where the Wild Wolves roamed. And the Wolves saw the slaves were wise. They gave them meat and water and led them to a great crater in the hillside.

From the centre of the crater rose a spur of black quartz whose root spread like a mantle beneath the land, and there the weary wounded travellers rested for the night, warmed by the breath of the beasts who circled them. And when the slaves awoke the next day, their eyes had become like emeralds flecked with gold, for they had drunk of the waters of the river Esh.

The Wise Wolves told him how each living world that floats upon the Wilderness is bound by threads of force that breathe the breath of life . . . but warned that men who drew upon this force must husband and replenish it, lest it weaken and wane.

And Seth saw that the fires fuelled by these forces burned brighter than any fires fuelled by the wood of trees, and he looked upon the landscape with new eyes. . .

When Seth saw that his people were settled, he went alone into the White Mountains and lived among the Wolves and drank deeply of their lore. When he returned he sent men to quarry a great crystal from a cave in the mountains and carve it into a dome, and raise it above the crater in the hillside to make a chamber filled with light.

Then he gathered the scholar slaves into the chamber and released the great treasure he had stolen from the race of warriors. It was a glowing Sphere as pale and delicate as a bubble of spun glass, and nestling within it, like life within a seed, lay a droplet of the pure and perfect essence of all things.

As the Sphere rose from the basket and floated up towards the crystal dome, its inner fires flickered and brightened until it shone like an infant moon. And Seth stood before the scholar slaves and told them all he had learned of its mysteries. How before the living worlds were born, a great star had floated on the void. And when it reached the number of its days, its fiery core erupted in a mighty burst of power, shattering the star into more pieces than there are raindrops in a storm. Like ripples on windless water, the power spread out across the void, wave upon wave, scattering the shattered pieces in its wake. And from those far-flung shards the living worlds were born. Some were great enough to harbour men and beasts and seas and forests, and some, of which the glowing Sphere was one, were small and smooth as rounded seeds. And when, with time, those ripples of power grew still, they stayed like fiery threads that circled and enmeshed the living worlds. And through them flowed the very force that gives and nurtures life.

Yet all between those threads and shards there was a nothing-place, a dark and dismal wilderness. And still beyond that nothing-place there lay a nether void that neither man nor beast could look upon and live.

And though the glowing Spheres were small and frail, they held a rare and precious power. For they could twine and twist the flows of force, and shape and turn the shifting tides of fate. So living world was linked to living world, and all were governed by the glowing Spheres.

And Seth was troubled in his heart, for he knew such power could tempt the minds of men. But he put aside his fears and bade the scholar slaves to trust in truth. And he built a gate upon the dome that opened to the web of fiery threads and through that gate he sent explorers to other living worlds in search of Knowledge.

And there rose up a band of the first slaves who had sought refuge in the Lands of the Wolf, and they called themselves the Manus Sacra. They were the greatest of the scholars and they travelled deep into the hidden realms of wisdom. They studied the mysteries of the Wilderness, and though they held the keys to many doors that were locked to lesser men, they yearned to know the secret of the Spheres. And they declared that they alone were noble enough in blood to wield the Wisdom of the Stars and strong enough in mind to control the flows of force that turn the tides of fate. For they believed that they alone had been chosen to use these sacred gifts to wield dominion over all the living worlds.

Among the most trusted of Seth's advisers was a man called Nessus, who studied the mystery of metals. He saw that in the mantle of quartz wherein they stored the Wisdom of the Stars there hung droplets of gold. He smelted those droplets in the Fires of Understanding, lit from the celestial flame that burned in the Sacred Sphere. And he wrought that gold into stars shaped as the ways of the winds and the cycles of the seasons. The stars cleaved to their bearers and no stranger could take them for his own. And with those stars they shared the mastery of numbers, music and tongues and spoke to one another with their minds. Seth named this bond of minds the Link of Light, and though the scholars laboured hard to fathom its subtle workings, they learned only that it was driven by the action of the Sphere. And Seth knew that the distant worlds that floated in the Wilderness were fraught with danger and he vowed that no man should journey through their depths to die alone. He commanded each wandering band of explorers to lay their stars one upon the other in the Fires of Understanding, and from that time until the days of their deaths those stars would pulse as one.

Wolfie, Tala and Zi'ib obtained an eight-point star from this magic square.

4	9	2
3	5	7
8	1	6

This is how they did it. They wrote out the numbers 1 to 9 along three rows like this:

1	2	3
4	5	6
7	8	9

Then they joined them up in the order they appeared in the magic square, in all directions – horizontally (i.e., 4→9→2), vertically (i.e., 4→3→8) and diagonally (i.e., 4→5→6).

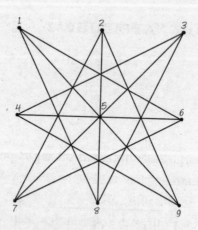

Finally they turned the shape so that the points labelled 3 and 7 faced north and south.

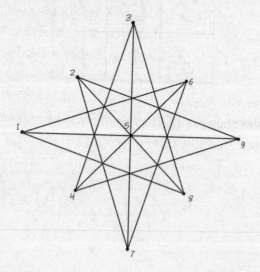

ACKNOWLEDGEMENTS

I would like to thank Dr Frank King, the diallist who designed the analemma in Paternoster Square, for his fascinating and helpful insights; the Megalithic Portal website for providing a continuous flow of intriguing information about ancient technologies; Merrily Harpur for her book *Mystery Big Cats*; my agent Stephanie Thwaites and Alice Swan, Anna Solemani, Gareth Collinson and the team at Scholastic for all their help. A special thank you to Marion Lloyd for her guidance, patience and inspirational meetings around her kitchen table; to my son Murdo for helping me to work out the codes; and to my husband James, who makes it all possible.

SAM OSMAN ANSWERS
READERS' QUESTIONS

Do ley lines exist?

Lots of people believe they do and there are hundreds of different theories relating to them. The pioneer of the idea was a man called Alfred Watkins, who spent years studying the locations of prehistoric stones, burial sites, sacred hills, holy wells, ancient churches and crossroads and discovered that such features often stand along straight lines that run for miles across country. Watkins claimed that these alignments marked the remains of a network of straight trackways used by Neolithic travelling traders. He did a lot of his work in the 1920s, but it wasn't until the 1930s that people began to claim that these ancient lines in the landscape might mark paths of invisible cosmic force or "earth energy".

However, many ancient cultures refer to similar lines of energy flowing through the landscape, often linking them to serpents or dragons. In China they are called Lung-mei, the paths of the dragon, and in Ireland they are known as fairy paths, which must never be blocked. The Aborigines of Australia believe that the gods of their Dreamtime traversed the country along lines that are still remembered in song and painting. Some years ago, pilots flying over the Nazca plains of Peru noticed curious geometrical patterns laid out across the landscape by a vanished pre-Inca race so that travellers walking down them at the equinox or solstice would see the sun or a star rising or setting straight ahead.

I loved the idea of mysterious channels of energy criss-crossing the landscape, hinting at a forgotten magic that had nothing to do with broomsticks and fairies and everything to do with the very real forces of nature. So, although *Quicksilver* and *Serpent's Gold* are fantasy adventures, the plots have their roots in some of the very curious facts and myths I unearthed when I was researching the many intriguing theories surrounding energy lines in the landscape.

Wolfie, Tala and Zi'ib, the children in *Quicksilver* and *Serpent's Gold*, have the ability to *dowse*. Can you explain what that means?
Dowsing is the ability to search for things, usually with the aid of a hand-held instrument such as a forked stick, a pair of metal rods or a pendulum. It is an ancient art, originally used to find water or precious minerals like gold, silver or

coal. Some dowsers claim to be able to find lost objects like keys and many say that they can pick up the energies in ley lines. No one is sure of the origin of the word *dowsing*, and it may be just a strange coincidence that during the reign of King Henry VIII a schoolmaster called George Dowsing was employed as a "hill digger" to search for buried treasure.

Although many people remain sceptical about dowsing, there are hundreds of professional dowsers who make their living searching for water and I have seen some of them at work. The US marines even experimented with using dowsing rods to detect underground tunnels and explosive devices during the Vietnam War of the 1960s.

The de Monteneuf family in the story are supposed to be descended from the Knights Templar. Who were these knights and did they really have anything to do with ley lines?

The Knights Templar were originally a band of monastic knights who came together around 1119 to protect the many hundreds of pilgrims who were flocking to Jerusalem after the first crusade. They took their name from their quarters on the Temple Mount in Jerusalem, which was supposedly the site of Solomon's Temple. Although they began as a charity, they soon amassed fabulous wealth through the creation of an early form of banking. Their power and wealth made them very unpopular and the sect was accused of all sorts of crimes, including blasphemy. Many were tortured and brutally massacred and the order was officially dissolved in 1312. However, the mystery surrounding the true beliefs and practices of the Templars has led to centuries of legends about them, including rumours concerning their links with the Holy Grail, questions about their association with the Freemasons and hints of their lost treasures and arcane knowledge being handed down through initiate families. Many Templar churches and strongholds are located on what are believed to be the intersections of powerful ley lines, and the curious symbolism found on these Templar buildings has fuelled much supposition about the order's mystical secrets.

In *Serpent's Gold*, the children strike a series of metal pots and pans, which causes some spilt sugar to form geometric patterns. Did you make that up?
No, not at all. The idea is based on the work of a German physicist and musician called Ernst Chladni, who performed early experiments with sound and vibration. He invented a technique that consisted of drawing a violin bow over a flat metal plate lightly covered with sand. The plate was bowed until it reached resonance and the sand formed a perfect geometric pattern. In the twentieth century, people achieved similar results by placing a loudspeaker over or under the plate. This technique of converting sound into patterns is so precise that variations of it are still used today in the design and

construction of acoustic instruments such as violins, guitars and cellos.

If you would like to find out more about the research behind my novels *Quicksilver* and *Serpent's Gold*, or share your views about the stories, visit my website: www.samosmanbooks.com. I would love to hear from you.

Find out how it all began in . . .

QuickSilver

1

Wolfie

When wasted lie the pathways of the wise
The Book of Light

Wolfie Brown awoke to the familiar smell of burnt toast and the grim prospect of delivering papers in the rain. No lightning flashed, no strange shadows played across his bedroom walls and no ghostly voices drifted through the floorboards. In fact, there was nothing to give him the slightest hint that this drizzly October Thursday had been awaited for a thousand years.

Ducking under the blankets, he pulled on the clothes he had been warming all night with his feet and ran downstairs. In the poky storeroom wedged between the kitchen and the sweet shop he found his mother bent over her easel, dabbing delicate white curls on to a portrait of a giant poodle.

"It's Mrs Poskitt's Monty. What do you think?"

Sarah Brown had a knack of making the pets she painted look just like their owners without the owners ever noticing. Wolfie stepped over a jar of brushes and a squashed tube of purple paint to get a proper look. He grinned. She had captured Monty's likeness to perfection – the doleful expression, the glint in his little black eyes and the dome of puffy fuzz perched on his head. With a few more whiskers and a headscarf it would have been the double of Mrs Poskitt.

"It's great," he told her, glancing at the clock. "Have you sorted the papers yet?"

"I've done my best, but that idiot at the warehouse sent all the wrong ones again." Sarah scooped her thick dark hair into a hasty knot and pinned it with a paintbrush. "I've burnt the last of the bread. Can you get yourself some cereal?"

"Don't worry, I've got to go. But, Mum . . . I need some dinner money. Yesterday they wouldn't give me any lunch. And I still owe three pounds for the school trip."

Sarah looked at him guiltily and felt in the pocket of her pyjamas. She pulled out a crumpled tissue, a rubber and stub of pencil.

"Can you see if there's any cash in the till? I'm a bit short this week."

This week and every week, thought Wolfie. He thrust aside the worn velvet curtain slung across the low doorway to the shop and banged open the heavy brass till. It was almost empty. As he scraped together a handful of coins he sneaked a look at the dog-eared accounts book lying on the counter. He knew things were bad, but not this bad. She was behind with the payments for the gas and electricity and hadn't paid the cash and carry for months.

Leaning against the sagging, half-empty shelves, he gazed around the shabby old shop where he had lived all his life. Maybe they could tempt some customers back with a themed week or a special promotion. One look at the jars of melted humbugs, the faded packets of tobacco and the greying slabs of coconut ice told him it would take more than Sarah dressing up as a liquorice allsort, or a two-for-one offer on bubble gum, to turn their fortunes around.

Sarah poked her head through the doorway. "Do you think the vicar will mind *Woman's Weekly* instead of the *Church Times*?"

"No problem," said Wolfie. "He could do with a makeover."

He was always saying things to cheer her up, though he knew it was Sarah who had messed up the newspaper order – she often did. Unlike her father and grandfather, she just wasn't cut out to be a shopkeeper.

Wolfie wheeled his bike through the back yard and round the corner of Stoneygate Street to the front of the shop. So much for *Thornham's Oldest Family Business*. The outside of the building was even more dilapidated than the inside. The gold letters spelling out the words *Stanley*

Brown & Son, Tobacconist & Confectioner were so faded you could hardly read them. Sarah had talked about repainting the sign for years but somehow she never got round to it. She said it reminded her of the days when Wolfie's grandparents, Stanley and Merle, were alive and the sweet shop was the pride of Thornham, filled with the smell of home-made fudge and the buzz of gossiping customers. He supposed he should be grateful. At least his mother's hankering for the past hadn't prompted her to call him Stanley. He rode away, fed up with everything: with the cold drizzle stinging his face, with his battered bike and with being the only kid in his class without a mobile phone and a computer.

They couldn't go on like this. He had tried telling Sarah to sell up, buy a flat on one of the new estates, and paint full-time. But she refused even to talk about leaving. It wasn't just that the shop had been in their family for generations or that she and Wolfie had been born there: it was as if there was something else that kept her tied to the dusty jars of peppermint creams, the dawn scramble with the papers and the growing mountain of debt.

He was speeding along Greyfriars Crescent, head down, pedalling hard, when a man in tweed plus fours carrying a stout walking stick stepped out into the road followed by a huge grizzled dog. They disappeared into the misty gloom of the common, hardly noticing as Wolfie slammed on his brakes and swerved into the gutter.

*

The clock of St Michael's Church struck seven. Beyond the far reaches of the now-known worlds something shimmered in the twilight: a fragment of a long dead star, a glowing sphere of gas and dust. Its inner flame began to flicker and flare and when it was blazing brighter than a tiny sun, a glistening wave of sparks erupted from its core, reawakening the age-old arteries of power that circled the earth.

Like a silent river bursting a dam, a quicksilver flow of primal energy trickled, then streamed, then surged across space and time and earth and sky, through oceans and forests, caverns and car parks, boulevards and bus stops, until it reached the ancient place of power once known as Thornham Magna, on the outskirts of London. With a tremor that rocked the gasworks, the deluge branched into three streams. Two flowed down the high street, past the dry cleaner's, and on through Norwood, Penge and Bromley in search of pyramids and deserts, cataracts and mountains. The third cascaded down Blackthorn Drive and swept across the common to the sweet shop, pouring up the drainpipes and through the plugholes in search of Wolfie Brown.